Catherine Mangan grew up in Ireland and studied languages at University College Cork.

Shortly after graduation she moved to Italy, which was the beginning of a life-long love affair with the country. Under another name, Catherine is an award-winning Irish entrepreneur. She now divides her time between Ireland and the USA.

Also by Catherine Mangan

The Italian Escape

One Italian Summer

The Italian Holiday

The Italian Castle

Catherine Mangan

SPHERE

SPHERE

First published in Great Britain in 2025 by Sphere

1 3 5 7 9 10 8 6 4 2

Copyright © Catherine Mangan 2025

The moral right of the author has been asserted.

All characters and events in this publication, other than those clearly in the public domain, are fictitious and any resemblance to real persons, living or dead, is purely coincidental.

All rights reserved.
No part of this publication may be reproduced, stored in a retrieval system, or transmitted, in any form or by any means, without the prior permission in writing of the publisher, nor be otherwise circulated in any form of binding or cover other than that in which it is published and without a similar condition including this condition being imposed on the subsequent purchaser.

A CIP catalogue record for this book
is available from the British Library.

ISBN 978-1-4087-3090-4

Typeset in Baskerville by M Rules
Printed and bound in Great Britain by
Clays Ltd, Elcograf S.p.A.

Papers used by Sphere are from well-managed forests
and other responsible sources.

Sphere
An imprint of
Little, Brown Book Group
Carmelite House
50 Victoria Embankment
London EC4Y 0DZ

The authorised representative
in the EEA is
Hachette Ireland
8 Castlecourt Centre
Dublin 15, D15 XTP3, Ireland
(email: info@hbgi.ie)

An Hachette UK Company
www.hachette.co.uk

www.littlebrown.co.uk

For Mom, for telling four-year-old me that I could be anything I wanted to be.

Just not the Queen of England.

CHAPTER ONE

The buzzer on Emma's apartment door rang shortly after six o'clock. She placed the knife next to the onion on the chopping board and padded barefoot through the kitchen to the intercom system.

Who shows up unannounced on a Monday evening? she thought, as she hit the speaker button.

'Who is it?'

'It's me. Who else would it be?'

'What are you doing here on a Monday night?'

'I was just passing.'

Emma laughed. 'Liar. You don't live anywhere near here.'

'Okay, so I lied. I wasn't just passing. Consider this an intervention. Hurry up and let me in. It's pouring with rain.'

'Did you bring wine?'

'Of course I brought wine. When do I ever show up without wine? I brought food, too. I stopped at the new Thai place.'

Emma buzzed her in and unlocked the door to her apartment. She tossed the onion back in the fridge drawer, along with the defrosted salmon fillet, and pulled out a previously chilled bottle of white wine. The bag of spinach leaves would remain unopened in the fridge for another day.

Another bag of spinach brought home to die in the bin, she thought.

Jo burst through the door, rain dripping from her umbrella and from the two plastic carrier bags in her hands.

'You wouldn't put a dog out in that tonight. This weather is brutal. Summer in Dublin is a joke.' She pulled a bottle of wine from her oversized handbag. 'This isn't cold. Please tell me you have wine chilled.'

Emma smiled and twisted the corkscrew down into the cork. 'When do I ever not have wine in the fridge? I was just opening a bottle. And what are you doing bringing Thai food? I'm on a diet for the wedding.'

Jo removed her coat and tossed it in the bathroom, pulled a hair clip from her bag and whipped her fiery red hair into a messy knot on her head. 'Emma, it's Thai food. Do you know any fat Thai people? No. And I told them to hold the rice, so it's practically health food.' She kicked off her shoes. 'I'm soaked. Did you just get home?'

'Yep, ten minutes ago. I thought I'd have to cook.'

'You cook on Mondays? It's bad enough having to contend with a Monday in its own right, but having to make my own dinner, too? Not a chance. I have to stare into people's mouths all day. That's enough torture in a day.'

'Yeah, but dentists make a fortune so I've no sympathy for you. I, on the other hand, work in a financial planning office and get paid to track and record the savings and investment plans of actual rich people: people on six-figure salaries. Do you have any idea how depressing that is on a daily basis? My salary barely covers my life here in Dublin. I'm not investing anything anytime soon.'

Emma poured the Pinot Grigio into two glasses.

'What's that?' Jo asked.

'Pinot Grigio,' Emma replied, confused.

'No, I'm referring to the amount you just poured into my glass. Top it up, lady. I'm gonna need a heavy pour to loosen the knot in my brain.'

Emma smiled and topped up both glasses while Jo pulled three small and two large plastic containers from the bag.

'I hate that they use all that plastic. Why hasn't someone figured out a compostable alternative to plastic takeaway containers?'

Jo picked up her glass. 'Easy there, Greta, you can put away your placard for the night. We'll sign a petition tomorrow if it'll make you feel better. Just be grateful that we don't have to cook. Cheers.'

'That's why I live in a city. Imagine if you had to cook your own dinner every night. No thanks. Cheers.' She raised her glass to Jo's. 'How was work? How's your new assistant?'

'About as useful as a chocolate teapot.' Jo sat down on a kitchen stool. 'I'm going to have to start interviewing again. There's no way she'll stay the course. She told me today that she's going to need a standing desk and that hot coffee scares her.' She sighed. 'I miss the part of the pandemic that made it illegal for people to come anywhere near me. I think I'd do fine as a recluse.'

Emma laughed. 'You're the least reclusive person I know. You just hate your job.'

Jo sipped the wine. 'Correction, I hate my *career*. And to think that I had the points for law.' She shook her head. 'The wine is good, though, and Monday nights are my favourite.'

'You like Monday nights? What's wrong with you?'

'Monday night is the furthest possible point on the calendar from next Monday morning, when another tragic day looms just out of sight over the horizon.'

Emma began to pull the lids off the plastic containers and grabbed two plates. 'You're extra dramatic tonight. Is that why you bought all this food? I could call the neighbours in if I liked them, and we'd have enough to go around.'

'Oh, is the woman next door still a psycho?'

'Yes.'

'How exciting; my neighbours are so vanilla by comparison. We should invite her over for a laugh. Talking to her is like turning on a loaded blender without a lid. She's a mess. And yes, I know that I over-ordered and I'm okay with it. I comfort eat when I'm stressed. Hence the five different dishes. You're welcome.'

'Smells amazing,' Emma said as she pulled the lids off a shrimp green curry and a chicken pad thai. She dipped a spring roll in orange sauce and took a bite. 'God, these are good. I haven't had real food in days. I'm sick of salads. What are you stressed over? Anything juicy? A man, maybe?'

'Oh, God, no, just work drama.'

'Jo, when was the last time you went on a date?'

Jo hesitated for a moment. 'The nineties, maybe, and I still have PTSD, so don't start. Did you know that dentists hold the highest suicide rate among white-collar professionals? Bleak.' She shook her head. 'I don't want to talk about it. Let's talk about the wedding instead.'

Emma groaned. 'Do we have to?'

'Emma! Don't be so mean. It's her big day.'

'I know, I know. I love her to death, but I just can't cope with all the wedding talk. It's non-stop, Jo. I mean, I'm sure all brides are the same, but normally you only have to deal with it in the run-up to the wedding. This has been constant for months now.'

'Well, maybe that's because those brides aren't one of your best friends, so you only see them on random occasions. Emma, this is Eve we're talking about, and the fact that the three of us get together two or three times a week means we're going to have to listen to the wedding stuff. It'll all be over in a couple of months and then she'll go back to normal, sarcastic, mundane conversations. The fairy tale has a limited timeline and she's just in her bliss phase.'

Emma sat down alongside her and sighed loudly. 'Yeah, I know. God, I hate even hearing myself talk like this. It's not her fault. It's just hard to be all bubbly and happy right now after everything that's happened.'

'Well, so, don't. Who said you have to be bubbly? When were you ever bubbly in the first place?' Jo teased.

'I know, I know. I've been second guessing the whole trip, to be honest. I'm not trying to be dramatic, but maybe I shouldn't even go to Italy.'

Jo paused; a spring roll held aloft in the air. 'Okay, I don't want to hear another word of you even *thinking* about not going to Italy. First, that's simply not an option. This is Eve's hen party and we are her best friends, so it's our obligation to go to a gorgeous Italian island and celebrate some of the last few days of single life with her. And second, well,' Jo let out a slow exaggerated sigh, 'Emma, it's *Italy*! An Italian island.' She gestured dramatically with both hands. 'Sunshine, warm water, beaches, boats, Italian food, Italian wine. What's not to love?'

Emma nodded. 'I know ... You're right, and of course I'm going to go. I just need to forget about the past few months and put it all behind me.'

'Yes, you do,' Jo replied. 'No offence, but you've done the sad self-pity bit for long enough. You're just wasting time on someone who doesn't deserve it. Paul's a cheater. He proved that and you need to let it go.'

Emma grimaced. 'No, I'll take it to the grave, thanks. I'm fully qualified at holding massive grudges.'

'Fair enough. You haven't heard from him, have you?'

'No, not a word. He gave up months ago.'

'Good, well it seems like he's accepted his fate. You're well rid of him; he's a stale ham sandwich of a man, and you need to accept your new reality. Quite frankly, I think you dodged a bullet. You were engaged, not married. Imagine, if you hadn't found out about him cheating when you did, this could have been a whole lot worse. You're single, Emma, not dead. Being single isn't the worst thing in the world.'

Emma sighed. She knew that Jo was right, and she desperately wanted to put the entire debacle behind her and move on. But saying it was one thing, doing it was another. She had reeled from the betrayal and the sense of loss that it had unleashed. The future she had envisioned was no longer possible. It was the loss of the relationship, her partner, the loss of the life she had imagined with him, and a loss of confidence in herself, because how could she have been so blind? How could she have been such a fool, not seen it coming, not read the signs? Surely there were signs; weren't there always signs in a situation like this? If there had been, she had missed them, and the consequences were abject shock and horror at how it had all gone so horribly wrong.

'Just because you've been single your entire life doesn't make you an Oprah-grade expert. It's going to take me some time to get used to this and forget about him for real. It was four years, Jo. We were engaged and talking about moving in together. It's not like I can just forget about it overnight and move on. I'm trying, but some days are harder than others, that's all.'

'Sorry, you're right. I know. I just hate what he did to you, that's all. You were in it for real. You gave it four years of your life and he threw it all away.' Jo leaned across the table and squeezed Emma's arm. 'It'll be okay. Look at it this way: you're starting over, right? A fresh start, newly single and where are you going at the weekend? To an Italian island! Grab life by the arse, Emma! Pack fabulous dresses and skimpy bikinis and get ready to let loose in Italy.'

Emma sighed. 'You're right, you're right. I'll get it together.'

She stared out of the window, the rain running in rivulets down the glass. 'This weather is tragic.'

'All the more reason to run away from life to a gorgeous Italian island.'

Emma picked up her phone. 'Is there going to be Wi-Fi in this place? What if we forget something? It's not like we can just pop out to the shops. I mean, just how small and remote is this island?'

'Dunno.' Jo shrugged. 'And don't care. I don't plan on contacting anyone while I'm away, and I'm sure they'll have all the essentials.'

Emma tucked her blonde hair back behind her ears. She topped up their wine glasses, desperate to change the subject and talk about anything other than Paul. 'Are we still meeting in Hugo's for dinner tomorrow night?'

'Totally. They do the best steak frites in Dublin. We need to talk about our packing lists because Eve is planning to travel like Grace Kelly, and I have no intention of looking like the poor relation. We all need to look fabulous. Channel Amal Clooney. And we need to talk about the itinerary. Eve is freaking out. All she wants is beach and chill.'

Emma frowned as she tossed the plastic lids into the recycling bin. 'Well, Eve told me to take the lead because she wanted to be surprised, and I've spent weeks planning the perfect itinerary for her. So, sorry, but there's a boat trip and a cooking class in her future. And what does Amal Clooney have to do with anything?'

'Don't you remember the week she got married in Venice? All the outfits? I mean, she had Anna Wintour giving sartorial advice and consulting on outfits, but still, she looked amazing. That's the level of fabulousness I'm striving for here.'

'Are you being serious right now? I've shopped at Penneys and ASOS for this trip, Jo. Don't give me outfit anxiety as well as everything else.'

Jo laughed. 'Doesn't matter what you wear. It's all about attitude, love. You'll look fabulous.'

The first bottle of wine disappeared along with the appetisers. As Jo stood to pull a second bottle from the fridge, Emma rooted in her bag for her phone, opened her fitness app and added the calorie count for the spring rolls and first two glasses of wine. The app advised that she had five hundred calories left for the day. She mentally deducted the two hundred and twenty calories for the next two glasses of wine she would have with Jo, which left two hundred and eighty calories for her Thai main course.

'Bleak,' she muttered at the phone.

'Go on, send her a text message. Throw her a bone,' Jo said, screwing the corkscrew into the cork. 'She's all excited about getting together tomorrow night.'

Emma sighed as she opened her iMessages and typed a message to Eve, who was notoriously unpunctual. She turned to Jo. 'What time are we meeting?'

'Six.'

Eve was still unaware that both Emma and Jo gave her fake, earlier meet-up times to ensure they wouldn't have to endure endless waits.

> See you at Hugo's at 5:30. We'll order without you if you're late.

> Can't wait! Gonna talk you out of at least half the adventures you've planned. This is a HOLIDAY! Beach, food, wine!

She added a smiley emoji and three bride emojis.

Emma stuck her phone back into her bag and turned to Jo. 'How many years ago did we graduate?'

Jo thought for a moment. 'Fifteen?'

'This is the happiest I've seen Eve in fifteen years. I'm not sure if all the years of disastrous dates were like a training programme that led her to this happy place, or if suddenly they just don't count. Either way, I've never seen her so happy.'

She pulled the pad thai dish closer to her. 'Okay, I promise I'll change my attitude. I'll be positive and this will be fun. Maybe if I pretend that my life is great, and the bad thing didn't happen to me at all, I can manifest myself into a better place. What do you think?'

Jo poured the wine. 'Gotta keep these glasses topped up. I think wine is the adult equivalent of armbands. Like, it's absolutely an essential survival tool. Seriously, though, I know your personal life sucks right now, but we're going to Italy, Emma, not jail.'

'You're right. I just need to change the conversation in my head. As in right now,' she agreed as they clinked glasses and toasted their Italian trip.

Jo twirled her chopsticks in the noodles as Emma read out their itinerary, and the carefully laid plans that took them from Dublin to Rome and onwards to the island of Giglio. As the conversation ran to boat trips and beaches, she couldn't help but feel a little excitement about the promise of a real holiday with the girls and the magical feeling of touching down in Italy for the adventure to unfold.

CHAPTER TWO

The three girls hauled their carry-on cases down the narrow, windowless, interior staircase of the ferry, bumping from one wall to the other as the ship listed and swayed on its approach to the dock. The intercom played a recorded announcement advising in Italian and English that they were arriving at Isola del Giglio. Standing among the throng of people impatiently awaiting their turn to disembark from the sweltering airless hull, the girls were giddy in anticipation of the fresh sea air and afternoon sunshine. As the crowd inched its way along, Emma shuffled behind Jo, her eyes peeled on the narrow metal exit door ahead and her first glimpse of Giglio.

She stepped onto the stone marina and gazed around, taking in the assault of colour and the cacophony of Italian sounds. She tipped her face up to the sun, a smile spreading slowly across her face. Jo had been right. How could she have even for a moment considered missing this? She moved to one side, backing up to the port wall next to Jo as the ferry continued to disgorge its remaining passengers.

'Sorry, I got stuck in the crowd,' Eve said, eventually catching up with her two friends. She twisted her long blonde hair into a knot and secured it on the top of her head. 'I hate being stuck inside like that with no windows. I think I might be a bit claustrophobic.'

'You're always a bit something,' Emma mocked. 'Today's malaise is claustrophobia. I'll add it to the list of things you think you might suffer from.'

'I'm serious!' Eve exclaimed. 'I get the same weird feeling if I'm stuck in a lift for too long. Okay, where do we go now?'

'Yes, where's the hotel, Emma?' Jo asked, turning to look left and right.

'Why are you asking me? You're the one who booked it, Jo!'

'Only because you gave me that job, and that was months ago. I haven't looked at it since. I haven't had a minute! I do know my room has a sea view, though.'

Emma rolled her eyes. 'Helpful. A sea view. Yep, that really narrows the search seeing as we're practically standing in the bay right now.'

'Sorry, can't help,' Eve added. 'I'm just here to be surprised and astonished.'

Jo sat her shoulder bag on top of her case. 'This is why we made you our Chief Planner years ago, Emma. You do such great work! All we've gotta do is show up. I can look it up on my phone. What's it called again?'

Emma lifted her sunglasses off her face. 'Oh my God, you two are killing me. You don't even know the name of the place, do you?' She sighed. 'The website said it was literally a five-minute walk from the boat towards the end of the marina. It's called Hotel La Guardia. The address said *Giglio Porto*. Look! There it is,' she said, pointing straight ahead. 'That's it. I recognise it from the photos I saw online.'

The building, the last on the marina, stood four storeys tall and jutted out over the harbour and the small beach directly below, its open-air deck facing the wider bay beyond.

Emma adjusted her hat on her head. 'And to think I almost didn't come.' She strode off in the direction of the hotel, the other two scrambling to keep pace.

The marina stretched the length of the village, beginning at the central piazza and continuing down as far as Hotel La Guardia. The girls made their way slowly down the crowded, pedestrian street, their cases rattling behind them as they bounced over centuries-old flagstones. On the right, the bay lapped gently against the harbour wall, a smattering of boats tied up at intervals bobbing gently to and fro. On the left was a series of ticket offices, cafés and bars, each of them spilling onto the street with colourful clusters of tables and chairs. Halfway down the street, five restaurants sat on the bay side, their dining areas jutting out over the water, offering prime sea views. Their kitchens, tucked away across the street, were evident only by the waiters who darted in and out of five narrow doorways to retrieve steaming plates of food. Lunch was in full swing, and every table was full.

'Looks like we're going to need some reservations,' Emma said, leading the way through the crowd. 'These places are all packed.'

'I'm starving,' Jo said. 'How is that even possible? We just had breakfast a couple of hours ago. I think I have CHS.'

'What's that?' Eve asked. 'I'm hungry, too. Maybe I have the same thing.'

Jo turned to look at Eve. 'You don't have it, Eve. I just made it up: Constantly Hungry Syndrome.'

'Oh, shame. That would have been convenient.'

'There's nothing wrong with you, Eve. You just like food. It's one of life's terrible travesties.'

'Anyway, to hell with food, I'm ready for an Aperol Spritz.'

'Shocker,' Emma said with a grin.

'Ooh, I've been daydreaming about having an Aperol Spritz on this island since I booked my flight. How do you say Aperol Spritz in Italian?' Eve asked.

Emma looked sideways at her friend. 'Seriously? Eve, Italians invented it. It's Aperol Spritz in Italian.'

'Really? How come I didn't know that. That's easy!' Eve grinned.

Within minutes the girls arrived at Hotel La Guardia, its presence denoted by a single, simple brass plaque. They stood in the small piazza, catching their breath and taking in their surroundings. A small croissant-shaped beach sat directly in front of the hotel, a collection of locals and tourists sunbathing and swimming in the calm waters of the bay. The simple grey building towered over them, in stark contrast with the surrounding, typically Tuscan, architecture.

Emma pulled open the door to the lobby and stepped into the air-conditioned interior, a welcome respite from the afternoon heat. Poured-concrete floors and unadorned off-white, plastered walls created a contemporary, chic vibe. Staff uniforms were biscuit hued, each perfectly tailored to fit. A greyscale map of Giglio sat in pride of place on the wall behind the long wooden reception desk, upon which a simple wooden box hosted an array of flyers from boat rental companies and local restaurants.

The girls waited as the receptionist finished checking in the people ahead of them, an American couple with two teenage daughters, both of whom slouched against the wall scrolling on their phones as their father peppered the receptionist with questions. Emma dropped her bag to the floor and tore off her top layer.

'Here are your passports,' the receptionist said, handing four passports across the desk to the American guests. 'Your rooms are on the third floor, and they are ready. My colleague will accompany you to your rooms now. You can take the elevator from here.'

'That's awesome,' the American said. He handed the passports to his wife. 'Thank you so much for your help. We're gonna need some restaurant reservations too, but I guess I can ask you about that later.' He turned to acknowledge the three girls. 'I don't want to delay these ladies checking in.'

'Yes, of course. If you want to come back later, I can tell you about the restaurants nearby and I can make some reservations for you. For now, just relax.'

'Sounds great. Thank you very much.'

He nodded to the three girls and shepherded his wife and daughters towards the lift. 'Have a nice day, ladies. Okay, guys, let's go.'

The receptionist tapped at her keyboard for a moment and then turned to welcome them.

'*Buongiorno*,' she said with a warm smile.

'*Buongiorno*,' Emma repeated. 'We're checking in. We have three rooms. I'm Emma Brosnan.'

'Ah, yes, Signora Brosnan. Welcome to Hotel La Guardia. You are here for your wedding party, no?' she said in a strong Italian accent.

Emma laughed. 'Oh, no, not me. That's my friend, Eve.' She leaned over and caught Eve by the sleeve, pulling her towards the reception desk.

'Hi, yeah, that's me,' Eve said with a grin.

'*Bene, bene. Allora*, we have given you an upgrade because you are the bride,' the receptionist beamed. 'Let me see ... your name is ... ?'

'Eve Coffey.'

Jo looked up from her phone. 'One of these days I may consider getting married just for the perks,' she muttered.

'You'd have to go on a date first,' Emma said sarcastically.

The receptionist tapped rapidly on her computer keypad. '*Va bene*. How was your travel from Rome? Everything was okay?'

'Yes, it was easy,' Eve replied.

'Good,' she replied, her eyes scanning the screen. She looked up at Eve. 'Your room is on the top floor and is ready now, *signora*. I am sorry, but the check-in is at three o'clock and the other two rooms are not ready yet, but it won't be long, maybe thirty or forty minutes. For now, you can relax at the bar with a view of the sea. My colleague Stefano is there, and he will prepare a welcome drink for you. I will come to find you as soon as your rooms are ready.' She printed out a confirmation of each of the reservations. 'If you can sign here, please. These are the dates, and this is the room rate. You can initial here and here.'

Each of the girls scribbled initials and a signature on the document.

'Now, can I have your passports please? I will take a copy and when your rooms are ready, I will finish the check-in. For now, you can leave your bags here and my colleague will take them to your rooms as soon as they are ready.'

'Great, thank you,' Emma replied.

'You have already prepaid your rooms so all I need is a credit card for any incidentals. I will just place a hold of two-hundred euro on each card. This is okay?'

The three girls each placed a credit card on the desk in agreement.

'Where's the bar?' Jo asked, looking in the direction of the stairs.

'The bar is up the stairs on the first floor. There you will also find the restaurant, *signora*. The restaurant will open at seven p.m. for dinner. In the morning breakfast is served from seven to ten. If you need any recommendations for local restaurants, I will be happy to assist you, but for now I invite you to go to the bar where you will find my colleague Stefano and you can relax after your travel.'

'Sounds divine,' Eve said. 'Can I go to my room first and drop my bags?'

'*Sì, signora*.' She handed Eve her key card, walked to the lift and hit the call button. 'You can go to the third floor and my colleague will meet you there.'

Eve stepped into the lift, grinning at Emma and Jo. 'See you in a few minutes at the bar. I'm loving this already!'

Emma and Jo tucked their bags behind the desk at reception and took the stairs to the first floor. They gasped instinctively when they rounded the corner into the vast, open-plan space that morphed from lounge to dining area, the colour scheme replicating the soft tones in reception and providing a perfectly neutral backdrop for the jaw-dropping view. The room was open to the outdoors with breathtaking one-hundred-and-eighty-degree sea views, and only a covered awning separated the space from the bay beneath. The vast seating area was populated with multiple oversized chairs and sofas. Thick glossy picture books were stacked on wooden coffee tables and black-and-white photography adorned the walls.

The bar ran along the length of the back wall, its long wooden structure facing the sea. Jo pulled out a bar stool and turned it sideways as Emma leaned her back against the bar, not taking her eyes off the view. To their right, they could see all the way back down the street with the shops and restaurants they had just passed, and beyond it to the marina. Straight ahead was an unadulterated view of the Tyrrhenian Sea, the odd boat cutting a frothing wake through the otherwise perfectly blue canvas.

'*Buongiorno.*'

The voice came from behind them. Emma turned to see a tall, uniformed barman carry a case of wine from a back room into the bar. He placed it on the floor, rubbed his hands down his black apron and smiled.

'*Buongiorno,*' Emma replied. She pulled out the bar stool alongside Jo, the sea view temporarily forgotten.

Jo simply stared, unapologetically.

'*Benvenute a Giglio.* I am Stefano. You would like a welcome drink, no? You have just arrived?'

'Yes, we literally just got here,' Emma replied as Jo remained mute. 'I'm Emma, this is Jo.'

'You would like an Aperol Spritz? Is good for this time of the day.'

'Sounds great. Oh, can you make it three please? Our friend is just dropping her bags to her room.'

Emma guessed that he was at least six foot tall. The inside of his left wrist had a simple tattoo in a script she didn't recognise, partially covered by three dark brown leather bracelets. His hair was dark blond and dishevelled, and she couldn't be sure if that was by design or accident. But it was his eyes that pulled her in. Not the usual deep brown that you would expect of an Italian man, but instead a piercing, limpid blue.

He reached down into a fridge for a bottle of prosecco. '*Certo.* I make three. Is your first time in Giglio?' he asked.

'Yes, we love it already. It's beautiful.' Emma nudged Jo.

'Yes, beautiful,' Jo repeated. She tilted her head in towards Emma. 'He looks like he should be modelling men's aftershave or cologne or whatever you call it.'

Emma frowned in confusion. 'How exactly does someone model aftershave?'

'Wearing very little,' Jo whispered loudly. 'Maybe just those classic Italian tiny little shorts, laying back bare-chested and prone on the bow of some boat, with one arm folded under his head, just lying there gazing sultrily at the camera.'

'*What?*'

'Just sayin',' Jo said, not taking her eyes off him.

He placed three glasses on the counter in front of him. 'Where you are from?'

'Ireland. Dublin,' Emma replied. She always felt the need to clarify that she was from Dublin; it was an automatic follow-on comment whenever she said she was from Ireland.

'Ah, yes, I have been to Ireland,' the barman exclaimed. 'I like it very much. Guinness and green fields. Very, very green.'

'Yeah, lots of fields.' Emma smiled. 'But we're die-hard city girls.'

'I have been to Dublin and to Galway. I would like to go back one day. The countryside in Ireland is very beautiful.'

'It is, but there's not a lot going on in the country. It's too quiet for us. It's pretty, but Dublin is where all the action is.'

'How long you will stay in Giglio?' He poured the bright orange liquor, unmeasured, over the ice before adding prosecco.

'Just a few days. Our friend Eve is getting married, and this is her hen party. Do you know what a hen party is?' Emma asked, unsure if the term made sense to him.

Stefano smiled. 'Yes, of course. We have these parties every year. Lots of crazy women.'

He cut two slices of orange and stuck them into the top of the glasses. 'You are very welcome in Giglio. *Ecco*,' he said, as he placed both glasses on the bar in front of the girls. '*Salute*. The third, I will wait until your friend arrives. Is better this way.'

'Is *salute* cheers in Italian?' Emma asked, putting the straw to her lips.

'Yes, *salute*,' he repeated.

The girls clinked glasses and repeated it loudly in unison. '*Salute!*'

'Ooh! Wait for me!' Eve shrieked as she ran towards them and pulled out a bar stool, pausing as she caught sight of Stefano at the other end of the bar. 'Holy shit, who's that?'

Emma grinned. 'That's Stefano, the barman.'

'God, he's gorgeous. Do you think he was sent here to test me.'

'Stand down, Bridezilla. It's over for you,' Emma said. 'You, on the other hand, are definitely a candidate for a holiday fling,' she said, turning to Jo as she circled her straw in her drink.

Jo rolled her eyes. 'I'm not here for a fling. I'm here for a long weekend with you two. Emma, you're the one who should be on the lookout. I can't think of a better way to shed the shackles of break-up sadness than a fling with a hot Italian.'

'Not a chance, ladies, and don't go getting any notions about trying to get me to hook up with this barman either. I know what you two are like. Anyway, we don't know the first thing about him.'

Eve's eyes followed Stefano as he placed an Aperol Spritz in front of her. She leaned in towards Emma and whispered, 'I'm not sure what there is to know that could be of any importance right now. He looks like he's been pulled out of the pages of a magazine.'

'Aftershave model,' Jo repeated.

Eve frowned. 'What's she talking about?'

'Don't listen to her,' Emma said. 'Again, thank you both, but no. I'm not ready to be pimped out yet, so you two just worry about yourselves.'

Emma turned to face the bay, the gentle sea breeze wafting through the open space. Here she was in this glorious place, the kind of place most people only dream of visiting, but she couldn't just give in to it and feel it. A long weekend on a stunning Italian island lay ahead of her, but she still couldn't shake the faint shroud of sadness that settled around her shoulders. She hadn't thought about Paul all day, but now here he was, sneaking back into her thoughts again. She hated him for what he had done, to them and to her, and she hated that he still had the power to creep back into her consciousness. She was feeling better than she had in months, but she desperately wanted to get over these feelings of wistful longing. Longing for what, she wasn't sure. He had taken enough from her in the past few months, and she had wasted four whole years on him.

She sat there watching the ferry they had arrived on reverse out of the port, taking holidaymakers back off the island, their trip over. She decided right then that he had taken enough. She wasn't going to allow the memory of him to steal even a minute from these few days with her friends on this gorgeous outcrop in the Tyrrhenian Sea. She turned back to the girls with a determined smile, the three of them clinking glasses together.

'*Salute!* Here's to living our best lives for the next few days. This starts now!'

CHAPTER THREE

Two Aperol Spritz and a light lunch at the hotel restaurant later, the girls were back in their rooms to unpack, shower and change for dinner. Emma peeled off her travel clothes and tossed them in a pile at the bottom of the wardrobe. Locating a laundry bag so that they would be freshly laundered for the return journey home was tomorrow's problem. All she wanted now was to shower and head back downstairs for her first aperitivo. She unzipped her suitcase, stuck her swimsuits and underwear into a drawer and hung up the five dresses she had brought. Her one concession to exercise was a pair of yoga pants and T-shirt, packed to satisfy Jo's insistence that they partake in the hotel's free yoga class one morning. It was easier to pack the outfit than convince Jo that the likelihood of any of them making it to a yoga class at 8 a.m. any morning was slim to none.

She checked the time and smiled. It was almost 6 p.m., which made it 5 p.m. in Dublin. People were still at the office back home. She texted her work friend Maeve.

> Made it to the island! Fab! Getting ready for aperitivo hour and dinner.

The ellipsis pulsed immediately.

> Jealous. Stuck in projections mtng. My ears are bleeding.

Emma smiled. Maeve probably hated her job even more than she herself did, but they did a good job of consoling or distracting each other daily.

Maeve typed again.

> Bring me back something nice from Italy . . . Like a hot Italian guy. Doesn't have to speak English. I can use my hands to communicate ;)

Emma laughed and tossed the phone on the bed. She turned off the air-conditioning and opened the window. Her room looked directly out over the bay and the crescent-shaped beach below. The small crowd of sunbathers on the beach caught the last of the sun's rays, each of them already sporting a golden-brown tan. She leaned out, breathing in the sea air, and watched as another ferry reversed slowly out from the port. Further out in the bay, a sailboat traversed towards the open sea, and another hovered at the entrance to the marina, waiting for clear passage once the ferry had departed.

Church bells rang out, the sound echoing across the water signalling six o'clock, the church itself tucked away out of sight. Another followed suit just seconds later, adding a line of harmony in answer from the other side of the hill. Turning back to her room, Emma looked at her reflection in the mirror.

'You could do with a bit of sun,' she said to her reflection. 'Pasty, white, Irish skin.' She leaned in and looked at her face. She looked tired, with grey shadows under both eyes. She couldn't remember when she had last had an uninterrupted night's sleep. She brushed stray strands of hair from her face and peered at her reflection. 'Charlotte Tilbury to the rescue.'

She pulled on a simple red sundress and beige wedge sandals. The memory hit her like a slap in the face. Boom! A week-long holiday in Tenerife with Paul was the last time she'd worn this dress.

'Nope,' she said aloud as she applied a slash of cherry-red lipstick, refusing to let the memory of him dampen her mood. 'I'm done thinking about you.' She shook her head, grabbed her purse, room key and wrap, and pulled the door shut behind her. She took the stairs down to the first floor and pulled out a stool at the bar alongside Jo.

'Oh boy, what happened?' Jo asked.

'What do you mean "what happened"? Nothing happened.'

'*Buona sera, signora.* What can I get for you?' Stefano asked, placing a monogrammed coaster on the bar in front of her.

Emma glanced at Jo. 'What are you drinking?'

'Gin and tonic.'

'Hmm,' she paused. 'I'll have a negroni please.'

'*Subito.*'

'The first clue was the bright red lipstick. The second was the negroni order just now. What's going on?'

Emma sighed. 'Oh, nothing. I swore that I wouldn't think about Paul on this trip, but the last time I wore this dress was in Tenerife with him.'

'Oh, fuck Paul,' Jo snapped. 'He doesn't deserve a place in your head. Not after what he did, the lying piece of shit.'

'I know, I know. It's just the dress triggered the memory, and it all came back to me. I've already decided that he's not allowed back in my head. I'm not going to let him ruin this trip for me.'

'Good. He's a dirtbag and I don't want to hear you mention his name one more time this weekend. Once a cheater, always a cheater. Do you hear me?'

Emma nodded. 'I know, and I won't.'

'Look, don't get me wrong. If you need to talk about any of this stuff anytime, I'm totally here for you, but you deserve this break and you owe it to yourself to have a good time. Fuck it, find a hot Italian and have a fling. Anything!' She threw her hands up in the air. 'I swear to God, I'll condone anything if it gets you over Paul once and for all.'

She gestured down the bar. 'Stefano here is hot. What more could you ask for?'

Emma swivelled on her stool and faced Jo directly.

'Okay, I promise not to mention Paul's name again if you promise to stop trying to set me up with random strangers. You're starting to sound like my pimp.'

'You don't know what's good for you and you know what they say: if you want to get over a man, you've got to get under another.'

'Jo. Really? Can you not?'

'All right, all right. I'll stop. Just promise me that if the mood takes you, you'll jump on the opportunity and right into bed with your recovery man.'

'If it will make this stop, then yes, I promise.'

Emma turned to look back behind her towards the door. 'Now can we please change the subject before Eve gets here? This is supposed to be a happy weekend and we don't need her starting in on how my life got so off track and where it all went wrong. No offence, but I could do without either of your therapy sessions right now. I'll take my therapy in a glass this week.'

Stefano placed the cocktail on the bar. *'Ecco. Salute.'*

'Perfect timing, Stefano,' Jo said. 'It's like you just appeared out of a bottle.'

'I appear out of a bottle. I don't understand,' he replied, a confused look on his face. 'You need a bottle of something?'

'No, like a genie … in a bottle. You know, like Aladdin?'

'No.' He looked from one to the other of them, shaking his head.

Emma smiled. 'Don't mind her, Stefano. It's just an English expression. She just meant that you showed up with the drink right on time.'

'Ah, okay. I don't understand, but okay.' He shrugged. *'Allora*, so where you will go tonight?'

'We don't have any plans,' Emma said, relieved to change the subject. 'Is there some place you recommend for dinner? We passed all those restaurants down by the marina on the way here and they all looked great.'

'Yes, there are many good restaurants here in Giglio. You would like seafood?'

'Yes, I'm tired of my Lidl vacuum-sealed cod fillets,' Jo said. 'I want the real thing.'

'The real thing?'

'Yes! Good, fresh fish, Stefano. None of this conveniently packaged bullshit we deal with at home. I want just-hauled-from-the-water fish.'

Emma put a hand on Jo's arm. 'She means yes, Stefano, we would love some good seafood tonight. The lady at reception told us that she could help us with some reservations, but we never made it back down there.'

'Yes, yes, she can make reservations, but it depends on the type of place you would like to find. You will not find the real local place this way.'

'What do you mean?'

'Oh my God, sorry I'm so late. What did I miss?' Eve came rushing into the bar. 'Hi Stefano, can I have an Aperol Spritz, please?'

'*Certo*. I make this and then I explain.'

'Explain what? What did I miss?' Eve asked again.

'Not sure exactly, but it feels like he was about to tell us something profound about seafood.'

'Ooh, exciting! Anyway, sorry I'm late. I had to deal with a situation at home.'

'Oh good, please do share,' Emma said sarcastically. 'I'm dying to get out of my own head.'

Eve leaned in towards her friend. 'Why? Did something happen?'

'No, nothing,' Jo interjected. 'Leave it at that and tell us your situation.'

'Okay.' Eve shrugged. 'So, Barry is managing the two Airbnb apartments while I'm away because I told him I couldn't deal with it on another time zone.'

Jo looked at Emma and raised her eyebrows. 'We are

literally one hour ahead, Eve. That barely even counts as a time zone change. It's an hour's difference.'

'Okay, well, I didn't want to have to deal with it on my hen do, so basically I just blamed the time zone thing and said he'd have to cover for me.' She grinned. 'It's not a big deal, we have one check-in today, another tomorrow, and then that apartment is rented again in three days, so all in all, Barry has to deal with three check-ins. No biggie. So, anyway, we had a new family check in this afternoon. I kind of had an inkling that she was going to be a pain because she asked about four hundred questions before she even arrived and she's the only person ever to ask me to reduce the price.'

'Reduce the price of what?' Emma asked.

'The apartment. The price per night.'

Emma let out an audible sigh and took a sip of her cocktail. 'She does realise that this isn't a bazaar stall in Turkey, right? That Airbnb is an apartment rental service, not a bargaining platform.'

'She's just cheap,' Jo surmised. 'You should have rejected her arse from the get-go.'

'I can't afford to reject people. We need the money. This is my job now! We have a massive mortgage on the two apartments, so I need the bookings. Anyway, I didn't give her a discount and she showed up today and she's already moaning. Apparently, the apartment has an unusual feel to it, and the cereal bowls are too big for the children.'

'What? An unusual feel? Is she some sort of reiki-healer-type chick channelling vibes in her rental? That's ridiculous,' Jo scoffed.

'What's wrong with the bowls?' Emma asked. 'I don't get it.'

'Neither do I and I'm not going to get involved. Barry's going to have to deal with it.'

'Good. Here's Stefano. We need a dinner plan,' Emma said, gesturing to catch his attention.

Stefano place the Aperol Spritz in front of Eve and leaned one arm on the bar counter.

'What were you saying about booking a restaurant for dinner?' Emma asked.

'*Allora*, I will explain. You stay here in a five-star hotel, no? And you go to the reception to ask for the recommendations for the best restaurants here. Because you stay here in a nice hotel, my colleagues they tell you only the good restaurants that have the five stars, because they think that this is what you want. But . . . ' He gestured with one hand in the classic Italian manner. 'But these are not the only good restaurants in Giglio. There are many more, some that are not the five stars, they are more – *come si dice?* – not too fancy.'

'More local?' Emma suggested.

'*Sì, esatto*. This is the word: local. Many of these restaurants are simple, but the food, it is the best on the island. This is the place that the local people eat. They live here on the island, so they do not worry about how it looks, the restaurant. They do not worry about having the best view of the sea, because every day they see it. They worry only about the food!' He gestured again dramatically, but the movements worked in perfect sync with his words and expressions.

The phone on the counter behind him rang.

'*Scusate, un attimo*,' he said as he turned to answer the call. The girls watched as he spoke rapidly, transfixed, each of them deciding that Italian was undoubtedly the most beautiful language in the world.

Jo nudged Emma. 'Just sayin'.'

'Stop it!' Emma hissed. 'Give it up, for the love of God.'

Eve downed the last of her Aperol Spritz. 'I'm with Jo on this. He's divine. Look how strong he is too. I can just imagine—'

'You two are like pimps. We don't know the first thing about him. He could be married with kids or a stalker or an axe murderer.'

'I love how you put married with kids into the same scary category as axe murderer,' Jo teased.

Emma scowled at her. 'This is me changing the subject.'

Stefano ended the call and returned to the girls. He nodded towards Eve's empty glass. 'You would like another?'

'Yes please.'

Emma looked at Eve. 'Sucked that one down in a hurry.'

Eve feigned an indignant look. 'Yep, that first one tasted like a good time and I'm here for the party this weekend.'

'Touché,' Jo replied.

'Fair point,' Emma added. She turned to Stefano. 'So, where do you like to eat? Where do you recommend?'

He pointed to the string of restaurants down at the marina. '*Allora*, down at the marina are five restaurants. When you leave from here, the first four that you will see are very well known, all very good for the seafood. All five star. Fancy.' He gestured with one hand. 'The last one that you will see is not a fancy restaurant. The owner he does not care about this. He does not spend the money on expensive things like ... ' He paused and pointed at the clusters of tables and chairs in the dining area. 'These things.'

'The tables and chairs?' Eve asked.

'Yes, how do you call these in English?'

'Oh! Furniture,' Eve said excitedly.

'Easy, Eve, it's not a quiz. There's no prize for guessing the right word,' Jo quipped.

'*Brava*. Yes, this is the word I could not find. Furniture. The owner, Mario, he does not care about spending money on these things. But he is always the first man to arrive at the marina every morning to get the best fish and he is happy to pay the fishermen what they will want for this fish. Not all restaurants do this. Some of them they will want to pay less, pay a lower price.' He raised a finger in the air. 'And his mother, she is in the kitchen, so here you will have the best fish in Giglio. She was born here in Giglio, and she cooks in the old style of Italian cooking.' He placed a second Aperol Spritz in front of Eve and turned to Emma and Jo. 'You would like one more?'

'I'm switching to wine,' Emma said. 'If I have a second negroni I'll be on my ass.'

Jo sighed. 'So many ways I could respond to that right now, but I feel like I've been silenced. Such a shame.'

'You would like to try the wine from Giglio?' Stefano asked.

'They make wine here?' Eve asked. She turned to the girls. 'I didn't know that. Did you know that?'

Stefano smiled. 'They do many things. The people, they learn to create many things because is not so easy to get to the mainland of Italy at some times of the year.'

'That makes sense,' Emma said. 'So, they learned to be resourceful and self-sustainable.'

'*Sì, l'Isola del Giglio è sostenibile.* For this we have won many awards in Italy.'

'Can I taste the wine, please? White.'

'Me too, please,' Eve piped in.

'*Certo.*' He pulled a bottle from the fridge. 'This is one of my favourite wines from Giglio. Tell me what you think.'

The wine was almost transparent in colour.

'There is a word in Italian, I do not know how to say it in English. *Abbandonato.*'

'Abandoned?' Eve suggested.

'Yes, there are many vineyards here in Giglio and they are very, very old. These vineyards they were abandoned for many years and the people they decide that we need to make wine here on the island, so they decide to bring back to life the vineyards. The soil here in Giglio is unique and so the wine that we make is unique. You like it?'

'Oh, that's good,' Emma said. 'Delicious.'

He poured her a glass. The vineyard for this wine is high up on the mountain, this helps the grapes to stay cool in the summer, which is good for the wine. You can go to visit this vineyard and taste the wines that they make. Is not so far from here.'

'Oh, that sounds fun!' Emma said. 'We should add that to our list.'

'You mean our already jam-packed agenda?' Eve said. 'I don't think we've got any room. In fact, we might need to schedule some time to just chill for an afternoon.'

Emma rolled her eyes. 'I'm just trying to make sure that we don't miss anything. You can do a beach holiday any time, but we're in Italy. We have to explore!' She turned back to Stefano. 'So, can we call to get a reservation at that restaurant tonight?'

'No, is not possible. They do not take the reservations.'

'It's just walk-in?'

'Yes, you just go there and if it is busy you wait, and it is always busy every day.' He checked his watch. 'Soon they will open. I suggest to you to go early, then when you arrive, tell Mario that I send you. He will look after you. You will charge these to your room, no? I bring it for you to sign in a moment.'

He turned to greet the couple who had just pulled up stools at the bar. *'Buona sera.'*

The girls sipped their wine and signed the room charge.

'Maybe after dinner you can come back here for one more drink. Today is quiet in the hotel so there is not so much to do. I will tell you about the beaches here and give you some advice about where to have lunch in these days. Maybe I can teach you some Italian words,' Stefano suggested with a grin.

Jo winked at Emma. 'Language lessons have never sounded so appealing.'

'Sounds like we need to add nightcap to the already full agenda,' Eve agreed.

Emma tried to hide the smile. The last thing she wanted was a man in her life right now, but she couldn't deny that Stefano's charm was a little addictive. He was good-looking in that classic, ridiculous Italian way, but he was one of those men that made you feel like you were his entire focus when speaking to you, his deep blue eyes piercing right through you. She was determined not to be a cliché and fall for the good-looking Italian on the island holiday, but damn, he was hot.

She picked up her purse and her cashmere wrap. *No harm in a drink,* she thought, a smile finally breaking across her face.

CHAPTER FOUR

The narrow flagstone street that led to the marina was alive with energy. Couples and families mingled and wandered slowly from shop to shop, pausing to peruse the local artisan goods on offer, each shop competing for the attention of tourists with eclectic colourful displays. Clothing shops spilled out onto the street with rails of summer beach cover-ups billowing in the breeze, and jewellery shops added tables outside their windows with racks of beaded necklaces and earrings twinkling in the evening sun. Pottery pieces adorned in brazen colour slashes of reds and yellows were stacked precariously alongside delicate espresso coffee sets, while piles of linen napkins tipped sideways but never quite fell over.

Jo and Eve ambled arm in arm through the throng of people as Emma trailed behind, her iPhone poised to capture the golden glow of the slowly setting sun on the bay. The marina was flanked by three-storey buildings, their paint flaking from years of relentless battering from sea winds, their corners and sills crumbling in a slow demise from the grinding of salt water. Everywhere Emma looked was a picture, a potential painting, the setting sun only seeming to magnify the intensity of warm blazing colour everywhere.

As she stood capturing image after image, she tried to remember the last painting she had finished. It had been months. Not since the whole debacle with Paul, when her world had imploded with the discovery of his affair. Overnight, she had gone from painting almost every weekend to nothing. A hard stop. Her passion for painting had been subsumed in her distress, the crushing weight of her devastation having smothered this too. She looked around at the evening scene unfolding and breathed deeply as she admired the quiet, natural beauty of the island. Her artist's eye could envisage the scene before her depicted in paint, her version of the harbour in Giglio at sunset. She could imagine the first splash of paint on a white canvas, swathes of burnt orange, crimson and gold, as she tried to replicate the feeling that this warm, early summer's evening evoked. Layers of colour combined to recreate the golden glow that permeated everything.

Happy colours, she thought, her eyes darting left to right, the colours morphing before her eyes as the sun dipped lower and lower towards the horizon, deepening the glow that was imparted across the bay. She captured shot after shot, cataloguing the short walk towards the centre of the village, suddenly and abruptly pulled back into the world of colour, creation and art. She had lost sight of Jo and Eve, but the fact hadn't even registered. She was lost in the crowd, the sounds of spoken Italian acting as a harmony to the colourful symphony that was playing out around her.

The church bells rang out from the piazza, the sound

reverberating against the tall buildings, signalling to anyone who cared that it was eight o'clock. An approaching ferry sounded its horn in warning, exerting authority over the small, single-engine pleasure boat that sat in its way. Children darted in and out of the crowd with happy shrieks and calls, their parents blissfully ignoring them on their evening *passeggiata*, the time-honoured tradition of the gentle evening pre- or post-prandial stroll, a community affair that was simultaneously taking place in every town and village across Italy in the company of family or friends.

The thought struck her that nothing was missing. The low-level ache in her heart had lifted. She didn't miss or crave anyone or anything. She realised that for the first time in a long time, she felt perfectly okay. She didn't know where her friends were, but that was okay too. She'd find them. For now, it was just her, lost in her thoughts, lost in the moment, safe in a bubble of foreign sounds and smells. Her eyes scanned the crowd for the girls. She spotted them in the distance, Jo's long auburn hair piled in a loose, messy bun on top of her head, the colour like a siren in a sea of dark-haired Italians. She passed the first three of the five restaurants, noting that they were already more than half full, and caught up with the girls.

'Hi, sorry; I got carried away taking photos.'

'I bet! It's so beautiful,' Eve exclaimed.

Jo was leaning over a table display of jewellery: coloured beads and baubles glittering in the sun.

Emma tapped her on the shoulder. 'C'mon, Jo, we can come back here after dinner. The restaurants are already filling up.'

'Coming, coming. The prices on these things are amazing. God, we're really robbed in Dublin, aren't we? So much cute stuff. I might need another suitcase at this rate.'

The three girls made their way to the last restaurant. A weather-beaten wooden sign hung crookedly overhead, the letters in faded black spelling out the name: *Il Pescatore*. Two men dressed casually in T-shirts and shorts stood one in front of the other blocking the doorway, the first engaged in a conversation with the waiter, running his hand through his already dishevelled dark hair, the second, leaning against the doorframe patiently waiting for the dinner plan to be finalised. Emma stepped up behind them, waiting to cross over the threshold.

'*Grazie, a dopo,*' the first said to the attending waiter before turning back to the second. 'About a half-hour,' he said in a strong Irish accent. 'We can get a beer next door. He'll give us a shout when the table's ready.'

The accent caught her attention. It was the first Irish accent she'd heard since they left Dublin. The two men stepped out through the doorway, the dark-haired guy catching her eye as she stepped aside to let them pass. He smiled at her and nodded.

'Irish?' she asked.

Surprise registered on his face. 'Yeah, was it the accent or the bad sense of style that gave it away?'

She glanced at the black polo shirt, khaki shorts and black flip-flops and had to concede that he looked quite smart for an Irish man. Not the usual heavily logo'd GAA or soccer jersey and runners. He paused in the doorway, standing several inches taller than her, his dark hair tossed in different directions, one section hanging down as far as his eyelashes, moving as he blinked. His eyes hadn't left hers.

'It's a tough call, but I'd have to go with the accent.'

'That's a relief,' he said with a grin.

'You speak Italian?'

'Just enough to get by. The important stuff.' He shrugged. 'Enough to be able to order food and wine. You know, life's necessities.' He nodded back towards the restaurant. 'It'll be a bit of a wait here, but not bad. It's worth it, though. One of the best spots in town.'

'You've eaten here before?' she asked.

'Yeah, a few times. I come to Giglio every year. It's hard to beat this spot, to be fair. It's always packed, and for good reason. Try the whole fish baked in sea salt, if you can. It's the only place on the island that does it.' He pushed his hair back off his face. His skin was lightly tanned, and she was close enough to notice a small scar that ran down one temple. She caught his scent, a woody, musky smell. *Decidedly masculine*, she thought.

'You come to Giglio every year?' she asked.

'Yeah, just for a few days. For the art festival.'

'Oh, I saw a poster for that when we got off the ferry, but I didn't realise it was on now.'

'Tomorrow's the first day. We just got in today.' He gestured in the direction of his friend. 'It runs until Sunday, up at the castle. Actually, its inside the castle walls. Great location.'

'Inside the castle walls?' she repeated.

'Yeah, there's a whole hamlet inside there. It's a pretty cool set-up and they host the art festival every year. It's not on during the day, just the evenings. All the restaurants participate.'

'There are restaurants inside the castle walls?'

'Yeah, it's like a small village up there. The festival started years ago to help promote the restaurants up there, cause otherwise people didn't bother going all the way up. It's a bit of a trek so tourists used to just stay down at the marina or at the beaches. Now it's a whole thing and the restaurants are well known.'

'Sounds fab!' she exclaimed.

'If you go up there, check out the pizzeria. There are a few good restaurants up there, but only one pizzeria and it's one of the best in Italy. Wins all kinds of awards.'

'Oh, wow. I will. Thanks.'

'Jack!' his friend called in a British accent. 'I've got two seats over here.'

The Irishman stepped forward to join his friend, smiling as he brushed passed Emma, his arm lightly grazing her shoulder. 'See ya later.'

'Bye, thanks for the tip,' she replied, turning to watch him leave.

Emma stepped inside and waited for the waiter to turn his attention to her. The small room was completely packed. Emma counted eighteen tables, each of them full, adorned with ice buckets and wine, or multiple menus in anticipation of the same. Waiters scurried to and fro carrying plates of steaming shellfish, platters of grilled fish and bowls of salads. A selection of breads and olive oil was delivered to each table.

'Smells amazing,' Eve said from behind her.

The waiter turned to greet her. *'Buona sera, signore.'*

'*Buona sera.* Um, do you have a table for three?' Emma asked.

The waiter raised both eyebrows and gestured to the three girls. '*Tre?*'

'Yes, three,' she repeated, holding up three fingers. 'We're staying at the hotel. Stefano told us to come here.'

He glanced at the hardback daily planner on the counter. '*Va bene.* Okay. You must wait a little. He scanned the room and looked back at the list of hastily scribbled names. 'Maybe thirty minutes. Maybe a little more.'

'Okay.'

'Your name?' he asked, looking up at Emma.

'Brosnan.'

His pen hesitated over the page.

'Emma.'

'*Bene.*' He added her name to the list. 'You can take a glass of wine and sit there while you wait.' He gestured to the wooden bench that ran along the outside wall of the restaurant.

'Perfect.'

'*Allora*, white wine?'

'Yes, thank you.'

He didn't offer her a wine list, but merely stepped behind the bar and pulled a bottle from the fridge, pouring three generous glasses. '*Questo è fatto in casa.* This wine, we make here in the house.' He handed the glasses to Emma, who passed them back to the girls. The waiter gestured to the hill behind them.

'Oh, cool. Okay, thank you. So should we just come back in thirty minutes?'

'No, no. Relax. I will find you when your table is ready.'

The girls took a seat on the bench, breathing in the briny sea air, the last of the sun's rays warm on their faces. They sat in silence, sipping wine and watching the boats slowly navigate the narrow channel from the marina out into the bay. Emma's phone flashed up with a text message from Maeve.

> OKG. How's Italy?!?!
> Just getting home n0w. Drinks after wrk.
> Will need 2B resusssitatd in the AM
> Cnt tpye. Going 2 bed xx

Emma smiled and turned her phone around to the girls. 'What's OKG?'

Jo squinted at the screen. '"OMG" after a few drinks, I'm guessing.'

'Who were you talking to at the door?' Eve asked.

'An Irish guy. He said this is one of the best restaurants in town and that we should try the whole fish in sea salt. Apparently, they're the only place on the island that does it.'

'Funny to find another Irish person on such a small island in the middle of nowhere.'

'This is good,' Jo said as she sipped the wine. 'We should see if we could visit a vineyard like Stefano said. That would be fun.'

'I never got that whole thing about spitting out the wine,' Eve said. 'I mean, isn't the whole point to actually *taste* the wine? How can you taste it if you just spit it out?'

'Dunno.' Emma shrugged. 'I don't spit it out. I did a wine tasting tour in France once and they had the bucket to spit in, but none of us used it. Left the place with a lovely wine buzz!'

Eve turned towards her. 'Well, those wine tours cost a fortune, so I'd better be leaving with a wine buzz. I'm starving now. Fish. I want some Italian fish. What's the Italian for fish?'

'Why are you asking me?' Jo asked. 'Hang on, I have that translate app thingy on my phone. Fish . . . fish.' She opened the app, selected Italian and tapped her phone. Fish . . . I've no idea how to pronounce this.' She spelled it out: 'P-E-S-C-E.'

'I'm gonna ask the waiter. I want to learn a few words while I'm here,' Emma said. 'I think we should make a bit of an effort.' She thought back to the conversation she'd just had with Jack. He was just a regular Irish guy, and he made the effort to speak some Italian, so why couldn't she? 'Just the important words,' she clarified.

Jo sipped her wine. 'That waiter was cute.'

'Jo, they're all cute.' Eve sighed. 'I mean, Stefano isn't even cute, he's just hot. It's like Italians have some unfair advantage over other men. They're all good-looking, just various degrees of good-looking. Like, there's your basic good-looking Italian guy, then there's the really good-looking ones, followed by the smoulderingly good-looking guys, and then finally there's the guys who are so good-looking that you're already taking off your clothes just looking at them. That's the ultimate level of hotness, when your clothes just come off without thinking about it.'

'Is that your scientific analysis?'

'Yep, it's like the litmus test for men.'

Jo and Emma laughed and the three of them spent the

next thirty minutes discussing their dating history, being careful to avoid Emma's most recent disaster.

'*Signore!*' the waiter called.

'Yes!' Eve exclaimed as she stood up. 'I'm starving! Our first Italian dinner. I'm so excited!'

Emma followed the girls into the restaurant. The room was alive with the hum of happy chatter, the air filled with competing aromas of fresh seafood and decadent pasta sauces. She felt a tingling sensation of excitement at what was about to unfold. Their first dinner, their first night on the island, days of unwinding in the sun, punctuated with food and wine, a castle, a vineyard, an art festival. The familiar feeling of anticipation at the beginning of a holiday, when everything was fresh and unknown and layer by layer you discovered the hidden secrets of a new place. Every meal, every outing, every adventure revealed something different, and day by day the place began to feel more and more familiar.

They followed the waiter to their seats, scanning the tables as they passed, the various dishes and aromas an indication of what was to come. Emma pulled out a chair and sat facing the bay. The boats bobbed gently in the light evening breeze; the water glistened in the softening light. Jo had been right, she thought. It would have been foolish to miss this. She smiled across at her friend, grateful that she had insisted that she come. This trip was about the three of them and an Italian island adventure to celebrate Eve's upcoming wedding. She tugged her chair in closer to the table and took a deep breath. She was in Italy. On an island for a long weekend and she finally felt ready to throw off the shackles that she had been held in for the past few months.

Yep, she thought, as she accepted a menu from the waiter. *I've had enough of being sad. I'm ready to let loose.*

She decided right then that her normal rules about being responsible no longer applied. *The hell with that*; it was time to get back to her real self.

This trip was going to be fun.

CHAPTER FIVE

The first night on Giglio did not disappoint. The waiter had offered them a glass of dry prosecco as a welcome aperitivo and had recommended some of the more popular dishes, explaining that the restaurant was known for simple local fare, and as a result families had been returning for over fifty years. After much debate they settled on two starters – clams sautéed in white wine, garlic and chilli and crudo of sea bream – followed by *spaghetti alle vongole* and sea bass baked in sea salt, with lemon-and-oregano-infused, oven-baked potatoes.

Maria, who had started the restaurant fifty years earlier, still manned the kitchen each evening. Now seventy-five, she had handed the running of the restaurant over to her son, Mario, who ran front of house, but she ardently refused to relinquish control of her kitchen. Most of her kitchen staff had been with her for close to twenty years, but she still insisted on showing up each evening to govern the creation of her now renowned dishes, the most popular, as Jack had mentioned, being the fish baked in sea salt.

The specials menu changed daily, determined by that

morning's catch. Each morning Mario would wait for the fishing boats to arrive back at the marina. The fishermen, with decades of experience, would identify the best of the catch and Mario would pay their asking price, returning to the restaurant with his fresh fish packed on ice in the back of his pickup truck. The specials menu was handwritten daily and was entirely sold out by 9 p.m.

Giglio, like other Italian islands, enjoyed a bountiful array of wild fish, served in a variety of ways, but Maria's preference was to bake whole fish in sea salt. Fish baked in salt wasn't unusual in Italy, but the difference was in Maria's insistence that sea salt imparted a brinier flavour. It cost a little more, but in her estimation, the difference in flavour far outweighed the higher cost. The result was countless awards garnered year after year and a fiercely loyal, and predominantly Italian, clientele keen to enjoy the simple, light Gigliese cuisine.

Over the course of two hours, they had made their way through two bottles of crisp, dry local white wine. The vineyard was so small that it had a maximum production of only nine hundred bottles per year. This was the case with most of the vineyards on Giglio, of which there were only a handful. These small production levels explained why the local wines were not found on wine lists outside of the island. Instead, only locals, and tourists willing to make the journey to Giglio, got to enjoy the fruits of the unique granite soils and high-altitude locations of the vineyards. When he poured the wine for Emma to taste, the waiter had explained that the most unique feature of Gigliese wine is the fact that all of the wines produced on the island were cultivated by hand. The main reason for this being the vertiginous heights and steep climbs to reach the vineyards (many only accessible by foot,) making Gigliese wines all the more rare and special.

Two hours later, sated and content, they paid the bill and made their way back out to the street, with Emma trailing her two friends, each of them fully intent on perusing the selection of shops on their way back to the hotel.

'So, did you get the fish?'

Emma turned in the direction of the voice. Jack was seated at a corner table, tucked away inside the front door.

'Oh hi, yes, it was delicious. I'd never have ordered that, so thanks for telling me. I don't think I've ever had fish like that.'

'Yeah, it's good stuff. Maria's famous for it now,' Jack said. 'Sorry, this is my friend, Blaine. And you're ... ?'

Blaine stood to shake her hand. 'Pleasure to meet you,' he said in a soft London accent.

'I'm Emma. Nice to meet you, Blaine,' she replied. 'And you're Jack.'

'Yep. How long are you here for?'

'We just arrived today. We're here for a hen party for a long weekend.'

'You won't want to leave,' he said confidently. 'No one ever does.'

'Yeah, I can kind of tell that already.'

'First time in Giglio?' Blaine asked.

'Yes.'

'It will get under your skin in a way that nowhere else has ever done. I'm willing to bet on it.'

'So, this isn't your first time either?' she asked Blaine.

'No, I'm lucky enough to have a job that requires me to come back each year for the art festival. I think this is . . . ' He turned to face Jack. 'How many years is it now?'

Jack hesitated. 'Seven. No, it's eight this year, I think.'

He did some mental maths to confirm. 'Yes, eight. Are you girls staying at the hotel?'

'The one at the end of the marina, yes. Is that the only hotel on the island?'

'Yeah. There's an *agriturismo* on the other side of the island. We've stayed there a couple of times. It's nice, it's got kind of a rustic charm. Good hikes around there. Do you like to hike?'

Emma laughed. 'No, I'm not the outdoorsy type and definitely not hiking. I'm more . . . *outsidey*. I like brunch on a nice terrace with a view of the mountains, as opposed to actually climbing them.'

Jack laughed. 'Outsidey. Right. A city girl then, I'm guessing?'

'Yep, guilty. I'm a bona fide city girl. Dublin. I'm guessing you live in the country.'

Blaine laughed. 'Emma, there's country and then there is deep country. Jack here lives in the latter. It takes about twelve hours to reach him from any point in Ireland, and that's if you can manage to find the place at all. Poor Jack, all alone in the depths of the Irish countryside.'

Jack rolled his eyes. 'Kerry is not deep country.'

'No, Kerry in general is not, but the part you chose to reside in, all the way out there in the far west, hanging off the edge of Ireland, that is most certainly deep country. I stand by my statement.'

'First of all, it's south-west, not west. West is Galway or Mayo.' He looked up at Emma. 'Second, it's a five-hour drive from Dublin, not twelve. Nowhere in Ireland is a twelve-hour drive from Dublin, so please feel free to ignore Blaine, he does love to exaggerate. And third,' he said, giving Blaine a shove, 'you forgot about Bentley.'

'You drive a Bentley?' Emma asked, unable to hide the surprise in her voice.

Jack laughed loudly. 'No, my dog's name is Bentley. I don't think there are any Bentleys in Ireland – maybe one or two in Dublin, but definitely none in Kerry.' He ran his right hand through his hair. 'Sorry, what were we talking about? Oh yeah, accommodation here. There are a few guesthouses, but just the one hotel. There are a lot of Airbnb properties here, though. Really good value.'

'For when I come back again, you mean?'

Jack smiled. 'Exactly. Unless of course you're one of the people who fall so in love with the island that they return to buy a house. That happens more than you'd think.'

'Yeah, that's not happening. I could barely afford the flight here,' she replied.

He laughed again, an infectious, throaty laugh. She found herself laughing back.

'Emma!' Eve called out.

'I better go. Nice chatting to you both.'

Jack leaned back and hooked one arm over the back of his chair. 'Enjoy the rest of the evening. If you girls are going to shop, do it in the evenings. They're always keen to offer a bargain and negotiate on price towards the end of the day.'

'You're just full of useful titbits of information.'

'One of many useless talents that I possess,' he said with a grin.

'Well, now I'm just dying to know what the other talents might be,' she said, surprising even herself.

'Stick around and find out,' he said with a wink.

Blaine sat in silence, an amused look on his face. He raised his wine glass to his mouth. 'I feel like I'm on the set of Hugh Grant's next rom-com,' he teased.

Eve stood at the door of the restaurant. 'Emma!' she shouted, oblivious to the stares of the other diners. 'C'mon, the shops are closing in half an hour.'

'Okay, gotta go. Bye.'

She gave a small, awkward wave and followed Eve out the door.

'Who were they?' Eve asked.

'That was the Irish guy I was chatting to when we got to the restaurant earlier, and a friend of his.'

'They're cute. Is he from Dublin?'

'No, he's definitely not the city type,' she replied as they made their way down the street towards the string of shops. 'He lives somewhere in Kerry; don't know where but his friend called it "deep country".'

Eve glanced sideways at her. 'Hmm, interesting. I don't know about deep country, but it seemed like you were in *deep* conversation.'

'Eve,' Emma replied, her tone serious, 'he likes to go on hikes. *Hikes*, imagine! For *fun*.'

'He sounds perfect. Right up your alley,' Eve joked.

'Yeah, right. He's the exact opposite of my idea of the ideal man.'

'Is there such a thing? What does that even look like in real life – the ideal man, I mean?'

Emma turned to face her. 'Um, aren't you about to get married?'

'I'm a realist, Emma. Barry is my forever man, yes; I adore him, but he's not perfect. No one is. You're just lucky if you get to meet someone who's close enough to your own idea of ideal. I mean, I'm self-aware enough to realise that I have my flaws and Barry has his, but I accept that, and I love him regardless. The fact that we've renovated two apartments and raised a four-year-old without killing each other is all the evidence I need.'

'No, I get that, no one is perfect, but that old saying about opposites attract is nonsense. You have to have some qualities in common if you're going to stay the course. That guy Jack is one hundred per cent a country boy, and his idea of an ideal weekend is hiking up the side of a mountain for fun. My preferred weekend activity is a bottomless brunch in the city. Can you imagine someone like him being persuaded to swap one for the other?'

Eve looked at her with a smug grin. 'He's in Italy, isn't he? So, it's not like he's too provincial to travel.'

'Eve, if I'm going to have some kind of wild holiday fling, it's going to be with a hot, suave, well-dressed Italian who'll whisper in my ear all kinds of things I don't understand, and then fling me onto the bed with the prowess that they're renowned for. *That's* what my holiday fling looks like, not an Irish boy with mud on his boots, chopping wood for the fire and going on walks across the field with a bunch of dogs. *And* he didn't even dress for dinner tonight. I mean, he wore flip-flops to the restaurant.'

'What a *travesty*,' Eve said in mock horror. 'The absolute audacity of him to show up at a casual, wooden restaurant on a tiny island whose sign is battered and crooked – the kind of place that uses paper napkins – wearing flip-flops. Red flag! Red flag! *Run away!*'

Emma thumped her on the arm. 'If you want to find me a recovery man, as you keep saying, then focus on the Italians, please.'

'I thought you'd never ask. Emma Brosnan, I'm going to make it my personal mission to find you a man this week; it seems that Jo has sworn off dating for ever, so I'll have to direct my matchmaking skills towards you.' She smiled. 'And being limited to Italian men certainly won't be an obstacle to that goal. This place is literally crawling with hot specimens.'

Emma laughed. 'Operation Italian Recovery Programme! I think you're right. It's time I moved on, so do your best work!'

CHAPTER SIX

Emma woke up to a missed call from Maeve and a series of text messages, this time correctly spelled.

> Am in immense danger of sobering up soon.
> Gonna be a fun day @ work
> Send updates xx

Smiling, she typed back a quick response and tossed her phone in her bag. After a leisurely breakfast, the three girls got ready for their first beach day, deciding to follow the advice Stefano had given them over a nightcap the night before: do the walk and get some steps in ahead of lunch.

An avid runner and fitness fanatic, Jo was without doubt the most athletic of the three. The thirty-minute walk to the beach didn't cost her a thought. For Emma and Eve, however, it was entirely another story.

It had started off easily enough, with the girls following the path beyond the marina that wound up past the church, but the extent of the trek became apparent as they left the small village behind and faced a steep incline up and around the side of a hill. As Stefano had said, there was a path, but he had failed to mention that the path was almost vertical.

'Are you serious?' Emma asked, as she eyed the hill before her.

'I thought it was an easy thirty-minute walk to the beach. This is *not* that,' Eve grumbled.

'Oh, come on, you two; it's fine,' Jo insisted as she started off ahead of them.

They took to the hill at an ambitious speed, one that was soon tempered as they reached the curve in the road only to see another incline laid out ahead. Fifteen minutes later, Emma and Eve were out of breath, hauling themselves slowly towards the top of the second hill, trailing behind Jo.

'Show off,' Eve mumbled. 'She could at least wait for us.'

'I'm not talking right now,' Emma said, breathing deeply. 'I can only do one of the two, climb or talk, so talking is out. This is why I live in a city. Public transport options.'

'Right. Same.'

They climbed the rest of the hill in silence and were rewarded grandly for their efforts with a spectacular view of a beach nestled into the curve of the cliffs several hundred metres below. The small strip of sand looked like a golden croissant; the turquoise water lapped gently, its blue hues punctuated by a half-dozen white sailing boats. The cliff face was covered in dense, lush green growth, peppered with clusters of brazenly coloured wildflowers. The sea breeze whispered as it coiled up and around the curved arc of the tall, granite cliffs. The girls stood in silence, transfixed, words held captive by the sheer natural beauty that extended before them.

Eve was the first to speak as she and Emma caught up to Jo. 'Is this for real?'

'Wow,' Jo said quietly.

Emma stared out at the horizon, the water morphing from iridescent turquoise to a deeper blue, with slashes of frothy white wakes cutting through as boats traversed over and back. 'It's raw, that's what it is. Totally, and unapologetically wild.' She breathed in the sea air. 'What did Stefano say last night about the beaches? I was only half listening. Something about one of them not having a restaurant?'

'Yeah, it looks like that's the first beach down there, the one without the restaurant. That means our beach is only another ten minutes away, or at least that's what he told us,' Jo said. She adjusted her sunhat. 'And from the looks of things, the rest of it is downhill.'

'Hallelujah!' Eve said appreciatively.

'Thank God,' Emma said.

The next ten minutes was painless as they made their way down the other side of the hill. As they rounded the bend towards the bottom of the hill, they could see flashes of blue sea through the thinning trees, like a beacon beckoning them forward. Local taxis buzzed in and out, each van emblazoned with the name of the proprietor and his phone number. Eve took a photo of one, declaring the return trek back up the hill later in the day unnecessary.

They made their way around the path to the other side of the restaurant, the view opening up to the beach below with four orderly lines of blue-and-white beach loungers and navy umbrellas, their ruffled fringes flapping madly in the sea breeze. Children darted in and out of the water, shrieking with delight, as their guardians kept a watchful eye. Couples and small groups of Italians stood ankle deep in the water, soaking up the sun and accelerating the tanning process with the sun's reflection on the water.

The dining area, with its bare, sun-bleached wooden floorboards and simple wooden tables and chairs, was empty. A waiter swept sand from the floorboards back out onto the beach with a long-bristled broom, as another wrote the daily specials on the chalkboard menu. The girls peered inside at the bar, and the restaurant beyond it, the whole place oozing casual, bohemian beach vibes.

Emma stepped inside to get a better look. A bartender was polishing wine glasses behind the bar, an element of finesse in such a casual environment that was testament to the serious nature of food and wine in Italy, regardless of the circumstances.

'*Buongiorno, signora.*'

'*Buongiorno.* Do you speak English?'

'*Certo, signora.* Of course.'

'Um, we're just going to get some beach chairs. What time do you open for lunch?'

The bartender nodded towards the restaurant. 'The restaurant it will open at twelve for the lunch. But the bar is open now.'

'Great, we'll be back in a little while.'

'*Va bene*, I wait you here,' he said with a smile, as he turned his attention back to the glasses.

Jo stepped down onto the sand and tugged her sundress

over her head, her auburn hair waving wildly behind her. Within moments, a beach attendant in a white T-shirt and red shorts jogged up the beach towards them.

His face broke into a wide smile as he blatantly looked her up and down, taking in every inch of her svelte figure. '*Buongiorno, signora. Un lettino?*'

'Oh, sorry,' Jo said. 'I don't speak Italian.'

'No sorry, *signora*. Is not a problem, I speak English. You would like the beach chair?'

'Yes, three, please.'

'*Va bene*. Okay, follow me. I have three chairs in front of the sea.'

He turned to walk down towards the sea, with the three girls following him across the warm white sand. He deftly flipped all three chairs on their side to knock off errant sand and reclined the backs. 'You want the umbrellas?'

'Just one is fine, thank you.'

'*Prego, signora,*' he replied as he erected one umbrella, casting shade over two loungers.

The girls arranged their bags in the shade of the umbrella and flopped back gratefully onto the loungers. Eve tutted as she answered her phone.

'Now what?' she mumbled.

'Hello?' After a short pause she continued. 'For God's sake, Barry, he's four. It goes with the territory. I told you to call me if it was an emergency. This doesn't qualify. Not even close. In fact, this whole conversation is a joke, and this is me hanging up on you. Figure it out. Bye.'

Eve rolled her eyes as she turned to face Emma. 'He's unbelievable.'

'What happened?'

'Life. That's what happened. My soon-to-be husband is totally hapless.'

Jo grinned. 'I know he's super intelligent, but the poor man is really bad at coping with life in general, isn't he?'

'Don't even start,' Eve said. 'He called me so that I could tell Robert to get dressed. Barry said he's refusing to put on a shirt. He doesn't like buttons. It's just his thing. The child doesn't like dealing with buttons. I don't know how Barry has gone four years without realising this.'

Jo handed her the bottle of suncream. 'Maybe that's because you deal with it on the regular and he doesn't have to. You're enabling Barry's reliance on you by not forcing him to cope with the domestic stuff more often.'

'Maybe,' Eve conceded. 'Anyway, so Robert is throwing a fit, refusing to get dressed, then starts sobbing, then Barry tries to rationalise the situation and insists that he put on the shirt, and Robert gets so worked up that he vomits, at which point Barry calls me to intervene. A normal person would just put a T-shirt on the child. It's not like he's going to Wall Street.'

She sighed deeply, lathering suncream on her face. 'I'm just telling you right now that I'm going to lie here for a minute to calm down and then I'm going directly to the bar to get a glass of wine. Don't judge me.'

'Girl, this is a no-judgement zone,' Jo said from behind her sunglasses.

The remainder of the morning passed in a blissful state of languor. Eve sat on the terrace with a glass of wine for 'medicinal purposes', while Emma and Jo alternated between relaxing on the loungers and taking a dip in the calm blue waters of the bay. By twelve thirty they were more than ready for lunch and made their way to the outdoor deck. A waitress showed them to a table, handed them menus and explained that food and drinks were to be selected inside, and if they ordered pizza, they would take a number back to their table to facilitate the delivery of the pizza in due course.

All three of them logged into the restaurant's free Wi-Fi but it soon became clear that with only one bar of signal, internet connectivity was not a priority on this Italian beach. They joined the long, snaking queue of people shuffling forward in bare feet or flip-flops towards the buffet counter. Not a single word of English was spoken; the crowd was exclusively Italian.

As they reached the first refrigerated buffet display, the girls craned their necks to see the food options. Bulbous balls of fresh buffalo mozzarella, bowls of ruby-red vine-ripened tomatoes, octopus salad, shrimp skewers, crisp, green salad leaves drizzled with extra-virgin olive oil and mini plates loaded with prosciutto and melon.

The hot plates were equally delectable, with options ranging from *spaghetti pomodoro* sprinkled with basil; penne with a rich aubergine sauce, served with grated *ricotta salata* cheese; seafood lasagne; golden breaded chicken cutlets and pork *scallopini* in a white wine and lemon sauce. Baskets of freshly baked bread sat on the countertop alongside heaped bowls of finely grated parmesan cheese.

The pizza oven stood at the back of the room, its heat cranking at more than four-hundred degrees Celsius, filling the air with the aroma of freshly baked pizzas. A large chalkboard overhead listed the daily options as two *pizzaioli* took turns to twirl the dough, layer the ingredients and haul thin-crusted pizzas with bubbling tomato and cheese sauce from the cavernous brick oven.

A second bottle of wine was ordered as they languished in the warm afternoon sun. Eventually returning to their loungers, Eve declared it the perfect time for a post-prandial nap, and the only necessary exertion for the afternoon was a refreshing dip in the bay.

Later, as they stuffed their belongings into their beach bags, they agreed unanimously that Italians had life figured out, that simple pleasures were underrated, and that all three of them were now fully considering blowing up their lives in search of the Italian dream.

Back at the hotel, after a quick shower and change, the girls reconvened at the bar. Eve sat down with a sigh. 'God, I could totally live here.'

'Except you have to go home and get married. Speaking of which ... ' Jo said, reaching into her bag. 'I think it's about time we got you decked out like the blushing bride-to-be that you are.' She pulled out a bright white, waist-length veil, adorned with a sparkly, plastic tiara clip.'

'Oh, Jesus, you didn't. I thought we were too old for this shit.'

Jo laughed. 'There was no way I was going to pass up the opportunity to make a holy show of you. Girl, you're gonna wear this veil loud and proud.'

Eve groaned as Jo stood up and plunged the tiara hair-clip into her hair. A cheer went up around the bar.

'Bar stools!' Jo shouted as she spied three vacant spots.

Stefano laughed as the girls approached. 'Is better at the bar, no? Eve, you look very beautiful.'

'Oh my God, you look ridiculous,' Emma said, laughing as she took a seat alongside Jo.

'Why do I feel like I'm going to be the source of entertainment for the next few days?' Eve asked.

'Because you are,' Emma replied frankly as the conversation turned to plans for the evening.

An hour later, having convinced Jo and Eve to check out the art festival before dinner, Emma signed the bill. She followed the girls as they dashed downstairs to an awaiting Ottavio, who sat patiently in his white minibus, promising to rejoin Stefano for a nightcap at the bar before closing time.

They left the bustling piazza behind them and took the only road out of the village, passing the old white church, its paint and plaster crumbling in patches. Its doors were still wide open, even at this late hour, a lingering invitation for prayer completely ignored by the group of local children playing an impromptu game of football under its auspices. The road began to curve and wind up and around the hill, the landscape become wilder and more desolate, with dust swirling among parched trees, the tarmacadam relinquishing its grip and morphing into a rugged dirt road. The castle, tucked behind protective walls, towered over the island, dominating the view ahead and looming ever larger as they approached. Twenty minutes later, Ottavio came to a stop in front of a small church. He pointed towards the narrow cobblestoned road that would lead them inside the castle walls.

The twenty-foot-tall walls seemed to engulf them as they entered the interior, their voices echoing against the thousands-of-years-old crumbling stone.

Immediately inside sat a fruit and vegetable shop, the faded lettering on its lopsided overhead sign impossible to read. Wicker baskets sat on display in front of the shop window, brimming with summer peaches, plums, apricots, a variety of tomatoes, plump aubergines and a selection of leafy greens. Across from it was the bakery, its shelves now empty, its proprietor closing the shutters and locking the door, deep in conversation with the greengrocer who leaned against his doorframe, both completely oblivious to the tourists shuffling by. It quickly became apparent that the area within the castle walls was residential, a warren-like hamlet completely invisible from the outside. Adults sat on doorsteps and leaned out of windows, while children kicked balls or chased one another in and out of neighbouring houses. Ground-floor kitchen windows were flung open as dinnertime got under way, the aroma of garlic and onions wafting out, and large pots of water bubbling furiously on stovetops.

The girls looked from left to right at the unexpectedly domestic scene, as they continued up the steep incline towards the base of the castle. An olive-green Vespa was parked haphazardly outside the window of a coin-operated laundromat with three out of the four industrial-sized machines in operation. They watched as a young woman piled freshly laundered clothes into a reusable blue IKEA bag, swung it over her shoulders and climbed back onto her Vespa.

Following the crowd ahead, they rounded a bend. The castle, previously obscured, now stood in dominant position, with a sweeping view of the island below and the bay beyond.

Towering several storeys above them, its gigantic, solid wooden doors firmly shut, the castle cast a shadow over the side of the hill. Obligatory group selfies were taken, with the expansive view of the island providing a stunning backdrop and several shots of Eve in front of the castle, proud bride-to-be, her waist-length bridal veil billowing in the wind behind her. On the other side of the castle, they stumbled upon a small bar with four outdoor tables, one of which freed up as the girls approached.

'C'mon, let's grab a quick drink here before we hit the art festival,' Emma suggested. 'This place is adorable.'

The building that housed the bar, just like every other building within the castle walls, was built entirely of solid stone.

Rustic would be a kind way of describing it, Emma thought as she stepped into the cool, dark interior; basic was more appropriate. Bar was also a stretch, as she was about to find out.

The old lady behind the counter stood up slowly as she approached. Emma ordered three glasses of white wine, astonished when she wrote six euros on a notepad, turning it around to face her. The lady poured from a large, unmarked glass bottle into three small tumblers before reaching under the counter to pull out a large battered baking tray loaded with roasted garlic crostini. The aroma of garlic wafted up towards Emma as the woman landed it heavily on the countertop, before scooping nine pieces of crostini onto a paper plate, drizzling them with extra-virgin olive oil and sprinkling them with sea salt.

'*Ecco*,' she said, as she pushed the paper plate across the counter.

Emma placed the three glasses and plate of crostini on a plastic tray. '*Grazie.*'

'*Prego, signora,*' she replied, before sitting back down.

'Okay, three glasses of very dodgy-looking wine here, girls, but it's only two euro a glass, so cheers to that.'

'Yeah,' Jo said, having taken a sip. 'Not exactly an award-winning situation either, but it's not the worst I've ever had.' She turned her chair sideways to face the view, the sound of metal scraping on the flagstones echoing against the walls. 'That's some view, though.'

'Stunning,' Eve said. 'Can I take this thing off before we go to the art festival? I'll look like an awful clown otherwise.'

'Only if you promise to put it back on when we go to dinner after.'

'Oh my God, are you serious? Can't you wait until later to make a fool of me? I'm not going to wear this every day, you know. Most people only have to wear these things for a night.'

'We'll determine that, thank you very much,' Emma said. She grimaced as she sipped the wine. 'What will we do for dinner? That Irish guy, Jack, said the pizzeria up here is insanely good. Fancy trying that tonight?'

'Pizza in Italy is never *not* a good idea,' Jo admitted. 'Sounds good to me.'

Eve scrunched up her nose. 'Jesus, this is dreadful. Are you really going to drink it?'

'It's grand, just a bit dry,' Jo said, tipping back the rest of the glass. 'I'll drink yours if you don't want it.'

'Well, there's no need to be dramatic. I didn't say that I wasn't going to drink it, just that it was kind of dreadful.'

'Stop talking about it and hurry up and finish it,' Emma said. 'I want to get to the art festival.'

Eve stood up, tipped back the glass of wine and tugged the plastic tiara from her ponytail, winding the cheap veil around her hand and sticking it in her bag. 'Okay, let's go and be cultured for a minute.'

CHAPTER SEVEN

At the top of the hill, a vast piazza opened in front of them, its entire perimeter lined with stall after stall of art displays. Emma gasped as she took in the sight before her. She had expected maybe a dozen or so artists displaying their wares, but not this. It seemed inconceivable that such a small island could play host to such an overwhelming number of artists.

The early-evening sun cast a warm orange glow over the piazza, the hum of the crowd combined with birdsong playing a happy soundtrack overhead. Her eyes roved the lines of art displays – paintings, sketches, pottery, sculpture, wooden creations, metal creations, traditional art, modern art.

Her face lit up as she took in the scene.

This was her true passion; a world that brought her absolute joy when she gave herself permission to get lost in it, a world she had been denying herself properly for so many years. Too many financial constraints, too much temptation to cede to the corporate world and trade her passion for a salary, trade joy for a guaranteed income. Her job in finance and the salary it provided afforded her the ability to live a comfortable life in the city: the nice apartment, the city-appropriate wardrobe updated with monthly Penneys runs and online ASOS orders, holidays with the girls and restaurants several times a week. She was a fully subscribed urbanite, but the trade-off was the deep sense of dread every Sunday, knowing that she had to show up again the next day to a job that she, at best, tolerated, at times, despised.

It made her heart sing to be surrounded now, in this moment, by all these various forms of art. A display of delicate watercolours caught her eye, abstract interpretations of classic European landscapes: fields of lavender in the south of France, towering cypress trees in Tuscany, tulip farms in the Netherlands. She chatted with the artist for a few minutes, a British woman who had been coming to Giglio on holidays for many years, and who was eventually inspired to participate in the art festival and showcase her own work.

'I've always been a painter; my house is full of canvases,' she said to Emma. 'I was just never brave enough to put my work on display for other people to see, or critique.'

'I think that's brilliant. I love to paint too, but I haven't in ages. I – I've been too busy with work,' she said, stumbling over the mistruth.

'I used to say the same thing, about not having the time to paint, until one day a friend pointed out that that was just a story I told myself. I was allowing myself to not feel bad about ignoring the call to paint because I was able to blame work. When I finally heard that, it felt so uncomfortable that I did something about it, and I picked up the brush again.'

Emma smiled. 'Yeah, that's probably what I'm doing too,

if I'm honest. But I'm not nearly as good as you. I'm not a professional, it's just a hobby.'

'Oh, this isn't my job, it's just a hobby and I make a holiday out of this trip every year. I'm a teacher so I get the summers off. That's when I paint.'

'Oh,' Emma replied. 'I just assumed that everyone here was a full-time professional artist.'

'Most of them are. Some of them are really good, but there are a few of us who just do it because we really love it. A group of us come every year.'

'Actually, I met someone down at the marina last night and he said he has been coming here for years too. Jack something, an Irish guy. Is he one of your group?'

She laughed. 'Jack Bourke?'

'I didn't get his last name.'

'Well, if he's Irish then it must be Jack Bourke. No, he's not one of our group. Jack is on a whole other level.'

Emma frowned. 'What do you mean?'

'Jack Bourke is the famous Irish sculptor. He goes by JB.'

Emma hesitated for a moment as realisation dawned on her. 'Oh my God, of course. I thought he looked familiar, but I didn't put two and two together. *He's* JB?'

'Yes, that's him. He's such a lovely person and he's not all that comfortable with the spotlight, but he's smart enough to know that he needs to put up with it in order to further his career and build a following. I'd say he's one of the most successful artists here by a mile.'

'Wow, I had no idea. I've been following his work for years.'

'Yes, he's an incredible talent. You should go and find him, see his new pieces. They're quite astonishing.'

'Do you know where his display is?'

'Of course.' She turned around and pointed to the furthest corner. 'There, right in the corner of the piazza.'

'Great, thank you. It's been lovely talking to you.'

'You too. Maybe I'll see you back here next year.'

Emma smiled. 'Now that would be the dream.'

She made her way down along the line of artist displays, passing jewellery artists, ceramic artists, photographers and portrait painters on her way to the corner of the piazza. She recognised his work instantly, his pieces exclusively modelled from the landscape of rural Ireland, a feature that had endeared him to the Irish public and afforded him the opportunity to build a strong following within the Irish art community.

There were no egos among those who had 'made it' in the arts in Ireland. In fact, the opposite was mostly true: most artists expressed a humility and a gratitude for the support shown to them in their early endeavours, which ultimately allowed them to build a successful career. Emma knew from reading several of his interviews that no one was humbler than the famous Irish sculptor, JB. His work had been commissioned by luminary figures across Europe and displayed in prominent galleries in Paris, Madrid, Milan and beyond. His works took pride of place in Irish embassies around the world, and he generously donated pieces each year to Irish charities in support of their fundraising initiatives.

Standing as close as she dared to his display, she leaned forward to examine one of his latest pieces up close, a three-foot-long, alabaster sculpture of a wild Irish hedgerow, resplendent with wildflowers, bending in concession to the ever-present Irish wind.

Her eyes followed the soft curve of the grasses, the tilted heads of the ubiquitous Montbretia wildflowers that graced ditches and hedgerows along country lanes in the west of Ireland from July through September each year. The level of detail was exquisite, the sense of reality unparalleled, something for which JB was renowned.

The voice came from alongside her. 'Hard to believe that you can make a living from ditches and hedges, isn't it?'

She turned to see him standing over her. His eyes locked with hers. 'Oh, hi,' was all she could think to say.

He wore shorts and flip-flops and a Japanese Manga character T-shirt. He sipped from a bottle of water. 'I wasn't sure you were going to show up. I thought you three would be hanging out on boats and beaches for the next few days.'

'We did the beach thing today, and we probably will again tomorrow, but I wanted to see the art festival. I thought it was just some kind of local, summer thing. I didn't realise I'd be in the company of art royalty,' she teased.

'Ha! Far from royalty,' he laughed loudly.

'I didn't know you were *the* JB when we met down at the marina. Here I was thinking you were just this ordinary guy called Jack, not the internationally renowned sculptor.'

'Well,' he said, twisting the lid on the plastic bottle, 'that's precisely the reason I don't introduce myself that way. Plus, I'd feel like such a knob. It's bad enough being known as JB. Sounds totally pretentious, but I'm stuck with it now.'

'What do you mean "stuck with it"? You didn't call yourself JB as an artist name?'

'Jesus, no. Are you joking? Go around calling myself

by my initials just for the hell of it in County Kerry? I'd be shot. No, there were two Jack Bourkes in school. The other fella's surname was spelled B-U-R-K-E, I had the letter O in my name, so I became known as "Smelly Jack" with the BO.' He shook his head. 'If I was ever in therapy, I'd refer to that as a really bad period of my life.' He grinned.

Emma laughed. 'That's mean. Kids are the worst.'

'Yeah, so one of my friends started calling me JB. He was bigger and stronger than the other Jack, the one without the O, so it was kind of accepted and thankfully that one stuck.'

'You should use that in one of your interviews. You'd go viral.'

'Ah, stop.' He shook his head again, staring directly into her eyes. 'I can't think of anything worse.' He gestured to the neighbouring stalls and displays. 'These things are grand – these art exhibitions and festivals. The people who come here do so because they *want* to, because they're curious or interested in art, but the online stuff is brutal. I do as little as possible and only because I have to. My agent, Blaine – the guy I was having dinner with last night at the marina – gives me grief every few weeks for not being online. I hate it, but it's kind of expected, so I just do the bare minimum to keep him happy for another while. The internet can be a cesspit, especially Twitter, or whatever it's called now. People can be downright mean on that thing. I gave that one up.' He grinned again. 'I've no time for that kind of negative shit.'

She forced herself to focus on his words as he smiled at her. He stood so close that she could smell his scent again.

He pushed up one sleeve and scratched his arm, his skin beginning to flake over an inky black tattoo.

'Sunburn,' he explained. 'You think I'd know better by now. Irish skin.'

'What's the tattoo?' she asked, surprising herself at the personal question.

He laughed. 'It's a long story. When I started getting into sculpting properly, like, getting into it as a career, I got the piss taken out of me by the lads back at home. They told me I should go and get a real job. So, I started going to the gym and working out and got a tattoo to prove to someone … them and probably myself, that I was still tough. Kinda stupid, but I was only twenty-three at the time and I still gave a shit what other people thought.'

'You don't now?'

'God, no. That's exhausting. I gave up caring what other people think years ago. Now I do what I love, I take care of the people in my life, and my dog, and I engage with the people who like and appreciate my work. After that, they can all go to hell.'

She hung on the words 'people in my life' and found herself wondering who they might be. He didn't wear a wedding ring, but then many men didn't. She'd have to Google this fact later.

An older lady in a black linen sheath dress and black sandals shuffled towards them and came to a stop in front of his display.

'*Buona sera, sempre bellissima. Bellissima!*' she exclaimed.

'*Buona sera, Signora Rossi. Come stai? Tutto bene?*' He put his arms around her in a gentle, warm embrace. 'How's everything? All good?'

'Yes, yes, all is good. I am happy to see you again. Every year I am happy to see you and the work that you do. So beautiful. One year you will return here to Giglio, and I will be dead.'

'Nah, sure you're only a young woman yet.'

'No, I am too old,' she said with a smile. She placed a hand on his chest.

'You are strong, Jack. This is good. You must stay strong.' She turned to face Emma and looked back at Jack inquisitively. 'This is your friend?'

'Oh sorry, Emma, this is my dear friend, Signora Rossi. She lived in London for ages, so her English is great. She moved back to Giglio years ago and has been coming to see me here every year. Emma and I met yesterday at a restaurant down at the marina.'

The old lady turned to look at her directly. 'You also like art?'

'Oh, yes, I love it. I know Jack's work from back home in Ireland.'

'Ah, an Irish girl. The Irish people they are great artists, great writers. You are an artist also?'

'No, no. I love art but I'm not an artist. I mean, I love to paint, but it's just a hobby, not my job. I don't have time for it, but I love it, and I appreciate other people's art.'

The old lady tapped her arm. 'If you love it, then you must make time for it. You must make time for the things that you love in life before it is too late. God gives us talents to share with the world, not to hide. If you are good at it, then you must do it. Many other people would be very happy to have a talent, so it is a great disrespect if you have one and do not use it.'

'I hadn't thought of it like that, but there's no way I'm as good as Jack. I just like to sketch, and I do some watercolours.'

'Comparison is the thief of joy, my dear. You must not compare yourself to other people, you must be yourself and do your own work. Nobody else can.' She leaned forward and inspected Jack's hedgerow piece, gently touching the curves and edges.

Jack turned back to Emma. 'What kind of stuff do you sketch?'

'Mostly landscapes. Kind of abstract.' She shrugged. It felt uncomfortable to talk about her art efforts in front of someone so accomplished.

'Can I see some? Do you have any pictures of your work?' he asked, genuinely curious. 'I can't sketch to save my life. Too detailed for me, too intricate. I get away with much more in sculpture.'

'Oh, I don't even know if I have any photos,' she said shyly.

'Wait, I do,' Jo said, as she came to stand alongside her. She pulled out her phone. 'Looks like I showed up just in time; Emma here is the worst self-promoter I know. This is one of my favourites. Here,' she said, extending the phone to Jack.

He took the phone and zoomed in on the photo. It was a black-and-white sketch of a woman's head, the whole upper part of her face and her hair obscured by a cluster of butterflies. He looked up from the phone at Emma, and back down at the photo, zooming in further.

Emma turned to look around her. 'Where's Eve?'

'Over there buying something, I think,' Jo replied. She nodded her head to the left. 'Here she comes.'

'This is good,' Jack said, his eyes not leaving the screen. 'This is *really* good. Was this your idea? I mean, was it your concept?'

She blushed at the compliment and the attention. 'Yeah, I just thought that it was like her mind was full of beauty, or beautiful thoughts.'

'I like it. I like the piece itself, but I also like the concept behind it.' He handed the phone back to Jo and extended his hand to her. 'Hi, I'm Jack.'

'Oh, I know who you are,' Jo said, shaking his hand. 'You're the famous sculptor. I saw you on *The Late Late Show* one night.'

He grinned. 'Jesus, yeah, you know you've made it in Ireland when you're on *The Late Late*. I'll never live that down in Kerry. So, are you the bride-to-be?'

'Oh, God, no. There's another one around here somewhere. That's her life sentence, not mine.'

Jack laughed loudly, something that Emma noted he did often and easily. Signora Rossi patted Jack on the arm. '*Bellissima. Veramente bellissima.*' She looked up at him and smiled. '*Bravo.*'

He smiled at the gracious compliment. '*Grazie.*' He leaned down and gave her an air kiss on both cheeks. 'Make sure you come back and see me again. *A dopo.*'

'I will be back every evening. *Arrivederci.*'

'Your Italian is brilliant,' Emma said. 'What did you say to her just now? What did that mean?'

'*A dopo?* It kind of means "see ya later".'

Three British women approached Jack's display and asked him about his latest piece.

He turned to Emma. 'I better get back to work. Maybe

I'll see you guys down at the marina again one evening. There's another restaurant you should try before you leave, La Vecchia Pergola. It's close to your hotel, and they do really good shellfish dishes. Hang on, I've got their number in my phone.'

The British women waited patiently as Emma made a note of the restaurant on her phone.

'Okay, thanks. We'll let you get back to work.'

As they strolled away, Emma turned back to see Jack engaged in small talk with the women. It was clear that they were already charmed.

'Well, knock me down with a feather. What was that?' Jo asked.

Emma looked at her, confused. 'What was what?'

'I mean, I've heard of sparks between people, but that, my friend, was a full-on flame. Holy shit!'

'Oh, my God! You noticed it too?' Eve squealed.

'What are you talking about?'

'Jack! And *you*!' Jo continued. 'I'll be damned if that guy couldn't take his eyes off you. The temperature got about five degrees warmer just standing there.'

'Oh, don't be ridiculous,' Emma replied. 'You two are just so determined to see me move on from Paul you'll happily invent a man's interest in me.'

Jo pursed her lips. 'Oh no, sister. You mark my words. Either mercury is back in lemonade and I've got this all wrong or you've not seen or heard the end of Jack Bourke just yet.'

Emma continued in silence, not wanting to fan the flames of the conversation any further, but secretly delighted that Jo and Eve seemed to believe that they had witnessed some sort of chemistry. Jack was confident, but not cocky, worldly but not obnoxious. He was clearly a Type-A Alpha male, used to being in control, used to being in charge.

She glanced over her shoulder again and watched as the British women laughed at something he said. He most definitely wasn't her type, a bona fide country man who knew his place in the world and didn't need another human being for anything. Emma, in contrast, needed to be needed. She needed someone to need her, like Paul had. She knew that about herself by now and knew that there was no way she could be with someone as independent and confident as Jack Bourke, who was content to live a quiet life in the country. But that aside, she was damned if there wasn't something very compelling about him.

Just then he looked in her direction, caught her eye and winked. That was all it took. Her face flushed and her stomach gave an automatic upside-down flip. There was no denying it and it was hugely inconvenient, but she knew that despite all the logical reasons against it, it wouldn't take much for Jack Bourke to get under her skin.

CHAPTER EIGHT

The pizzeria was full and had a waitlist of at least an hour. Emma pulled rank and announced that they should return to the marina and plan a trip to the pizzeria another evening, so they hopped in a taxi, rattling and bouncing back down to the bottom of the hill. Emma dialled the number for La Vecchia Pergola, delighted to secure a table in thirty minutes' time.

Eve chatted animatedly about her wedding to-do list, while Emma sat quietly for the remainder of the journey, her thoughts racing. Had she been wrong not to have pursued her passion for painting? She thought of all the people she had seen exhibiting their art, and apart from the group from the UK who made it a holiday each year, for whom it was a passion project, the majority of the exhibitors were making a serious living out of the arts.

Questions swirled in her mind.

Why had she given up on it all those years ago? Why had she been so convinced that there was no future in it? Was she even any good?

Jack had responded positively to the photo Jo had shown

him, but was he just being kind? How could she tell? Was it worth pursuing now? How would she even begin?

She couldn't afford to quit her job, so she'd need to put some sort of plan in place if she were to even consider it in the next few years.

Or was it all just a pipe dream? In the middle of this Italian island, which was in itself magical, it was hard to discern reality.

She sighed loudly as the taxi slowed to a stop in the piazza.

You're such a bloody cliché, Emma, she thought. *You go on holiday to Italy and want to change your life.*

It was just like that movie, with the American actress – what was her name? – Diane Lane. She went on a gay bus tour of Tuscany, even though she wasn't gay, saw a villa she couldn't afford, which would require a total renovation, bought it and found a bunch of Polish lads to renovate it for her, and magically ended up living the dream in her magnificent Tuscan villa.

She shook her head and stepped from the taxi.

Nonsense, she thought. The castle walls had clearly spun some wizardry and got her all worked up. Now that she was back down at sea level she could see straight again.

'Madness,' she mumbled.

'What's madness?' Eve asked.

'Oh, nothing. Just thinking about stuff.'

After a swift glass of wine, the girls checked in at the restaurant. The owner greeted them warmly, sat them at a table in the corner and gestured towards a waiter who poured them each a welcome glass of prosecco. Emma looked around the room. Every other table was full.

Ravenous now, they quickly settled on some shared appetisers: grilled red shrimp, clams oreganata and mussels sautéed in garlic and white wine. Eve, determined to maintain some level of control over her pre-wedding diet, ordered the warm lobster salad, while Emma and Jo opted to share *spaghetti alle vongole* and *spaghetti allo scoglio*, which the waiter had said was a house special: a mixture of shrimp, clams, octopus and calamari cooked in a spicy tomato sauce. He didn't ask their opinion on wine, but merely showed up tableside with a bottle of white from the hills behind them. Light, fragrant and dry, it was the perfect accompaniment to the seafood feast and the girls powered through the first bottle with the appetiser courses alone.

The atmosphere was festive as groups of locals and tourists alike devoured steaming bowls of seafood and bottles of ice-cold, crisp dry wine. Laughter and conversation filled the air, the volume increasing by the hour. The girls' conversation ran the gamut of wedding outfits and plans for the remainder of the trip.

Eve raised her two hands and looked from Emma to Jo. 'Okay, I have something to say.'

'Oh God,' Emma said.

'Can't wait,' Jo said sarcastically. 'Are we going to need another bottle of wine for this conversation?'

Eve shook her head, leaned forward and picked up her wine glass. 'No, I'm serious, and I think I've had just enough to drink to be able to have this conversation with both of you. I've wanted to say this for *ages*, but I didn't.'

Her words were slurring ever so slightly.

'Okay.' She turned to face Emma. 'Emma, I know what

happened with Paul was terrible. Awful. He's a total prick and I'll never forgive him, but I think it's time that you moved on. I know you're still all sad over the way things ended, but honestly, I think it's time you put it behind you and forgot about him. Look,' she said. She put her glass back onto the table and leaned towards Emma. 'You need to meet someone else. You need a hook-up, a fling, something ... *anything*. I don't care who it's with, but you've got to put another man between you and Paul and that whole fucking mess.'

She turned to Jo. 'And you. I know you say you're quite happy on your own, but I don't believe you. I think that's a story that you're telling yourself, and us too, to make it okay that you're not making any effort to meet anyone. Jo, you don't go out in Dublin unless it's with us. Look at you!' She gestured with her hand up and down. 'I mean, you're gorgeous. You're totally stunning, a fiery redhead, and what are you doing about the fact that you're still single? Nothing.'

'Maybe she's fine with it,' Emma argued, draining the last of her wine. 'Not everyone wants to get married, Eve. I'm happy for you, but I'm definitely not in the running for marriage anytime soon, and maybe Jo feels the same way. Not everyone ends up in a happy-ever-after twosome. Some people are single most of their lives and totally fine with it.'

She looked to Jo for a response and frowned. 'What's that face for?' she asked.

'What face?' Jo replied, her cheeks flushing.

Emma squinted at her. 'That face; that smug smile that you're trying to hide. I know you. What are you not saying?'

Eve gasped. 'Have you met someone?'

Jo allowed the smile to cross her face. She nodded.

'What the—' Emma stopped herself from swearing out loud. 'Who? When? How long has this been going on and when were you planning on telling us?'

'I was going to tell you on this trip. I was just waiting for the right moment.'

'Well, now's as good a time as any!' Eve shouted.

Diners at the next table turned their heads.

'Shh, keep it down,' Emma said. She squinted at Jo. 'Wait, why were you waiting for the right moment? What gives, Jo?'

'Oh my God, is it someone we know? Someone *famous*?' Eve squealed.

Emma hissed at her. 'Will you for the love of God stop squealing and let her speak!'

'Sorry, okay, go on. This is all just too exciting!'

Jo looked down at the table, her face serious now. 'It's actually kind of serious. I've known him for a couple of years through work, but we got together about four months ago.'

'*Four months!*' both girls shrieked.

The diners at the adjacent table looked their way again.

Sorry, Emma mouthed, as she caught one woman's eye. 'You've been seeing someone for four months and you've not told us about him? Is he in jail or something?'

'No,' Jo said. She looked directly at Emma. 'But he's married.'

It felt like the scene in a movie when the camera zoomed in and the room began to spin around the protagonist, right before she passed out.

Emma's mouth went dry. She heard Eve make a sound alongside her, something like a gasp, but more audible, more guttural. She blinked twice, three times. She couldn't form any words; it was as if her brain had frozen still and emptied. She stared at Jo but couldn't find – couldn't grasp – the words.

Jo spoke first. 'Emma, I know what you must be thinking, but honestly, this is completely different. It's nothing like what happened to you. I'm in love with him and he's in love with me and we're going to find a way to—'

'He's *married*?' Emma repeated.

'Yes.'

'But how can you be with him if he's married?'

'Neither of us meant for it to happen. It just did and it was the most natural thing in the world, as if it was meant to be this way.'

'So, you're having an affair.'

It was more of a statement, rather than a question.

Jo nodded slowly. 'Yes.'

Eve put her hands to her face. 'Oh, God. This is bad.'

'You're having an affair with a married man. Actually, no, you've *been having* an affair with a married man for four months. Do we know him?'

'No.'

'Does his wife know?'

Jo's face flushed. 'No. Emma, I—'

Emma cut her off and continued. 'Does he have children?'

Jo took a deep breath and nodded.

'How many?'

Jo looked down at her hands.

'I said, how many?' Emma repeated, her voice cold as steel.

'He has two-year-old twin girls.'

Eve leaned forward in her chair. 'Oh God, this is bad, this is so bad. Emma, we should just—'

'Affairs destroy lives,' Emma said. She spoke slowly, enunciating each word. 'They destroy lives, and they destroy people. They break everything. Affairs break everything, including the people. Everything.'

'I know, I know that, but this is different, honestly. He hasn't been happy for a long time, and we've been friends for years and then—'

'And then you fucked him.'

Jo didn't dare to meet her eye, but continued to look down at her hands. Eve signalled for the waiter to bring the bill, knowing intuitively that they were on fragile, borrowed time before Emma lost her grip completely and exploded.

'You fucked him even though he is married to someone else, and you've continued to fuck him for four months even though he has a poor, oblivious wife who is presumably at home raising their twin baby girls, while you fuck her husband around town.'

The waiter placed the leather-bound bill fold on the table and retreated rapidly. The atmosphere could be cut with a knife.

Emma leaned across the table towards Jo and hissed, 'How could you do this? How could you do this to anyone when you know how it destroyed me? You watched me fall apart when I found out that Paul had been fucking that other woman. You watched as I tore off my engagement ring and flung it across the room. You sat next to me when I called him and told him that I knew, and that the engagement was off. You held me while I cried. No, wait, I didn't just cry, I *wailed*. I bawled and I sobbed because my whole life had just shattered, everything was gone. Poof! Just like that. All my dreams, my plans, gone in an instant. Up in smoke. Shattered and broken and unfixable.'

A tear coursed down her cheek, but her eyes never left Jo's face. Her hands gripped the edges of her chair. She could no longer hear the ambient noise around her. She was utterly oblivious to the crowd, but she continued, her voice low and determined. 'You were the one who told me that he didn't deserve a second chance, that he was a cheater and a loser and that he didn't deserve me.'

A second tear followed the first. 'He broke me, Jo. You sat and watched, so you know first-hand the kind of devastation something like this brings, and now you're sitting here in your sexy white summer dress, drinking wine and telling me about this guy who's like the fuck of the century or something; some guy whose marriage you're about to blow up, whose home you're about to wreck, whose wife you're about to destroy, some poor unsuspecting woman busy at home with her toddlers and whose children's lives you're going to alter irrevocably for ever. And for what?'

She turned and faced Eve for the first time. 'What was it she said? Some bullshit like "we fell in love, but we didn't mean to"? Some Hollywood tripe like that?' Eve stared at her but didn't dare to speak. Slowly, Emma turned her head to face Jo again. 'You didn't mean to. Like, oops, I spilled the ketchup. Didn't mean to! Or oops! I spilled my wine. Didn't mean to! Oops, he fell into my vagina. Didn't mean to!'

She shoved her chair back from the table, the legs grating loudly against the floorboards. She wiped her cheek angrily with the back of her hand and stood up. Eve scribbled a signature on the bill and quickly followed suit.

'I thought I knew who you were. I thought that I knew the kind of person you are, but obviously I didn't. No good person would watch me fall apart, witness all the pieces of my life fall apart, then turn around and inflict that same pain on someone else. You were all about the phone calls, the chats, the pizza nights, the endless conversations and questions. How did I not see it coming? How did I not see the signs? Were there signs? Should I have known? Did he just make a mistake? Did he just fuck up or was it more than that? All of that, all the rambling, the questions, the self-doubt, you sat listening to it all. And the whole time you were fucking someone else's husband. You were no better than Paul was. You were thinking only of yourself. You didn't give anyone else a second thought, especially not his wife or kids. You were selfish and you just went for it, regardless of the consequences, regardless of the fact that you'd just had a front-row seat to how this exact same situation destroyed me.' Emma gestured with her hands. 'Over here, you watched for six months while I lost my mind, while over there, you were busy taking your clothes off and creating the exact same set of circumstances, getting ready to light the fuse and blow up someone else's life.' She shook her head slowly. 'I thought I knew you. I thought you were better than this, but I was wrong.'

She turned to Eve. 'I'm sorry, Eve, I know you didn't want any of this drama and this trip is supposed to be all

about you, but I can't condone this, it hurts every bone in my body, and I can't believe that we've been lied to all this time. I can't be here right now. I have to get out of here.'
She turned and walked out of the door.

CHAPTER NINE

Emma weaved through the crowds back towards the hotel, grateful that the reception desk was unmanned and the foyer empty. She took the stairs two at a time, fully intending to go directly to her room. She rounded the corner on the first floor and ran face first into Stefano, landing on his chest.

'*Mamma mia*,' he exclaimed in surprise.

'Oh, sorry. I'm so sorry, Stefano! Are you okay?'

Stefano laughed. 'Yes, yes, I am fine, but where you are going in such a big hurry? You run like someone is chasing you.'

He looked over her shoulder, but the corridor was empty.

'Everything is okay?'

Her face crumpled.

Don't cry. Don't cry. Don't cry, she repeated in her head. 'No, it's not okay. It's a really bad situation and I really don't want to talk about it.'

'But your friends, they are here?' he asked, looking around again.

Emma shook her head, a strand of hair falling over her face. 'No, I left them at the marina.'

Stefano looked at her face intently and nodded. '*Capisco.* I think that I understand. Come, the bar is empty.' He took her hand and led her through the lounge and into the bar. 'Sit.'

She did as she was told and sat on one of the sofas. He ducked behind the bar and arrived back moments later with a glass of water which she accepted gratefully. She drank it in one go.

'Stefano, I'm going to need something a little stronger. Do you have tequila?'

'Of course, this is a bar, no?'

He disappeared behind the bar again and returned with two shots of tequila. 'This one is the best tequila. Is ... I don't know how you call it in English. I think you say top step.'

Emma took the shot glass. 'Top shelf. It means that the best stuff – the most expensive stuff is kept on the top shelf and the cheaper bottles are kept on the lower shelves.'

'Ah,' he said. 'This makes good sense. So, the other not so good bottles, I can call them lower shelf?'

She smiled despite her mood. 'No, it's just "top shelf" for the good stuff.'

Stefano shrugged. 'I will never fully understand English. *Allora,* now I finish work, my colleague he will work for the rest of the night, so I join you with this drink. *Salute.*'

'*Salute,*' she said, clinking glasses with him.

They downed the shot.

'So, you want to tell me what happen tonight? Or you don't want to talk about it like you say?'

She leaned forward, her elbows resting on her knees. 'I really don't want to talk about it.'

'*Va bene*, I understand.'

'It's just that I had a huge row with Jo at dinner.'

Stefano frowned. 'Sorry, but what does this mean? I don't know this word.'

'An argument.'

'Ah, okay. *Vai*. Continue.'

Emma sighed. 'I just found out something really bad, something that she's done, or actually, something she has been doing for months and she never told me.' She turned to face him. 'And the reason she didn't tell me is that she knew exactly how I'd react and how it would make me feel.'

Stefano ran a hand across his chin, making a scratching sound against his stubble. 'This bad thing that she has done, she has done it to you or to someone else.'

Emma hesitated. 'It's not that simple. It's complicated.'

'Friendships they are complicated. Friendships are complicated because there are many people involved together, and the people, they are not all the same.'

'Exactly! See, I'd never do what she has done. And frankly, after seeing what happened to me a few months ago she should have *known* better.' She glanced up at the bar. 'Could I please have another shot of tequila? We had a lot of wine with dinner, but I swear to God the situation back at the restaurant sobered me up totally and I need something to take the edge off my nerves.'

Stefano gestured to the barman for another round.

'God, what a mess.' She put her hands to her face. 'Poor Eve, this is supposed to be her fun, hen party weekend, but I can't stay here tonight. I can't be anywhere near her.'

'Why you can't stay here?'

'Because I might break into Jo's room and kill her while she's asleep.'

'Okay, this would be bad,' he said, a serious expression on his face. 'You don't want to go to the jail in Italy. They don't have any wine there.'

She smiled for the second time. 'I'm sorry to dump this on you.'

Stefano reached out and gently tucked the errant strands of hair back behind her ear. 'Is never a problem to sit and have a drink with a beautiful woman. Even if she is angry. I think that you forget that I am Italian. Is normal for Italian women to act like this when there is something that they don't like.'

The barman placed the two shots on the table in front of them and left without a word. They clinked glasses and pounded the shots.

'I have to get out of here, Stefano. I can't stay here now. No way. I know Jo. She won't leave me alone. She'll be all about the apology. I don't even want to see her right now.'

He shifted in his seat to face her. 'You can stay in my apartment.' He stared at her, waiting for her reaction.

She smiled. 'Stefano, under different circumstances that would be a great idea, but I'm so fucking mad right now that you don't want me spending the night. No offence.'

'But you can't leave the island. There is no ferry until tomorrow morning. Anyway, I think that you are thinking too much about this. Maybe tomorrow you can talk to your friend and fix this problem.'

She pulled out her phone. 'Not a chance.' She opened her Airbnb app. 'If there aren't any other hotels on the island, surely there's some sort of Airbnb option. We've only got a couple of nights left here until we go back to Rome for our flight home.'

'*Dammelo,*' he said, extending a hand. 'Give it to me. My friend, she has an Airbnb apartment up at the castle. I will see if it is available tonight. Is perfect for you.'

She handed him the phone. He typed in an address and scrolled. '*Sì.* Is available. Wait, I call her. He pulled out his own phone and dialled his friend's number, speaking in rapid Italian.

'*Va bene, sì, sì, capito. Sì, si chiama Emma.*'

'Okay, is done. Here, I send you the link and the address. Is cheaper this way than to book with the Airbnb. She is a big friend of mine.'

'Really? Thank you so much, Stefano. So, is she waiting for me, or do I meet her somewhere or how do I get in?'

'No, I give you the code for the door. Write it down.'

She opened her notes app and noted the four-digit code.

'Brilliant. Okay, I'm going to run up to my room and grab my stuff. Thank you again.' She threw her arms around him in a quick hug, put a twenty-euro note on the table and stood up. 'I can at least buy the drinks.'

Stefano smiled. 'Now you have my number. If you need anything you call me, okay? I call Ottavio to come now to get you, *va bene?*'

'Okay. Thank you.'

She ran up the stairs. She stuffed her clothes into her suitcase, swept her arm across the bathroom vanity and tipped her cosmetics into her bag, yanked her phone charger from the wall and pulled the door shut behind her. The hotel corridors were still and silent as she hurried back down the stairs and out into the night air, making her way cautiously along the street towards the piazza.

Ottavio was sitting in his minivan, and she waved in his direction. She showed him the address on her phone.

He read the address, glanced at her luggage and frowned. '*Ah, sì.* This is inside of the castle walls. I will take you to the same place that we go tonight, the place I take you and your friends. Then, you go inside and is easy. Five-minute walk.'

'Okay, great.' She jumped in and slid the door shut.

Twenty-five minutes later, Ottavio pulled up outside the castle walls and dropped her off at the foot of the piazza. It was almost 11 p.m. but the place was still teeming with activity and lit by the soft golden glow of streetlamps. Emma dragged her suitcase along behind her as she followed the same path she had taken just hours earlier with the girls. She followed the directions Stefano had given her, but minutes later she came to a stop at the top of a cul-de-sac. There was no sign of an apartment, just a shuttered butcher's shop. She checked her phone. No service.

'Shit,' she muttered.

Reading the address aloud, she retraced her steps back towards the piazza, but ended up at the bar they had sat at earlier.

'Dammit,' she said.

She held her phone aloft, hoping to pick up even one bar of signal. Nothing. She looked left and right. Stefano had said that it was near the laundromat but there was no way she could guess which direction that might be. The walls inside the castle were confusing enough by day but resembled a medieval maze by night.

She stopped a couple walking by. 'Excuse me, do you know where the laundromat is?'

The man shrugged his shoulders and said something in Italian.

'Great,' she muttered. 'Suddenly no one speaks English.'

She turned around in a full circle, retracing her steps from earlier that evening in her mind. We came uphill and found the bar, then the laundromat was further up the hill. Or did we see the laundromat first? She continued further up the hill and checked her phone again. Still no service. She reread the address and checked the streets that ran to the left and the right of where she stood, but neither of them had any street names. Her rage began to bubble again inside of her as snippets of the conversation with Jo ran through her mind.

Dragging her case to the crest of the hill, she had a flash of recognition, and suddenly knew where she was. She could hear the noise of the crowd from the pizzeria, which was around the corner ahead on the left.

Maybe they have Wi-Fi, she thought, her suitcase bouncing along awkwardly over the cobblestones.

She stood at the corner of the pizzeria, trying her best to look inconspicuous as she opened the settings on her phone.

The Pizzeria Wi-Fi was password protected.

'Dammit,' she muttered softly.

She glanced around the room. There were at least four empty tables, but it looked like the place was still open as waiters were bringing out pizzas from the brick oven at the back of the restaurant. She would just have to order something, get the password and leave.

A waiter approached her and gestured to a table. *'Buona sera, signora.'*

'*Buona sera.* Um … can I order just a glass of wine?'

He smiled and pulled out a chair for her to sit. '*Certo, signora.* I bring you the wine list.' He looked at her like it was the most natural thing in the world to sit in a pizzeria after 11 p.m. alone, with a suitcase, and order a glass of wine.

She ordered a glass of house red wine, typed in the password and connected to the Wi-Fi network. Her phone lit up with over thirty WhatsApp messages and missed calls from Eve and Jo. Jo beseeching her to call her back, Eve frantically asking where she had gone and if she was okay.

She felt a twinge of guilt at having left in such a dramatic fashion. It was, after all, supposed to be a few carefree, happy days celebrating Eve's last days of freedom, but she couldn't bear the thought of having any further conversation with Jo. She typed a short response to Eve saying that she was fine, that she was moving to an Airbnb, and that she'd call her in the morning.

The room was buzzing with chatter and laughter, happy couples and groups of friends, tourists and locals alike. The cheerful scene only served to make her feel worse. She was neither part of a happy couple, that having blown up months ago, nor among friends, having abandoned them in a fit of rage. Now, the rage weighed heavily on her shoulders as she sat alone. She knew it had been rash to storm out as she had done, but the rage she had felt at Jo's confession was instant and volcanic.

How could she? she thought again. *How could she do that? And with two babies at home.*

The waiter placed the glass of red wine and a basket of garlicky pizza bread on the table in front of her, disappearing without a word.

It was incomprehensible. Jo had been there and witnessed first-hand the devastation that Emma had felt when she learned of Paul's affair. Had she been sleeping with the guy even back then? Was she immune to guilt? Or was she so wrapped up in this guy that she simply didn't think about the consequences or the fallout for everyone else involved.

Or did she just not care?

She licked garlicky butter from her fingertips, the red wine slipping down her throat.

Fucking delicious.

Reaching for another slice of garlic pizza bread, she pondered her options. Find this Airbnb and stay there until she needed to return for her flight home, or stay there tonight and then head back to Rome in the morning.

No, Rome would definitely be a more expensive option than Giglio, and there was no way she could change her flight. Every flight this time of year was full. She'd have to wait it out in Giglio and then worry about dealing with Jo when it came to flying home. Maybe she could change her seat. At least that way they wouldn't have to sit together on the journey back.

Opening the Google Maps app, she typed the address.

The icon swirled three times then flashed up a visual. She entered the name of the pizzeria to take note of the directions. According to the map it wasn't far, but she was going to have to memorise the directions as none of the streets had names on them.

Screenshot it, she decided.

The waiter stood at her table. 'You would like one more glass?'

'Yes, please. And thank you for the pizza bread. It's delicious.'

'*Prego*,' he replied. 'Here we make the pizza since forty-two years. Is the same family. Is the best pizza here in Giglio. I bring you your wine.'

He disappeared towards the bar as she returned her attention to her phone.

The voice came from over her left shoulder. 'Well, it's good to see that someone listens to me.'

She looked up to see Jack Bourke and his friend standing over her. She saw Jack's eyes go to her suitcase and watched as a flicker of *something* registered on his face.

She felt like shit; she guessed that she probably looked like shit too. She was tired, angry and had the beginnings of a dull ache at the base of her skull. Everything had gone wrong. Again. She wasn't supposed to be sitting here alone looking for some random apartment. She was supposed to be sitting in the hotel bar enjoying an after-dinner drink, laughing with the girls. But, as with everything else in her life for the past six months, things hadn't turned out the way they were supposed to.

Don't cry. Don't cry. DO NOT CRY, she admonished silently. Not now. Not in front of him.

The waiter returned with her glass of wine. Jack spoke to him in Italian and turned to his friend. What was his name? Blake?

'I'll catch up with you tomorrow.'

He put his hand on the back of the chair opposite Emma. 'Mind if I join you?'

He didn't wait for her to answer and sat down as the waiter placed a glass of wine in front of him. 'You know, you're getting this holiday vibe all wrong. This is not how it's supposed to go.'

She stared at him as he lifted the glass. 'No offence, but you cut a pretty sad figure, sitting here all alone with your suitcase. You do realise that you're on an Italian island in the middle of summer, and sitting in the best pizzeria north of Napoli, don't you? But for some unknown reason, you're not radiating joy over there.' He held the glass across the table. 'Problem shared?'

Emma tipped her glass to his and gave a reluctant smile. 'You've no idea what you're getting yourself into.'

'I have three sisters, so I grew up with female drama, and not to be a smart arse here, but I'm guessing that's what this is, seeing as you're here with your suitcase instead of your friends. Anyway, I'm not that easily scared.' He winked at her. 'So, I'm game if you are.'

CHAPTER TEN

Emma knew nothing until she heard a door slam in the distance, the sound pulling her from her slumber. She opened one eye, squinting in the bright sunlight that seeped in through the half-closed, wooden shutters. She sat up slowly, her eyes darting around the unfamiliar room. The spacious bedroom was minimalist and decorated in neutral tones. The walls were off-white, decorated with black-and-white photographs of what she assumed were shots of the coves and bays around Giglio. Under the window sat a small white desk and chair that held a single white vase with wild white roses.

The door to the bathroom was ajar; it too was decorated in white, oversized white stone tiles with a pale blue border. The white coverlet on the bed lay crumpled in a heap on the old stone floor tiles beside her, the linen sheets wrinkled beneath her. From her vantage point, she could see down the hallway towards the front door, a small galley kitchen leading off to one side. She pulled the sheet up towards her chest, noticing only then that she wore a white T-shirt that wasn't hers.

'Good morning,' Jack said with a smile, appearing from

the galley kitchen. 'I brought breakfast, otherwise known as resuscitation remedies. On a scale of one to ten, ten being up for a five kilometre jog, one wanting to lie back down and die, how are you feeling?'

'Is zero an option?'

'I figured as much. Here.' He handed a takeaway coffee cup to her.

She gasped. 'You got coffee?'

'Yeah, I only realised when I got to the café that I didn't even know what kind of coffee you liked, so I took a chance on cappuccino with normal milk. I figured you'd be okay with the dairy option. You don't strike me as the alternative milk kind of girl.'

'God, no. Imagine coming to Italy and having a dairy issue and not being able to eat the cheese. That would make me sad. There was a woman at the hotel who said she travels with these lactose intolerance pills so that she can eat pizza and cheese here. Imagine. Thank you. This is giving me life right now.' She closed her eyes as she took a sip. 'I must look a state, sorry. Probably a bit of a mascara situation.' She ran an index finger under her eyes. Every woman's defence mechanism against morning panda eyes.

'No.' He smiled.

She noticed that he did that a lot. Smiled. He put a paper bag on the bed between them.

'You look cute. Dishevelled, but cute.'

She ran a hand through her hair. 'I can't imagine, but I also kind of don't care. I'm just focusing on inhaling this coffee right now.' She raised a hand to shield her eyes. 'I'm not able for daylight today.'

Jack laughed. 'You look a lot less city this morning. Not all put together with your make-up done right, like you've been the few times I've seen you.'

'Are you saying that country girls walk around every day looking like morning-after catastrophes? That's how I feel right now.'

Jack threw his head back and laughed. 'No, it's just a lot more casual in the country. I'm sure they all still have mascara emergencies, but I dunno, it's just a different vibe.'

'How do you know about mascara emergencies?'

'I have three sisters. I told you that last night.'

She pulled her knees up to her chest and sipped the cappuccino. 'You did?'

'Yes, here, I bought these too.' He handed her the paper bag with one plain and one almond croissant. 'I wasn't sure which you'd like, so I'll just have whichever you don't want.'

She pulled off a piece of croissant. 'Thanks. This was very sweet of you.'

He shrugged. 'So, how do you feel about everything this morning? You were pretty upset last night.'

Snatches of the previous night's conversation and random memories flashed through her brain; the two of them sitting at the pizzeria until late. *Very* late. They had been the last ones to leave. Pizza. Did they order pizza? She remembered something about pizza, but she couldn't be sure. Walking in the narrow, empty, dark streets. Her crying.

Oh God, she thought, had she cried for real in front of him? Her face flushed at the thought.

'I know. I'm sorry to have unloaded all that on you. I

was a bit of a mess,' she said, tearing off another piece of croissant.

'No, that's not what I meant. I just meant with you and your friend. I mean, you're here on holiday with her, but then you had that big blow-out argument, so how do you feel about it all in the cold light of day? Still mad?'

'Mad as hell,' she snapped.

'Fair enough. Do you want to talk about it?'

'I desperately don't want to talk about it. I don't even want to *think* about it.'

'Great. How about I take you out to lunch at the beach instead? I don't have to be at the festival until this evening. I'm one of the judges in the competition, so I have to be back before five o'clock.'

'Really? But wait, last night ... did we, I mean did anything, you know, happen?'

'Jesus, Emma, I'm not a predator. If anyone took advantage of you in that condition they deserve to go to jail. You were a mess. I brought you back here, gave you a T-shirt and put you to bed. You passed out in seconds.'

'So, where did you sleep?'

'Right there, next to you.' He pointed to the other side of the bed.

'But we didn't—'

'No, we didn't. You did throw your arms around me at one point at dark o'clock and told me that you loved me, but otherwise it was uneventful, run of the mill even.'

'I'm so sorry,' she groaned. 'I shouldn't be let out. I shouldn't drink.'

Jack laughed. 'Don't worry about it. You had a bit of a blow-out with your friend: it happens. No biggie.'

She took a long sip of the coffee and looked around the room. 'I thought I was booking a small, pokey little Airbnb; this is nice.'

'You probably did, but this is my Airbnb. We couldn't get into yours last night.'

'Oh, Jesus. Sorry. *Again*. So, I just crashed at your place? That's lovely. Was that my idea?'

'No, it was mine. You must have written the entry code down incorrectly. At one a.m. I gave up trying to play Jack Reacher and hack the code to get into your place and the host wasn't responding, so I made an executive decision to bring you back here. Don't worry, I found out who he is, and I already sent him a note to say you'd check in today instead. It's not a big deal.'

She put one hand to her face. 'I'm mortified.'

'What for? You worry too much. Now, forget about it. Look, you've got this shitty situation with your friend, so the way I see it you've got two choices: option one, you go back to the hotel and hash it out.'

'No, what's the second?'

'You drink your coffee, take a shower and I take you to my favourite beach for lunch.'

'I like option two better.'

'It's a bit of a trek, but nothing extreme. You up for it?'

She looked at him warily. 'What do you mean by "trek", exactly?'

'We have to cut through a bit of forest, nothing too dramatic. You can get there by boat too, but I'm not much of a boat person.'

'You come to an Italian island every summer, but you're not much of a boat person. How does that work?'

'A, I come here for work, and B, much and all as I'd prefer to stay on dry land, if the best restaurants require a boat ride, then I'm going to suck it up.' He glanced over at her suitcase. 'Did you pack anything athletic or outdoorsy in that bag? What did you call it . . . ? Outsidey?'

'Outsidey, yes. I have a bikini.'

'That's not athletic.'

'It's outsidey.'

'Shorts?'

'Oh, actually, yes, I did pack a pair of shorts.'

'Okay, good. You can keep that T-shirt if you want, that'll do for the walk to the beach, consider it a souvenir. What about sneakers?'

'Well, I've got my cute white leather ones.'

'That'll do. It's not like we're climbing The Bones.'

'What's that?'

'It's one of the highest mountain peaks in Ireland. You know . . . the country you come from. You've never heard of The Bones?'

'No, I've never heard of it. Why is it called The Bones? Are you just making this up?'

'*No*, I'm not making it up. It's an actual mountain. I think The Bones is a translation from the original Irish name.'

'They probably called it The Bones because so many people died trying to get to the top,' Emma muttered. 'This lunch isn't at the top of some mountain, is it?'

Jack stared at her. 'Didn't you hear me saying beach lunch? Beaches are usually found at sea level.'

'Okay, fair enough. Like I said, I'm not that outdoorsy, so this stuff doesn't exactly come naturally to me.' She sipped her coffee. 'So, no mountain, that's good.'

'There's a bit of an incline down to the beach, but there's a path, so you'll be grand.'

Emma looked at him warily. 'Better be a really good lunch.'

Jack crumpled up the paper bag. 'Right, I've got to meet Blaine for about half an hour before I disappear off for the day, then I'll come back here and change. That work?'

'You're not one of these extreme sports people, are you? Like, you're not going to be wearing spandex for this hike or anything, are you?'

He shook his head and grinned. 'Do I look like the kind of guy who wears spandex?'

Emma laughed. 'No, but you're just so outdoorsy I bet you have all the appropriate gear.'

'I do back home, hiking gear and stuff like that, but not here, and no, no spandex under any circumstances. I'm Irish. We don't go in for that shit. Okay,' he said, standing up from the bed. 'Are you good?'

'Yep, I'm good.'

'Right so, see you in a bit.'

He looked good this morning in a white T-shit and pale blue jeans. Her eyes ran the length of his body as he turned away from her. He was fit. She watched as he grabbed a key and opened the door, turning to smile briefly as he pulled it softly shut behind him. That wink again.

Fuck, she thought.

She let her breath out in a puffing sound through her lips. He was hot, and he didn't seem to have the first clue that was the case. He had just winked at her, and it had elicited a physical response.

Does he do that on purpose? she wondered.

She swirled the coffee, downing the last dregs of caffeine. Everything about the way he moved seemed slow and considered. He had been totally easy-going again this morning. Had she imagined the flirtatious vibe from the night before? Had she read the situation wrong? She recalled him sitting down to join her, and her determination to not talk about the reason behind the argument. He had placed one hand on hers at one point. She couldn't remember what he had said but she remembered the touch, and the butterfly feeling it had sent through her. But she'd slept in his bed, and nothing had happened. Had she imagined the feeling that there was some sort of spark between them? He certainly gave no indication of that this morning, but then again, she'd been a hot mess, so she'd likely doused water on any potential spark.

She jumped out of bed, unzipped her suitcase, and pulled her cosmetics from her handbag. She leaned in close to the mirror and pulled at her skin.

'Drastic rescue remedy needed here,' she muttered. Failing to figure out the hot water configuration, she took a cold shower, rinsed her face and lathered on moisturiser and sunscreen. She used a generous amount of concealer to hide the unexplained red blotch on her forehead and the dark circles under her eyes and applied a lick of mascara. She tied her hair up in a messy bun and rooted in her bag for her bikini and the one pair of shorts she had packed. She checked her phone. It was plugged into the wall and fully charged. She wondered if she'd done that or if Jack had thought to do it for her. Four missed calls from Eve, six from Jo and a string of text messages. She typed a text to Eve.

> I'm sorry I bailed on you, but I just can't believe that Jo would do that.
> I can't see her right now and I don't want to get into it.
> I need to calm down before I see her again.

The ellipsis pulsed immediately.

> Totally get it. Don't worry bout me. TBH I'm delighted to have no plans.
> Cxld the cooking class! Gonna chill @ beach for the day.
> FWIW, she feels awful, but I know you don't wanna hear that rn.
> Just text me later xx

Emma responded with the love heart emoji and flicked the phone to silent.

She sighed. *Have I overreacted? Should I have stayed and argued it out with Jo? Is it really any of my business what Jo does?*

Her mind flashed back to the last conversation with Paul. At first, he had been adamant, he had denied it all furiously. She scoffed. He didn't even have the balls to own it like a man. Once he knew that she had proof, his story changed, but again he continued with the excuses, the lies. She shook her head now, trying to dislodge the memory, to shake it out of her head. She could feel the anger swell in her stomach.

She felt guilty that this was all happening on what was supposed to be Eve's hen weekend away. She stopped and looked at her face in the mirror. She hadn't even wanted to come in the first place. The only reason she gave in to Jo's insistence was out of sheer guilt. Guilt for letting Eve down.

'No,' she said to her reflection. 'You didn't start this. You didn't create this shitstorm.'

She screwed the top back on the tube of toothpaste. She wasn't going to try to make things right with Jo just because she felt guilty that Eve had got caught in the middle. Eve was a big girl. She could choose to have a good time here on the island. And the hell with Jo. She didn't want to talk to her, to listen to her excuses, her warped rationalisations of this totally fucked-up situation. She didn't want to deal with any of this right now.

No, she was going to put the whole mess on Status Ignore, go on some kind of hike to some beach with a guy she barely knew, someone who apparently put her to bed last night and who she'd drunkenly professed her love for. She was going to put last night's debacle out of her mind for the day and worry about it later. She was damned if she was going to waste a minute of her time in Italy pondering Jo's poor choices or her decision to lie to her and Eve for the past four months.

She was on an Italian island and a hot Irishman had just offered to take her to a beach for lunch.

She was done with people lying to her and letting her down, done with being roped in to other people's messy situations, situations that they'd created for themselves. No, she was going to the beach with Jack Bourke, the sculptor with the great ass and the killer smile.

She slicked some lip gloss on her lips and grabbed her wallet and sunglasses. She didn't care if he wasn't in the least bit interested in her. So what? It felt good just being around him, so the hell with it all.

Jack opened the door and stuck his head inside.

'Hey! You ready to go?'

She stuck her phone in her bag and placed her sunglasses on her head, quite sure at that moment that she'd follow him into hell if he asked.

CHAPTER ELEVEN

The first fifteen minutes of the walk was easy, and Emma was lulled into a false sense of confidence. They made their way down the hill and out beyond the walls of the castle, through the small village towards the opposite side of the island. They chatted easily as they walked, Jack regaling her with stories and gossip about the locals. The owner of the laundromat, who started the business when his wife threw him out and he was forced to rent a tiny apartment that didn't have laundry facilities; the bakery, whose original owner was a raging alcoholic who burned the place down twice, but which was now owned by his son and hadn't been subject to arson in twenty years; and the café owner, a cat lover who suffers from terrible allergies so can't have one of her own, but instead puts out the café leftovers to feed the population of feral cats and their kittens each evening.

As soon as they left the paved path and started the descent down through the forest, she knew things were about to change. Jack took the lead and warned her about the route.

'It gets kinda steep about halfway down, so take your

time. No prizes for first down or anything, and if you go flying here, you'll get a nasty scrape from all these branches.'

'I thought you said there was a path the whole way down.'

He turned to look at her. 'This *is* a path.'

'Not where I come from. In Dublin a path is paved ground, like a footpath. This is a strip of dirt that appears to be going down in a very steep incline. It is most definitely *not* a path.'

Jack laughed. 'You'll be grand. Just take your time.'

She followed him, keeping pace down and around the series of switchbacks, which Jack explained were cut into the hill in a zigzag manner to make descending and climbing easier.

'If this went straight down, we'd just die. That's why they have the paths go slightly horizontal, so it's not a flat-out, steep descent. They have a lot of these in the hills in Kerry, too. Built them years ago when they had to rely on donkeys to take trailer loads of stuff up and down the mountains. Nowadays, machinery can go anywhere, but back in the day, they had to cut out the tracks in softer inclines so the animals could make their way up and down and haul a load at the same time.

'Well, if they're anything like this, it sounds like cruelty to donkeys to me. I'm surprised the ISPCA wasn't all over that.'

Jack paused and looked sideways at her. 'Okay, first, it was probably sixty years ago, and second, it was the opposite of animal cruelty. They were doing it to make life *easier* for the donkeys. You really don't understand life in the country at all, do you?'

She shook her head. 'No, nor do I want to. What part of Kerry do you live in, anyway?'

'Valentia Island.'

'Where? That's not even really in Ireland.'

'*What?* What are you talking about? Of course it is!'

'No, that's an island in the middle of the Atlantic Ocean. Ireland is an island. But you're saying that you live on another one.'

'Ireland has several islands; you do know that, don't you?'

'Yeah, of course I do, but, like, they're for lighthouses and stuff.'

Jack paused and turned around again, looking at her blankly. 'Are you taking the piss right now?'

'About what? Not understanding why someone would want to live on a rock in the Atlantic Ocean? No, I'm not.'

Jack laughed. 'Emma, it's a normal place. I have a house, and land, a studio, a shed, a car, a driveway, walls, a sofa, books ... just like any normal house. It's not just a rock in the middle of the ocean. It's an actual island where people live normal lives. There are other houses, farms, sheep, two pubs, a small hotel, cafés, *people*. Here, look.' He pulled his phone from his pocket and opened Google Maps.

Emma looked at the phone and then back at him. 'It looks like a rock in that picture.'

'Well, yeah, of course it does, it's a map. You really don't know Valentia Island?' He stuck his phone back in his pocket and continued down the path.

'No, I *do*,' she insisted, beginning to laugh now. 'But I thought it was, like ... the kind of place that they'd film a movie and Tom Cruise would play the lead role with a bad Irish accent. You know what I mean, uninhabited, barren land, all stone walls and green fields and mad big waves crashing off the Atlantic.' She paused. 'Oh, and a lighthouse.'

'You sound like you're on a National Geographic programme describing some wild, unpopulated island miles off into the ocean, as yet to be discovered by mankind. Leave the city much?'

She picked up a stone and threw it at him.

'Well, Emma, it is all that, but Valentia Island is not uninhabited, although I do think there are actually more sheep than people on the island. I think the ratio is something like three to one.'

She shook her head. 'I just don't understand why anyone would want to live somewhere like that. I mean, what do you do all day?'

'I work.'

'No, I know you work, but when you're not working, what do you do?'

The questions came in a torrent now.

'I mean, don't you get lonely there all by yourself? I know you said there are people there, but what kind of people, like ... do you have actual friends there? How do you get coffee? Isn't it super quiet all the time? How do you not go mad?'

Jack stopped at the next bend and pulled off his backpack.

'Let me see,' he began, counting on his fingers. 'No, I never get lonely, and anyway I'm not there all by myself. Yes, many friends. I make the coffee myself. I even have a fancy coffee machine that can make cappuccino. In winter, yes, it is "super quiet", and it's magic. In summer, no, not for a minute, the place is packed with people, a lot of families who've been coming back every year, some of them their whole lives. What was the last one?' He frowned. 'Oh yeah, how do I not go mad? I could ask you the exact same thing. How do you not go mad all day every day in a concrete jungle? Noise, traffic, polluted air, sad-looking, spindly trees stuck in squares cut out of concrete footpaths, shopping in big supermarkets, commuting to work, commuting home from work, walking at a mad, frenzied, city pace ...' He paused for a second. 'Having to schedule down time, trying to keep up. Seriously, Emma; how do *you* not go mad?'

Emma wiped the back of her hand across her mouth. 'I do sometimes.'

'Touché.'

He pulled out two bottles of water, handing one to Emma. She stopped and looked around. They had descended more than halfway, and the further they went the more the trees thinned out – so much so that from this vantage point she could see glimpses of the aquamarine bay below them.

'But I wouldn't trade it for a second,' she continued. 'I love living in the city.'

'Okay, sell it to me.'

'What?'

'I want you to sell me on the notion of living in the city, but just hold the thought for a minute.' He pointed to the path ahead of them. 'This bit is a little tricky because the dirt is loose, so hold that thought and you can sell me on the joy of urban living over a glass of wine.'

'A glass of wine sounds great right now,' she said, peering down through the trees. 'How much longer until we get to the beach?' She wiped sweat from her forehead and took a sip of water.

'About twenty minutes. Are you doing okay?'

'Yeah, I think my heel is a bit cut from these shoes, but I'm fine.'

He placed his water bottle on the dirt path. 'Lemme see.'

'I think the socks are just too short.' She pulled down the heel of her sneaker.

He bent down on one knee. 'Yeah, they look like city socks to me.'

She looked at him dubiously. '*City socks?*'

He grinned up at her. 'Yeah, what's it they call them ... those invisible socks that are cute and don't stick up above the rim of the shoe, because God forbid someone might see the top of your socks?'

Emma opened her mouth to argue but laughed, realising that he was probably right. He plucked a dense green leaf from a bush and folded it in two.

'Here,' he said. He caught her ankle and tilted her foot, wrapping the leaf around the back of her heel and slipping her shoe up over it. 'That'll do in place of a plaster.'

'Jesus, you're like a real-life MacGyver.'

He winked at her then as he stood up, his face inches from hers. 'I'm a country boy. Gotta know how to survive in the wild.'

Her stomach did the flippy-over thing as his eyes met hers. He hesitated for a moment, and she caught her breath. His eyes were a deep dark blue, his irises wide and black. She knew that that was a sign of something, that it meant something, but she couldn't recall what.

'You have an eyelash there.'

He stood so close she could feel the heat radiate from him. She ran both hands across her eyes. 'Where? Did I get it?'

'No, here,' he said. He reached out and touched her face gently, the eyelash refusing to budge. 'Hang on.' He took a step closer and tried again. His fingers felt warm against her skin. He stood at least four inches taller than her and looked down intently. She could feel his breath on her face as she studied his. The faint scar on one side of his face, the only white mark on otherwise tanned skin, the stubble, at least two or three days' growth. Her eyes were drawn to his mouth, his lips full, sensual, slightly turned up at the corners, the hint of a smile ever present.

'Sorry,' he said, leaning in towards her, his gaze focused on the job at hand. His breath again, a hint of coffee and mint. 'It's being stubborn.' He licked the tip of one finger and touched it against the side of her face. 'There, got it. You're safe from certain death.'

His eyes met hers. He stayed there, inches from her, for a few seconds. Her pulse increased and her heart began to beat loudly in her chest. Everything slowed around her. It felt like minutes had passed. She didn't even think to answer, to respond in any way. For those few seconds she had stopped thinking. She knew instinctively that her next move, if she were to make one, would be physical, a primal instinct. It wouldn't be words. There was nothing to say. He stepped back. The spell broke. She blinked, her head spinning slightly.

'C'mon, nearly there. You're doing great. Will you make it?'

You're doing great. The words ran again through her head. She needed to say something, to answer in some way. Why did the compliment make her feel so good? Why did that little snippet of praise from him have such an effect on her? What part of her was craving and loving this approval from him?

'Yep,' she said as casually as she could. 'I'm good. Let's do it.'

They continued down the path for the next fifteen minutes. The breeze picked up as they got closer to the water. Stray strands of hair whipped across her face. Right at the turn, she stepped on some loose stones and her foot shot out in front of her. Jack turned to catch her, softening her fall as she landed on her arse on the ground.

'Shit. Are you okay?'

She stood up and brushed off her shorts. 'Sorry, yeah, I was looking at the view and not where I was going. I'm fine.'

'That was lucky. Sorry, I should have warned you about this bit. It's all these loose stones.' He held his hand out to her. 'Here, hold on to me, we're almost there.' He slowed his pace slightly and they continued the rest of the descent together. Emma held on tightly to his hand, determined not to fall for a second time. Her hand felt small in his. She knew nothing about this guy, but she felt an unnerving feeling of *something*. She couldn't put her finger on it. Security? Safety? Comfort? She couldn't find the exact word, but somehow, he made her feel all of those things as they walked hand in hand towards the beach.

You're being ridiculous, she told herself. *Overthinking things as usual, reading into things. Maybe you should just write fiction for a living*, she thought, *cause you're so good at making shit up.*

She chastised herself silently. *The only reason he's holding your hand is to keep you from landing on your arse again.*

She was so busy thinking and second guessing herself that she failed to notice that they'd come to a stop at the bottom. He still held her hand, the feel of his palm traced against hers.

'Oh,' she exclaimed. 'Wow.' She gazed at the water that stretched out infinitely in front of her, the sunlight streaking down, sending sparkles along the gentle ripples of the bay. The beach was quiet, half full at best. Half a dozen boats had dropped anchor and bobbed from side to side. Everything appeared to be stalled, paused, as if life itself had slowed down in the languorous heat of midday. They stood for several moments just staring, silently taking in the view. The only sounds were of waves lapping softly against the shore, the low groan of an outboard motor and strains of Italian music reaching them, carried on the breeze from somewhere close by.

He dropped his hand, she felt it leave hers, her fingers releasing one by one. Her palm was warm and clammy. She tucked stray wind-whipped strands of hair behind one ear. Did it mean anything? Was he just being kind, helping her along, ensuring that she wouldn't end up on the ground again?

She could smell his scent from her hand. Her mind raced. He hadn't given her any indication of anything. Okay, he had stood close to her and held her gaze, but that had only been a few seconds.

She breathed in the smell of the sea.

You're doing it again, she thought. *Overthinking everything, one of your default moves. He's a big-time successful artist in his late thirties and a die-hard country boy who prefers to live alone, or at least somewhere in the woods with his dog. He has shown no interest in you, nothing except just being kind. He helped you out last night and you slept in the same bed together and nothing happened. That should tell you enough. Get a grip, Emma, and enjoy the day for what it is,* she admonished silently. *Just because he rescued you last night doesn't make you Cinderella.*

A sleek, navy yacht had pulled into the bay. Emma watched the classic Italian summer scene as the elegant yacht dropped anchor, the sound of the metal chain echoing across the bay as it fell to the seabed. A tall brunette stood on the bow of the boat in a white swimsuit, a long, white cover-up flapping behind her in the breeze as she waited for the small, weather-beaten wooden boat to take her to the restaurant on the shore.

Jack put a hand to his forehead, shielding the glare of the sun from his eyes, and pointed to a wooden building, not much more than a shack, on the left at the water's edge. The doors and windows were flung wide open, the wooden deck, a promontory that jutted out over the bay, was filled with tables and chairs. Yellow umbrellas fluttered in the breeze, casting shade on the diners who sat beneath.

He pointed towards the colourful summer scene, turned to her and grinned. 'That's lunch.'

She caught herself staring at him, realising that on the walk down, her hand in his, she had managed to forget all about lunch.

She smiled to herself as she followed him towards the restaurant.

Well, that's a first, she thought.

CHAPTER TWELVE

They were greeted warmly and seated immediately, the waiter handing them menus and reciting the daily specials in Italian.

'White wine?' Jack asked.

'Great.'

He ordered a bottle of sparkling water and two glasses of white wine, all of which were downed in mere minutes, as he translated the specials for her.

Jack motioned for the waiter. '*Altre due, grazie.*'

'*Subito,*' he replied.

'Okay, can you teach me some Italian? Just something simple that I could use while I'm here.'

'You want to learn Italian from an Irish man? That's probably a first, but sure,' he laughed. 'I only know a few words and phrases. The important stuff.'

'Like ordering more wine?'

He smiled at her, the corners of his eyes crinkling up as he did. 'Exactly.'

She smiled back, her eyes following the curve of his mouth. She forced herself to look away. 'So, what did you just say to him? You didn't say *vino.*'

'No, I didn't need to. I just said *"altre due"*, which means another two.'

'*Altre due*,' she repeated, rolling the vowels on her tongue.

'I'm not that good, but it's like anything – just do a little, but do it well. It's not like I can get into a debate about Italian politics, not that I'd want to, but I can definitely order more wine. Now, you promised to sell me on the wonders of living in Dublin City. Let's have it.'

The waiter reappeared with two more glasses of wine and a plate of fresh anchovies marinated in oil and lemon juice.

This will be easy, she thought.

'Well, first off, as I'm sure even someone from Kerry knows, Dublin is a cool, contemporary city. It's got everything – culture, arts, restaurants, bars, cafés. You can walk to everything, so no, I don't have a dreadful commute to and from work. It's got great shopping and nice parks and green spaces. It's cosmopolitan, lots of different nationalities, lots of tourists, and Dublin airport has connections to all the other European countries so it's easy to hop on a flight for a holiday.'

She sat back, quite pleased with herself.

'Okay.'

'Okay what?'

'Nothing, just okay. It sounds like any other city to me. Cosmopolitan, lots of people, restaurants, bars, etc. But at some point, cities, or at least European cities, feel the same. They may look different, different buildings, styles, scale, but they all basically function in the same way.'

Emma interjected. 'Well, the same can be said of country life.'

'Not necessarily.'

'Oh, come on! The country? It's all the same – a bunch of green fields with sheep or cows, throw in a few hills or a mountain, a cosy pub and a church. That's basically your typical Irish countryside.'

'Agreed. That's the basic countryside description right there, but the beauty of rural Ireland is that no two villages are alike. No two regions are the same. They are all one hundred per cent unique. It's not like you visit one village in rural Ireland and think, *That's it, I've seen it all now.* They all have their own unique charm, they all feel different, or maybe you feel differently about each one.'

'So, you're saying that the place you live is different to anywhere else in the country.'

Jack smiled. 'It is; but hang on a second, I'm starving. Let's order some food. What do you feel like?'

Emma pursed her lips and looked around at the other tables. 'What's that?' She nodded to the table alongside them. 'That dish they're all eating?'

'I think that's one of their specialities. I've had it before. I don't know what it's called, but it's *cavatelli* with a white fish in a tomato sauce. It's simple, but delicious.'

'What's *cavatelli*?'

'A short, twisted pasta about two inches long.'

'Sounds good.'

'Great. How about some grilled calamari to start?'

'Perfect.'

Jack ordered the food and leaned back in his chair. 'What were we talking about?'

'You were going to tell me what's so special about Valentia Island.'

'Why don't you come and see for yourself?'

Emma hesitated for a moment. Was he *actually* inviting her to Kerry for real, or was he just being sarcastic? He was hard to read.

I'm going to have to go with sarcastic, she thought.

'Drive five hours to the other side of the country? No, thanks. Send me a postcard.'

'You don't even like *visiting* the country?'

'Well, I do, but in summer for a weekend or something. I'd have to plan it.'

Jack shook his head. 'Summer's great. There's nowhere like Kerry on a summer's day, the air is fresh and cool, the water is crystal clear; it would rival the Mediterranean on a good day, the way the colour changes from blue to turquoise.' He took a sip of his wine. 'My house is at the end of a road, at the foot of Bray Head, the last house on the island. You round this bend and the road curves to the left, about four hundred feet above sea level, with a sheer, vertical drop to the bay below and this tiny shale beach tucked into the curve of the cliffs. The only way to get down there is to abseil. The coastguard uses those cliffs to practise their rescue techniques, the drop is that extreme. Anyway,' he continued, 'the water is totally unpolluted. The only boats in and out are the few that go out to the Skellig Islands, where they shot the *Star Wars* movies, and the odd mackerel fisherman. Apart from that, the water is undisturbed. It's one of the most westerly parts of Ireland, so you can imagine the winds coming in off the ocean in winter, but on a summer's day there's only the whisper of a breeze. The only sounds you'll hear are the odd outboard motor, birds and sheep, lambs especially cause they're always getting lost and calling out. That's it. Sit outside for a few minutes on a summer's day and you'll taste the salt water on your lips. It's one of the most remote, unpolluted and magical places I've ever been.'

'I don't know,' Emma said, warily. 'The way you describe it, it sounds like something out of a book.'

Jack laughed. 'I'm not making it up.'

'But how do you live in a place like that? So remote, I mean. Isn't it a pain to get groceries or go for a night out?'

'Actually, no. So, across the way from the island, on the mainland, is a small fishing village called Portmagee. There's a church, two pubs that serve food, a couple of cafés and the Post Office that is also the local shop and butcher.'

'How can the Post Office also be the butcher's shop?'

'They've got a butcher's counter down the back,' Jack said matter-of-factly.

'That sounds mad.'

'It's brilliant. They sell everything ... fresh bread, fruit and veg, groceries, meat, newspapers, batteries, rope. I've never gone in there and they didn't have what I was looking for.'

'Why would anyone need rope? That sounds a bit murdery.'

Jack laughed. 'It's the country, Emma. It's no different to having a drill or a box of nails. You'll always find use for a length of rope.'

'How do you even buy rope?' Emma asked.

'What?'

'No, like, how do you actually go and buy rope?'

'You go into the shop with money, give it to the person behind the counter and take home your rope. *What?*'

'No, I mean, is the rope rolled around a big wooden wheel and you just say, "I'd like this much rope please"?' She stretched her hands out to her sides.

Jack laughed. 'Jesus, we lead very different lives. No, they don't have big wheels of rope. It's just the local shop. The lengths of rope are a standard cut, usually about eight or ten feet long, coiled or wound up like this, and tied in a knot.' He rolled his hands around to demonstrate.

'Oh, right. That's a little disappointing. Sounds almost normal to go into a Post Office and buy some rope, now.'

'It *is* normal!'

Emma laughed. 'In your world maybe!'

The waiter placed a platter of grilled calamari on the table, a whole squid cut into slices. Jack squeezed a half lemon over it and speared a ring. Emma followed suit, the smoky taste of charcoal melding with the acidity of the lemon in her mouth.

'I thought it was going to be the breaded rings, you know, the usual calamari you get back home. I haven't had it like this.'

'Yeah, this is the way they do it here, it's the grilled version. Do you like it?'

'Yeah, it's amazing,' she replied, spearing a second ring. 'I'm not much of a hike person, but this is already worth the effort of getting here.'

Jack smiled. 'Good. Yeah, sometimes it helps to have a reward to keep you going. On Sunday mornings at home, I bike across the bridge to Portmagee to get the papers. Having a coffee at the café after is my reward.

Helps convince myself to get on the bike instead of taking the car.'

Emma licked lemon juice from her fingers. 'I can't remember the last time I was on a bike.'

'Really?'

'Yeah, if you don't count spin class.' She grinned.

Jack rolled his eyes. 'No, I'm talking about bikes that actually go somewhere. That would drive me nuts, cycling like a lunatic and going nowhere.'

'Well, that's not actually the point,' she contested.

'I know, but still, wouldn't you rather be putting that effort into getting somewhere? Out in the fresh air, heading off to someplace nice? What's your reward at the end of spin class if you end up in the same place you started?'

'Finishing is a reward. Those classes are brutal. Plus, I go for coffee afterward, so it's kind of the same as you cycling to the village on a Sunday.'

'Yeah, exact same thing,' Jack said sarcastically.

The waiter cleared their plates and returned with two steaming bowls of seafood pasta.

'I have to judge this thing later on so I can't go mad, but are you up for another glass of wine?'

Emma speared a piece of pasta with her fork. 'Yeah, I'd love one. So, how did you get into sculpture in the first place?'

'By accident. I always thought I'd go into law. My dad and both of my uncles are solicitors, but this girl I was dating in college talked me into a weekend away in Dorset. I thought that the idea was just to get out of town for a few days, but she'd signed us up to this pottery thing that I didn't know about until we got there. I tried to get out of it, but she'd paid a stupid amount of money so I kind of just went along with it. Turns out I was good at it. So, the relationship didn't last but the love affair with sculpture did. What about you? What's the story with those paintings?'

Emma shook her head. 'It's just a hobby. I don't even have time for it these days. I haven't painted since my life blew up. Her face flushed as she cast her eyes down. She hadn't intended to mention it, it had just come out. She pushed her hair back from her face. 'I was in a relationship that sort of imploded and it threw me off for a few months. I haven't got back to it since ... painting, that is. It's a long story. It's complicated.'

'I'm sure it is,' he said with a kind smile. 'None of us get to our mid-thirties without racking up some complicated situations. We've all got a story, Emma.' He shrugged. 'So, you haven't painted in a while, that's okay. You'll get back to it when you're ready.'

She looked up at him and smiled. 'I suppose you're right.' She wondered about his life, his mid-thirties 'complicated situation', his story. She waited, but he didn't offer any insight.

'I'd love to see your work. Do you have any more photos?'

Is he changing the subject? Or does he really want to see photos?

She loved how he called it her work. It made it sound important, and it made her feel important too. Not just a hobby, but work.

She blushed. 'I don't usually show people.'

'Oh, come on. I'd love to see.'

'All right,' she said reluctantly. She pulled out her phone and scrolled. 'These are the ones I was working on before ... well, anyway ... '

Jack took the phone. He scrolled, tapped, zoomed and scrolled again, his attention focused entirely on the screen. 'Emma, these are good. I mean, *really* good. I'm not just saying that. You should paint. Like, for a living.'

She laughed. 'Not a chance. There's no way I could survive and pay Dublin rent as an artist.'

He looked up at her. 'So, move.'

She met his gaze, his blue eyes boring into hers. He looked back down at the screen. 'What's this one?'

He turned the phone around for her to see.

'Oh, that's the last one I was working on. It's not finished yet. It's another butterfly one.'

'This is incredible. Did you see something to spark this, or did it just come to you?'

'It just came to me. I've been doing butterflies for ages, they're my favourite thing to paint. That one is kind of abstract.'

'It's amazing.' He looked up at her again. The way he looked at her pulled her in, quietening everything else around her.

She wasn't used to hearing such praise. 'Thanks.'

'I'm telling you right now,' he continued, 'you should be doing this for real. Can you promise me something?'

Anything, she thought, still holding his gaze.

'Promise me you'll think about it – or even better, do something about it. Start sharing this stuff online, enter some competitions, just start doing something.'

She blushed at the implied compliment and extended her hand to take the phone back. 'I'll think about it.'

'Do you mind if I send some of these to myself on WhatsApp?'

'Sure.'

He tapped the phone and handed it back across the table, his fingers grazing hers as she took it.

The next hour flew by as they chatted animatedly and laughed loudly.

'We better be getting back. I've to be at the exhibition by five.'

Emma slouched back and sighed heavily. 'I'm dreading that climb back up.'

'Don't worry, I know a guy.'

He looked over his shoulder, signalling to a bare-chested, mahogany-coloured local in a boat docked at the small wooden pier. That's Flavio, he's got a water taxi service. He'll take us home. One way is enough, especially after a lunch like this.'

Jack pulled out two fifty-euro notes, placed them on the table and raised his hand. 'I don't want to hear a word from you. I'm buying lunch, no argument.'

'But—'

'You might be one of those feminist types who doesn't want the man to pay for lunch, and that's cool, but I insist. You can buy me a drink later.'

They thanked the waiter and the owner and took the steps down to Flavio's boat. He put out his cigarette and extended a hand to Emma to help her climb aboard. The sun, high in the sky, beat down on them as they pushed off from the pier.

It had been the perfect lunch, and she couldn't decide which she was happier about: getting to take a boat home instead of another hike, or the unspoken promise that Jack had made to see her again later that evening for a drink.

She had to admit that, even though she didn't know what he had in mind, the latter won, and as unappealing as the idea of another hike was, she'd deal with it for the chance to spend another evening with Jack Bourke.

CHAPTER THIRTEEN

Emma rolled her suitcase to one side, stood on the top step and keyed in the correct four-digit code: One Eight Six One, which, the Airbnb owner had informed her, represented Italy's year of independence. The solid wooden door clicked as the lock released.

I have no recollection of standing here last night, she thought.

She reached down to grab her suitcase, turned the door handle and leaned her weight against the door to push it open. Her footsteps echoed in the stone corridor as she approached the sweeping stone staircase that led to the first floor.

'Apartment 1B,' she read aloud, making her way up the stairs.

A yellow potted plant on the windowsill of the first floor hid a single key out of sight.

'Yay,' she said with a smile as she turned the key in the lock, and finally gained entry to the apartment. Sparsely furnished and simply decorated, the studio overlooked an interior, cobblestoned courtyard, a central fountain emitting pleasant water sounds as she threw open the wooden shutters and unhinged the old-fashioned locks on both windows.

She leaned out and breathed in the fragrant air. Flowering jasmine lined the courtyard and swathes of wild wisteria billowed up and over the walls in a purple cluster. At the end of the wall was a solid wooden door that presumably led to the outside; a black cat curled up asleep in its shadow, in the dead heat of the afternoon sun.

She turned to look around the room. While it was decidedly less glamorous than the hotel, it had a charming, homely feel that immediately put her at ease. The entire apartment was painted white, the dark wood shutters a stark contrast, almost a focal point. She wondered if the owner had done that on purpose. The tiny galley kitchen had a two-ring gas stove, a small, white ceramic sink and an under-counter fridge. The white drawers held IKEA kitchen utensils and cutlery, and the white cupboards were filled with IKEA pots, pans and tableware. The fridge contained a small carton of milk, ground coffee, a punnet of strawberries, two eggs and a jar of homemade jam. She popped a strawberry in her mouth and shut the door.

She peeped inside the neat bathroom; it too was painted white, and the shower tiled with a pale green accent. The living area held a two-seater sofa, a small coffee table, and an end table with a pretty stained-glass lamp. A single shelf was loaded with an eclectic selection of what appeared to be dog-eared or well-read books in various languages, leftovers from previous guests, she suspected. She flipped over the welcome manual and connected to the Wi-Fi, her phone pinging instantly with notifications.

Two texts from Jo asking her if she could please call her and if they could talk, one from Eve saying she had cancelled the planned day trips and was loving beach life, and one from Jack.

Her heart gave a jump in her chest as she opened his text.

> Hey, I'm done here by 7 p.m. You free for dinner?

She texted back immediately.

> Yes! Sounds great

Dammit. That exclamation point was unnecessary, Emma, she said to herself. *Talk about sounding enthusiastic.*

Jack's response flashed up on the screen.

> Good. Don't forget you owe me that drink.

He added a wink emoji before continuing.

> Meet @7 at the bar beside the church. Will book table for dinner. Best restaurant in Giglio

'What do I wear?' she said aloud.
She typed again.

> Is it fancy?

> Yep. As fancy as they've got here. See ya later x

'A kiss. How do I respond to that? Shit.'
Best to just avoid it, she thought.

> Good luck being judge!

Jack replied with the thumbs-up emoji.

She tossed her suitcase on the bed and pulled out the dresses she had packed. Her favourite and one she knew looked good on her was a teal-blue satin midi dress. She frowned as she shook it out and noticed the wrinkles, but she had worn it often enough to know that they'd fall out with a little steam exposure. She hung it on the back of the bathroom door and put the rest of her clothes in the narrow closet.

One power nap and hot steam shower later, she pulled the heavy wooden front door shut behind her and walked up the hill towards the church. Jack was already seated with his friend at an outdoor table when she rounded the corner towards the bar.

Oh, she thought. *Is the friend coming for dinner too? Why do I have such a mental block about his name? Are we all going to dinner? Did I misinterpret his invitation? I hope he won't ask me about the girls.*

'Oh hello, Emma. Lovely to see you again,' she muttered to herself. 'Why are you here alone with Jack? Aren't you supposed to be on someone's hen party? Your friends? Remember them?'

Awkward, she thought.

Jack waved and stood up as soon as he saw her. He was dressed smartly in black pants and an open-neck white shirt.

God, you look good, she thought as she walked towards them.

'Wow. You look great,' he said.

She pretended not to notice as he looked her up and down. He greeted her with a kiss on both cheeks. She breathed in his scent as he moved from left to right of her.

'Thanks,' she said with a smile. 'You clean up pretty good yourself.'

'You remember Blaine,' Jack said, gesturing for her to take a seat alongside him.

Blaine. 'Yes, hi.'

Blaine nodded courteously. 'Nice to see you again, Emma. I hear you went to my favourite beach restaurant today.'

'Yeah, it was amazing.'

'I'm jealous. I had to work all day. All these demanding clients.' He grinned at Jack. 'Still, beats real life back home in Ireland, right?'

Jack adjusted his watch strap. 'And tonight, we're going to Ristorante da Maria. You'll love it,' he said, ignoring Blaine's comment.

'That's quite the culinary line-up. Jack is pulling out all the stops.'

'Don't mind him. He's just jealous.'

'I believe I just admitted that,' Blaine said with a smile. He stood up. 'Emma, can I get you a drink?'

'Oh, that would be great.' She glanced at the table. They were both drinking beers. 'I thought she only sold wine. Is the beer any good?'

'Hard to believe, but it's actually worse than the wine,' Blaine replied.

'I'll have a glass of wine, then.'

'Wise.'

He disappeared inside.

Thank God, she thought. *No mention of the girls or of having abandoned my friends in favour of his client.*

Jack shifted in his seat so that he was facing her. He sat back and leaned his right ankle over his left knee. He stared across the table at her. 'I'm glad you came.'

She smiled in response. 'Me too.' It was all she could think to say, but it was the truth.

'You look good,' he said, his eyes boring into hers.

She felt a rush of pressure fill her chest. Her cheeks flushed with the compliment, heat rising to her face.

'Thanks.'

He held her gaze. She couldn't stand it. Tearing her eyes from his, she looked down at the table.

Get a grip, Emma, she thought. *Say something.*

'So, is Blaine coming to dinner too?'

Jack shook his head and smiled. 'No, I just had to catch up with him on a few things because I've got this exhibition in Dubai in a couple of weeks, so he's just here for a drink. Our table is booked for eight.'

She couldn't deny that she was pleased it would be just the two of them.

'Dubai sounds fun. I've never been. My friend Eve was there on holiday a couple of years ago. That's where her fiancé proposed.' She tried but failed to suffocate a giggle.

'What's so funny?' Jack asked, smiling in response to her laughter.

'Well, it's not funny really. Or I should say, it is now, to me at least, but it probably wasn't at the time. She was standing in front of that famous, massive, dancing fountain; you know the one where they make the water move to the rhythm of the music that's playing?'

'The Dubai Fountain. Yes, I know it, it's like, fifty storeys tall and it's synchronised to music, yes.'

'Synchronised. That's the word I was looking for. Well, anyway, she was standing there, and they started playing Andrea Bocelli and Celine Dion's "The Prayer", and she'd had a few drinks and got all emotional and was bawling crying and turned around and Barry was down on one knee with a ring, and he'd arranged to have someone video the proposal, and there she was ugly crying her way through the whole thing.' She put her hand to her mouth to suppress the laugh. 'Sorry, it just makes me laugh every time.'

'Jesus, women are mean,' he said, grinning. 'Poor guy. That's terrible.'

'I know, sorry, I shouldn't laugh. Anyway, what's the exhibition?'

Blaine appeared from behind and placed a small, stubby glass in front of her. 'Apologies for the glass. I tried to ask if she had a proper wine glass, but she just glared at me. I don't think English is her strong suit, but in her defence, she did give me this.' He placed a plate of garlic crostini on the table.

Emma smiled. 'Oh, I've had these, they're good. Thank you.'

Blaine sat back down. 'I heard you asking about Dubai. You should know that this one,' he nodded in Jack's direction, 'will almost never tell you the truth – not about his work, anyway. He's the worst self-promoter in the business and I say that with not a little chagrin, as his agent.'

'Why?' Emma asked. She sipped the wine. 'Not as bad as I remember. What's going on in Dubai?'

Jack rolled his eyes. 'Blaine, will you give it a rest.'

'Absolutely not.' He turned to face Emma. 'It's not just an average exhibition. Jack, here, has been invited by the government of Dubai ... ' He frowned. 'Were you invited or summoned? I'm not sure, but anyway, he has been, let's go with invited ... to Dubai to do a commissioned piece for the palace.'

'No way! That's amazing!'

Jack drained the last of his beer. 'I don't have the job yet, it's just a chat at this point.'

'A chat with the head of government,' Blaine corrected.

'Yes, a chat with the head of government. It's nice to be invited, but I don't like to think about these things in advance as you've no idea how they'll pan out.'

'I'm not sure Dubai's government is prone to inviting people over for chats. I think that this is a concrete indication of intent, but sure ... if it makes you happy, we can say that you're going to Dubai for a meet-and-greet.'

Emma laughed. The banter between the two of them and the easy way they had with each other was indicative of years of friendship and a solid working relationship.

Blaine stood up and brushed down the front of his pants. 'Now, if you'll excuse me, I'm meeting someone at the pizzeria.' He turned to face Emma. 'I hear you're somewhat of an artist too?'

Her face flushed. 'Oh, no, it's just a hobby. I like to dabble in it from time to time, but these days I have less and less time so I've kind of abandoned it.'

'That's a shame. Jack tells me that you're quite good.'

'He's just being kind. What I do is nothing like what Jack does. He's on a whole other level.'

Blaine pulled on his navy linen blazer. 'Never underestimate your own work, even if you do it purely for fun; and most definitely, never compare it to anyone else's. Only you can do what you do.'

It was the second time she'd heard this sentiment.

'But anyway, enough of the life lesson lecture. Pick it back up again when it feels right. According to Jack, it would be a shame not to.' He tucked his chair back under the table. 'Now, *arrivederci*, you two. Jack, I'll see you tomorrow morning. Don't forget that we have that meeting at ten a.m.'

'God, I hate those things.'

'Yes, I know you do, but you'll show up and pretend to enjoy it all the same.'

'Right,' Jack said with an exaggerated sigh. 'The JB dog and pony show.'

Blaine glanced from one to the other of them and smiled. He patted Jack on the shoulder and turned to leave. 'That's the spirit. *Ciao.*'

Jack shifted in his chair and turned to face her. 'How's the Airbnb?'

'Cute. Small.'

He smiled. 'I figured. One guy owns that whole building and he's as cheap as chips. Converted six great apartments into ten Airbnb studios, and apparently, they're all like shoeboxes. I wouldn't mind but he's worth a fortune. Inherited a bunch of land from his grandfather.'

'How do you know so much about everyone here?'

'Like I said, I've been coming here for years. You learn more every time. C'mon, finish that,' he instructed. 'Getting a table here is no mean feat and they'll turn us away if we're more than ten minutes late.'

They stood up together, barely a foot apart. He smiled down at her. It was intoxicating to be so close to him.

They strolled up the narrow winding path behind the church. When they reached the pizzeria, its tables full and a line already forming with people awaiting a table, Jack placed a hand on the small of her back and guided her to the left, along a narrow footpath that curved around behind the old stone building.

She felt the warmth of his hand burn through the thin fabric of her dress. It felt almost proprietorial, and she didn't want it to end.

She slowed her step, not wanting to lose the connection with him.

The narrow footpath continued in a steep, curving incline, before it petered out into a series of two dozen steps that loomed above.

'Okay, last hurdle. You good?' Jack asked.

'Yep.'

He smiled at her. 'I promise, it'll be worth it. It's just at the top of these steps.'

She stood on the top step, turning to take in the view as she caught her breath. The restaurant was situated on one of the highest peaks of the island, a rambling old building, its stone façade crumbling at the edges. The hostess stood at a desk inside the door and greeted Jack warmly, as an old friend would. She extended a hand to Emma and spoke in Italian, before self-correcting and switching to English.

'Welcome to Ristorante da Maria. Please, follow me. I will show you to your table.'

Jack gestured for Emma to step ahead of him, and as she did so he placed his hand on the small of her back again. With that simple gesture, it felt as if he was claiming her, a silent signal to the rest of the room, one that wasn't unwelcome.

As independent as she was, it surprised her how much she liked the idea of it. Was she overthinking things again? Did it mean what she thought it meant? *Was* he claiming her in some silent way? Or was it just a gentlemanly gesture? Did inviting her to dinner constitute a date? It certainly felt like one.

The questions swirled in her head as their footsteps hit on the old wooden floorboards, echoing through two elegant dining rooms, each resplendent with large crystal chandeliers and original works of art, before they reached a third. The hostess guided them to the last table on the left-hand side of the room, alongside a door cut into the stone, with a wrought-iron balcony just outside. The view overlooked the old church down beneath them and the entire west side of the island, before giving way to the vast Tyrrhenian Sea beyond.

The hostess indicated towards the table. 'Here, we face west, so you will have the best view of the sunset. Enjoy your meal.'

The three of them sat to dinner: Jack and Emma on opposite sides of the table, and Emma's fully developed overthinking capability perched on her shoulder.

As she picked up the menu, she resigned herself to the fact that, even though she was hugely attracted to him, Jack Bourke was probably not interested in her in the same way.

She looked up at him from behind her menu and decided that, regardless of how he felt, she was happy to spend the next couple of hours in his company. He caught her staring, his face breaking into a smile.

'You look good,' he said for the second time. 'That's a great colour on you.'

She blushed. 'Thanks.' Her mind spun with the compliment.

'How about a glass of champagne to start?'

'Sounds great.'

She took a slow, deep breath and tried to focus her attention back on the menu. Jack ordered two glasses of champagne and they read through the starters and the pasta options together. She stole a glance across the table as he translated what he could of the menu.

Her eyes took in every inch of his face, his jaw, the strong line of his shoulders. Her attraction to him was building at a ridiculous rate and she couldn't deny that in that moment she wanted nothing more than to close the space between them and feel his mouth on hers. She licked her lips unconsciously.

Jack put down the menu and held up his glass.

'To unexpected encounters.'

The evening progressed with a slow, comfortable rhythm. Over a bottle of local white wine they talked about his career and the many obstacles that he'd had to overcome in order to break through at a professional level. He talked at length about his love of Kerry and how he couldn't imagine living anywhere else, no matter what the circumstances.

Emma told him how she had always wanted to be an artist and that even as a little girl her favourite pastime was to paint. But the draw of city life had been too great, and she had wandered into a mid-level management career in finance, one that afforded her the ability to live life on her own terms in Dublin city. She talked about her sister, who lived in Paris, and her aunt, to whom she was very close, who lived in London.

'All the women in my life are city people, especially the girls, Eve and Jo.'

Her face fell at the mention of Jo's name.

'Sorry, I had momentarily managed to forget about that whole situation.'

Jack leaned over and topped up her wine glass. 'No, no, no, not that face. Pull that great smile of yours back out. C'mon, don't go down that rabbit hole right now. Don't let it ruin your evening. These things usually have a way of working themselves out. You'll figure all that out with her eventually. Just stay in the moment.'

'You're right,' she said with a sigh.

'Anyway, this wine doesn't pair well with sad. Look,' he said, turning the bottle around, 'it says it right there on the label: pairs well with happy.'

She laughed. The weight of the conjured-up negative memory of the argument with Jo dissipated instantly.

'Much better.' He smiled at her, his gaze holding hers for long enough to mean something. She felt a wave of heat rise inside her chest, a physical reaction to him again. He placed the bottle back in the ice bucket.

'What about you?' she asked, desperate to change the topic of conversation.

'What about me?'

'You said that you knew all about mascara emergencies because you grew up with sisters. Are they diehard country people too?'

He smiled. 'Yep. None of us are city material.'

'What about the rest of your family?'

He frowned. 'Hang on,' he said, reaching into his pocket. He pulled out his phone, tapped the screen twice and put it back. 'Sorry, just got buzzed. How about another bottle of wine? That one is just about gone.'

'Sure,' she said, delighted at the thought of extending the evening even further.

He motioned for the waiter, ordered a second bottle and launched into a story about how he got his rescue dog, Bentley.

Has he just changed the subject? she wondered.

One sunset, two glasses of champagne, two bottles of wine and three exquisite courses later, they thanked the hostess and stepped out into the cool night-time air.

She turned to face him and smiled. 'Thank you for dinner, that was—'

Jack ran his hand through his hair. He turned his head to look at her, his eyes flashing wide and wild. 'I can't take it any more,' he said, stepping in so close that she could feel his breath on her face. 'If I don't kiss you right now, I'm going to lose my fucking mind.'

He didn't ask for permission, and she didn't stop him. He moved her one step backwards, his body against hers, and pinned her against the wall. The kiss was as furious as it was welcomed and she responded hungrily, wrapping both arms around his neck and leaning into him. She didn't want it to end. She felt all the uncertainty, the anxiety, leave her body as she allowed herself to melt against him, responding to his kiss with the same passion.

He pulled back from her and stared intently into her eyes. 'I need to get you home.'

She looked at him questioningly, her eyes searching his, trying to decipher what he meant. Get me home? *Drop me off?*

He read the question in her eyes and shook his head. 'Oh no, baby, you're not going home alone.'

CHAPTER FOURTEEN

Her place was closer. They didn't stop until they stood on the top step at the exterior door to her apartment, both breathless.

'Shit!' she said, pausing at the keypad. 'Hang on, I don't remember the code.' She fumbled in her purse for her phone. 'I hate big handbags. It's on my phone. I made a note of it.' She looked up at him. 'It's the date of Italy's independence, one-eight-something-something.'

He put his hand around the back of her head and pulled her in toward him, his mouth hard on hers. 'I don't know, and I don't care. Just find the goddamn code.'

She pulled out her phone triumphantly and entered in the four digits, eliciting a happy squeal when the lock released. They virtually ran up the flight of stairs. She had the key ready when they reached the door of 1B; it had barely closed behind them when Jack pinned her against the wall again, kissing her hard.

'I want to know every inch of you.'

She kicked off her sandals and pulled her dress over her head. He tugged off his shirt roughly, a button popped free, skittering across the tiled floor, his shoes hitting the skirting boards as he yanked them off and tossed them aside. He unbuckled his belt. It slithered through his pant loops, and he tossed it to the floor. He put one hand behind her head and grabbed her hair, wrapping it around his hand.

'If you don't want this, you're going to have to tell me right now,' he said, his breath coming fast and heavy.

'Don't stop,' she said.

He didn't. They lay, folded into one another, limbs entwined, their mouths wet, kissing, searching. Breathing heavily, they wound around each other, pulling each other closer and closer, their bodies moving in sync. He lay on top of her, his weight pressing her down onto the bed. She relished the feel of his body, firm and taut on hers. She wrapped her thighs around his hips, the sheets bunching up beneath her. She ran her hands up the length of his arms and across his shoulders.

Her hands felt small against him. She felt every inch of him, his chest pressed against hers. With her eyes closed, she breathed in the smell of him. Beads of sweat formed across her stomach where he lay on her, their bodies slippery, moving against each other.

He rolled off her and pulled her up. She straddled him and sat tall. Her hands traced the line of dark hair that ran from his chest to his abdomen. He smiled at her; his eyes wild with lust.

He wanted her and she could see it. It felt good to be wanted. She felt powerful.

Her mouth tingled from friction. She held his gaze as he reached one hand up and flicked open her bra clasp.

'Impressive,' she grinned. She shrugged her shoulders and it fell to the bed.

'Years of research,' he quipped as he cupped her breast, stroking her nipple with his thumb. She groaned softly, tilting her head back, the sensation of pleasure trickling down through her in small waves.

'Okay, that's it,' he said. 'I want you right now.'

In one swift movement he flipped her over and was back on top again. He lifted her hips, hooked one finger underneath each side of her panties and pulled them down in one fluid movement.

This time he didn't hesitate. He nudged her thighs apart with his knee, his eyes not leaving hers. His expression was one of pure desire. She wanted him more than anything, in this moment, her hands reaching for him, grabbing the cheeks of his ass, pulling him down towards her.

They moved together in silence for little more than sixty seconds. Every ounce of attraction she had felt towards him was bubbling up inside of her, released in one long moment of intense pleasure. She neither wanted to nor cared to be quiet. The sound of her drove him wild with desire, his groans following, as primitive as hers.

He collapsed on her and they lay together, wet with sweat, their chests heaving. She felt powerless under the weight of him, pinned there, every inch of her skin against him. She didn't dare to move, not wanting to lose the feeling of him, heavy on her now.

He leaned on one elbow. 'Are you okay? Am I hurting you?'

She couldn't shake her head as her hair was coiled

underneath him. 'No, you're not. Don't move,' she panted.

He stayed for several seconds until his breath slowed, then lifted himself off her and lay back heavily alongside her.

'Jesus.'

'Yeah,' was all that she could think of to say.

She licked her lips; her throat was dry, her skin saturated with sweat. He leaned over and kissed her gently, feeling for the balled-up sheet with his foot and tugging it towards them. He reached over and pulled her in towards him, her head resting on his chest.

She could hear his heart beating. He pulled the sheet over her shoulders, his left arm wrapped around her.

She closed her eyes and drifted off into a deep sleep, knowing no more until they stirred in the still darkness of the early hours of the morning, reaching for each other once again.

Who had woken up first? Who had reached for whom? She couldn't remember, but could clearly recall the slow, rhythmic lovemaking in the dark, their hands assuming control in the weighted darkness of the night. She had wanted him even more the second time. He had traced his finger down her neck, her breasts, her abdomen, his fingers finding her still wet from hours earlier.

'God, that's such a fucking turn-on,' he had said. She had smiled at him, not that he could see it.

'Don't move,' he had instructed.

He had run his tongue slowly underneath her chin, her throat, down her chest. She had groaned as he'd licked her nipples. His tongue flicking lightly, teasing her. She had reached for his shoulders. Tried to pull him back up towards him. She'd wanted him again, wanted to feel him on her, inside of her.

'No. Not yet,' was all he had responded. He'd continued, desire mounting in her as his mouth felt its way down along her body in the dark.

'Oh God,' she had whispered, her fingers gripping the sheets.

They had fallen dead asleep for the second time.

Now, hours later, she felt him, curved around her back, one arm draped across her waist. She opened her eyes slowly, blinking against the light that poured in through the window.

The small room smelled of sex, the sheets smelled of sex, she *definitely* smelled of sex.

Her heart began to pound in her chest as images of the night before flashed through her brain. She sifted through the visuals, willing herself to remain still and not wake him until she could make sense of her thoughts. Images from the initial round of hot, frantic sex flashed in front of her eyes, then the feeling of falling asleep on his chest, before waking in the dark, early hours of the morning.

She moved her right hand now, pushing strands of hair off her face. She could smell his scent on her hand and breathed it in deep. Her thigh muscles ached, but she already wanted more of him. She ran a finger under her eyes, hoping to wipe away any smears of mascara. There had been no time to remove make-up or attempt any sort of bedtime rituals. Everything had been forgotten, cast aside as carelessly as their clothes had been in the heat of the moment.

Jack stirred behind her.

'Good morning,' he said sleepily.

She shifted around to face him. 'Good morning.'

'Did you sleep okay?'

'Yeah, you?'

'The first time or the second time?' He smiled. 'I was dead to the world. I think you put some kind of spell on me.'

She leaned up on one elbow. 'Yeah, I forgot to mention my magic powers.'

'I seem to recall one or two.' He looked around the room. 'Any idea what time it is? I've no idea what I did with my phone.'

'No, not a clue. It's bright out, though, whatever that means.'

She scanned the room for her phone, aware that she was naked under the sheet. Suddenly self-conscious, she was reluctant to leave the thin veil of cover that it provided.

'Hang on, it's here,' he said. He leaned down, picking it up from the floor. '*Fuck!*'

In one swift move he threw the sheet back and leapt from the bed. 'Fuck, fuck,' he muttered. 'Where's my pants?'

He rummaged under the blanket at the foot of the bed and unwound his pants from its crevices, a wrinkled ball of material.

'What? What's wrong?' She sat up and pulled the sheet towards her.

'It's nine forty-five. I have a meeting in fifteen minutes.'

'Oh, shit, the one Blaine mentioned last night.'

'Yeah, the one he warned me not to be late for. It's with this aristocrat dude who rarely grants meetings. He's a bit of a prick, but we're trying to confirm him as lead sponsor for next year's festival and the organisers thought I could help.' He stuck his arms in the shirtsleeves and pulled it across his chest, stalling as he fumbled for the missing button second from the top.

'What the fuck?'

Emma giggled. 'I think that went flying last night. A sex casualty.'

He looked up at her and grinned. 'Open neck it is, then.' He ducked into the bathroom. She heard the tap run. She ran her hands through her hair, a tangled mess, the result of hours of sheet friction. He stepped back out of the bathroom and stuffed his shirt-tails into his pants. He looked completely dishevelled.

'I'm sorry about this, but I've gotta run. Are you free for lunch later? Tonight is the last night of the exhibition, so I'll be tied up until late. There's the awards thing after we close for the exhibitors. I've to give some bullshit speech. But I'll be done with this meeting by noon and will be free until around five.'

'Yes, I'd love to. I've got no plans.'

'Where are my socks? Why have I only got one sock? Shit.' He bent down under the bed. He stuck his bare feet into his shoes. 'Will have to do without them.' He leaned over the bed and kissed her, stood up then bent down and kissed her again. 'I want more of that later. I want more of you. I'll text you.'

He grabbed his phone, tapped his back pocket feeling for his wallet and pulled open the door. He turned around to face her. 'You could just stay right there if you like. It'd be kind of sexy to think of you waiting in bed for me for the next few hours. I could come back and pick up where we left off.'

'Go! Don't be late,' she teased.

'Okay, see ya later.' He winked at her and hurried out of the door.

CHAPTER FIFTEEN

At four minutes past noon her phone pinged with the sound of a text message.

> Hey! Just finishing up here. Can you meet me at the marina in thirty minutes?

She typed back immediately.

> Sure. What do I need to bring?

> Dress casual. Wear a swimsuit (unless you fancy skinny dipping)

> See you in a bit.

She pulled on a black one-piece swimsuit and threw a short cover-up on over it. Her phone pinged again, and she picked it up, smiling to herself, but the message was from Jo.

> Emma, please call me. I don't know where you are or how to reach you other than this. Please.

She sighed and stuck her phone into her beach bag.

Not now, she thought.

She knew she was delaying the inevitable and would eventually have to face Jo, but she didn't want to deal with all the drama right now, not when everything was just so lovely.

'You made your bed, Jo,' she said as she pulled the door shut. The sky was cloudless, and she stepped out into the searing heat of the midday sun.

'Hat. Dammit,' she muttered, running back inside.

Thoughts swirled in her head as she made her way to the piazza outside the castle walls. Flashbacks to the previous night, the intensity she had felt towards Jack building, the kiss outside the door of the restaurant.

If I don't kiss you right now, I'm going to lose my fucking mind.

A smile crept across her face, a 'cat got the cream' kind of satisfied grin. Crumpled sheets, Jack hovering over her, the weight of him bearing down on her. Her face flushed with the memory. Laughing. Lots of laughing. The simple pleasure of falling asleep in someone's arms. The flashbacks and thoughts continued unabated until she stepped into a taxi.

'*Buongiorno.* Can I go to the marina, please?'

'*Certo, signora.*'

'*Grazie.*'

She sat back, her thoughts switching to the situation with Jo. Was she being dramatic in not speaking to her? Was she overreacting? She shook her head, dispersing the negative memories, not wanting to allow their argument to sneak back in.

I'll deal with it later, she thought. She stared out of the window at the landscape flashing by. They passed the dusty sign for the vineyard.

Maybe we could do that tomorrow, my last day, she thought. *When does Jack leave?*

She hadn't thought to ask him; in fact, she hadn't thought about anything but him for the past twenty-four hours, but tonight was the last night of the exhibition, so did that mean he'd pack up and go tomorrow? She'd have to ask him at lunch.

The taxi pulled up at the top of the marina.

'*Eccoci qui, signora.*'

'*Grazie.* How much?'

'*Venti euro, signora.*'

She handed the driver a twenty-euro note. '*Grazie.*'

'*Grazie a lei. Buona giornata.*'

She could see Jack ahead, standing at the edge of the pier, talking on his phone. He had changed into shorts, T-shirt and a baseball cap and looked every inch the casual tourist.

He hung up and pocketed the phone as she approached.

'Hi,' she said, as she stepped alongside him.

'Oh hi!' He leaned in and kissed her, before gesturing down to a tanned, super-fit, thirty-something-year-old. 'This is Pierpaolo. He's going to take us to lunch.' He placed one arm around her shoulders. 'This is Emma.'

'*Buongiorno, signora.*' He tipped his fingers to his forehead and looked back at Jack and grinned. '*Ora, capisco.*'

'*Buongiorno,*' Emma replied. She turned to look at Jack. 'What did he say?'

'He took one look at you and basically said that he gets it now. I told him that I wanted to take someone to lunch at the cove and he said he was booked for the day. I told him it was important and asked him to do me a favour. He got someone else to cover his other run so that he could take us. I don't go to the cove with anyone else. Only Pierpaolo.'

Her face flushed at the thinly veiled compliment. 'I thought you said you weren't much of a boat person?'

'I'm not, but when one of the best beach restaurants on the island is only accessible by boat, what are you going to do? I'm not going to miss out just 'cause of some irrational fear.' He nodded towards Pierpaolo. 'I've known Pierpaolo for years and I only go out with him. Look at him. Doesn't he look like nothing is gonna go wrong on his watch?'

Emma smiled. 'Yeah, he does.'

'*Allora, signori, andiamo?*' Pierpaolo asked.

Jack stepped down onto the pier and extended a hand back up to Emma. '*Sì, andiamo.* Let's go.'

They clambered into the wooden motorboat as Pierpaolo took up at the stern, one hand on the outboard engine, the other on his right thigh. He guided the boat gently away from the pier, turned back to face the mouth of the marina and slowly navigated his way past the lines of boats already docked. Jack pulled Emma in close to him, wrapping his right arm around her waist. As soon as they had left the marina, Pierpaolo cranked the engine and picked up speed. Emma stuck her hat into her beach bag.

'It's about a thirty-minute ride,' Jack said.

She turned to answer him, but he stopped her short with a kiss. She couldn't be sure if it was the increased speed or his kiss that took her breath away, but it caught in her chest as she kissed him back. As the wind picked up, her hair whipped around her face. Jack brushed it back from her face, pulling her in against his chest. They passed Hotel La Guardia, the last building on the marina. Emma looked up at the terrace as they sped by. Tables were occupied with lunchtime diners, but there was no sign of Eve and Jo. She sighed softly, wishing it could all be different, but a flash of Jo's confession caused her heart to pound in her chest again.

I'm just not going to think about it right now, she thought, leaning into Jack.

Pierpaolo made a sweeping left-hand turn around the arid, rugged granite rocks that bordered the hotel and formed a peak at the north end of the island. He turned around and shouted something in Italian to Jack, his voice bouncing over the wake.

'What did he say?' she asked, shouting to be heard above the noise of the outboard motor.

'He said when we make this turn, we'll face the wind, so it'll be rough for the next ten minutes.'

'Okay.'

Emma tucked closer into him, feeling the warmth of his body, loving the feel of his arm protectively cast around her. Pierpaolo hadn't exaggerated and they continued for the next ten minutes in silence, the wind whipping their faces and rendering any attempt at conversation futile. Tears stung her eyes as she tried to watch the towering, rugged landscape zip by. In the end she gave up, leaned against Jack and closed her eyes, enjoying the power of the wind, and the roar of the outboard motor. His hand squeezed her shoulder, and she looked up at him. He smiled down, leaned forward and kissed her gently, before pulling her back into his embrace. She sighed a happy sigh that only she could hear.

The boat followed the curve of the land, turning further left, around the top crest of the island. Once they had cleared the bend, they faced east, and the wind dropped as suddenly and dramatically as it had risen.

Pierpaolo turned back to face them. '*Ora va bene*,' he said as he reduced his speed slightly. 'Now is okay,' he translated for Emma's benefit.

With the wind diluted, she shifted slightly in her seat, her back curved into Jack. He leaned back against the boat and wrapped his right arm around her shoulder, brushing her hair from her face with his left hand. The island looked gigantic from the water, its granite rock face standing several hundred feet above them. Flocks of seagulls hovered offshore, trailing fishing boats that offered the potential of a fish carcass reward.

Wildflowers dotted the rugged terrain that whizzed by in bursts of burnt orange and bright yellow, while at the base of the black-grey granite rocks, crystal-clear water lapped against the stone, slowly and determinedly moulding the rock face as it had done for thousands of years. It looked to Emma as if the island of Giglio had been carved by the wind and moulded by the sea, such was its raw, rugged beauty.

Pierpaolo slowed the boat and navigated towards an arch-shaped cave carved from the rocks by centuries of wind and seawater. As the engine was reduced to a choking whimper, the only other sound was that of the clear, aquamarine water gently licking the interior walls of the dark, cavernous cave.

'Fancy a dip?' Jack asked. He stood up and pulled off his T-shirt.

Emma's eyes followed the line of hair that ran from his chest down to the waistband of his shorts, a flashback to the previous night searing into her brain.

'We can swim through the cave and Pierpaolo will pick us up at the other side.'

Emma looked from Jack to the mouth of the cave alongside them. 'Swim through the cave? It's pitch black in there!' she exclaimed.

'No, it's dark, but not completely black. You can see the whole way through.'

'How long is the cave? I mean, the swim. Is it long?'

'No, it's not long. Five minutes to the other side, maybe. It's cool in there.'

She hesitated. 'How deep is it? I don't want to sound like a scaredy-cat but I'm a bit nervous when I'm out of my depth.'

Jack glanced at the cave. 'It's deep enough. A few metres, probably four or five. But the water is calm the whole way through. Does that help?'

The truth was she was terrified. She knew how to swim but anxiety gripped her when she was too far out from shore, or too far out of her depth. But here was Jack Bourke inviting her to swim alongside him through a cave. She desperately didn't want to say no.

'Kind of, as long as you'll be next to me,' she said slowly.

He put a hand on her shoulder and leaned towards her. 'I'll be right there with you. It'll be fine, I promise.'

'What about sea creatures? Are there any sea creatures in there?'

He laughed. 'No, no sea creatures. The only thing that might be in the water is jellyfish, but it's still early in the year, so it should be fine.'

'Jellyfish? So, how do you avoid them?'

'You can't. You won't be able to see them, but if you get stung, I'll pee on you, don't worry.'

'That's gross, but thanks.'

'You don't have to do it if you're nervous.'

He tucked his T-shirt under the seat. It was clear that he was going in.

'No, I want to,' she replied. 'I'm just not the best swimmer, that's all.'

'I'll be with you the whole way. You'll be fine. Trust me.'

Jack dived overboard as Pierpaolo hooked a three-step ladder over the side of the boat. The usual Emma would have demurred and remained on the boat, reluctant to get into the dark waters of the cave, afraid to take her chances with any resident jellyfish. But this version of her was determined not to miss out. She pulled off her cover-up and tied her hair up in a knot. She climbed down the three steps, the water cold on her feet, then her thighs. Jack trod water at the mouth of the cave as she pushed off the bottom step towards him, the crystal-clear sea rushing up and over her shoulders.

She could taste the salt on her lips as she swam four strokes towards him, the shock of the cool water taking her breath away. Pierpaolo turned the boat and headed in the direction of the other side of the cave.

'Okay?' Jack asked as she reached him.

'Yes, it's beautiful.'

'C'mon, just stay by my side right here in the middle.

Don't touch the edges. Those rocks are sharp, and you'll get scratched up. It's going to feel like it's dark at first, but your eyes will adjust, so just give it a few seconds. Once you get into the cave the light will be behind you and your eyes will focus on the light on the far side. That's what's going to illuminate the water, okay? I'll be next to you the whole time.'

'Okay,' she replied. Her voice was tight, shortened by the chill of the seawater and the anxiety that bubbled inside of her.

Jack led the way, swimming slowly so that she could keep pace with him. His shoulders powered through the water, his strength propelling him effortlessly as they left the light and crossed into the dark, cold cave. Instantly plunged into darkness, Emma stayed close to his right side. She couldn't see him, but she could feel his movement through the water.

His voice came to her through the darkness. 'I'm right here, just give it a second and your eyes will adjust.'

'Okay,' she replied breathlessly.

He was right. The light that pierced through the darkness from the other side of the cave began to permeate the blackness, the dense impenetrable shroud that surrounded her giving way to a shadowy black-blue haze. The walls of the cave became clearer, the water that lapped up against her morphed from black to navy blue. The sounds of their arms cutting through the water bounced off the cave walls, the splashing, lapping sounds echoing around their bodies. It was at once unearthly and surreal, and she gazed up in awe at the jagged cave walls around her.

Time appeared to slow as they continued forward, each

of them lost in their own thoughts, their own reverie. She could make out his shape now, his skin luminous against the dark canvas of the sea, his shoulders cutting methodically, rhythmically through the water. True to his word he stayed by her side, remaining one stroke ahead of her so that she could both see and feel him. She continued in silence, not wanting to dilute the dark beauty of the moment with needless chatter. The shard of light ahead grew wider, stronger, the last ten strokes entirely illuminated by sunlight, revealing the deep blue of the water and the limpet-clad walls of the cave.

The sound of the outboard engine hummed out of sight as she approached the exit of the cave. Pierpaolo sat, patiently awaiting their return.

They swam to the boat, Jack treading water and gesturing for her to go first up the ladder. She hauled herself up, breathing heavily, seawater dripping from her skin as she stepped up onto the boat and into the warm embrace of the midday sun as Jack followed behind. Pierpaolo tossed a towel in her direction.

'*Grazie*,' she said, wrapping the warm, cotton towel around her body.

They sat side by side again as Pierpaolo put the boat into gear.

'Well?'

'That was amazing. There's no way I would have done that on my own.'

'It looks scarier than it is,' Jack said.

She patted the towel against her face. 'Thanks for pushing me. I never would have got in otherwise. Not a chance.'

He grinned and ran his towel over his hair. 'Sometimes

you just have to take a leap of faith.'

Pierpaolo shouted from the bow of the boat, over the rumbling sound of the engine. '*Andiamo? Siete pronti?*'

Jack gave him a thumbs-up and they nestled in close against one another. 'Ready for lunch?' he asked.

For the first time in a long time, she felt entirely and completely happy. She nodded her head in answer, not trusting herself to speak in that moment. The entire experience was overwhelming, and she felt more than a little bit emotional. He had just encouraged and helped her to overcome a fear, staying by her side, giving her the confidence to do it. This man she knew very little about was sweet, kind, caring, and she was drawn to him in a way that she'd never been drawn to anyone before. It was a little unnerving because the truth was, she wasn't just ready for lunch, she was ready for anything as long as it involved Jack Bourke.

CHAPTER SIXTEEN

Emma turned her face up to the sun as they continued along the coastline. Pierpaolo made a wide turn around the rock face, steering the boat to the left, towards a small cove and a bay with pristine aquamarine water. She gasped as the view unfolded before her: a small stretch of beach with two rows of yellow sun loungers, their yellow and white striped umbrellas flapping gently in the sea breeze that whipped towards the shore. The tall cliffs towered in an arc around the cove, providing shelter to the bay below.

On the right sat a metal structure, a dark grey colour that blended seamlessly with the granite cliffs. It was almost invisible but for the wooden deck and cluster of a dozen or so outdoor tables and chairs. Pierpaolo reduced his speed and guided the boat gently across the bay towards the restaurant. As she squinted from a distance, Emma could see that there was no interior to the restaurant. The small metal structure appeared to house a kitchen inside and the tables outside. It was easily the smallest restaurant she'd ever seen.

Pierpaolo pulled up to the pier and tossed a line onto the jetty. A shirtless old man, his skin a deep, dark brown, shuffled barefoot towards them, a cigarette dangling from his mouth. He looped the bow line around one of the iron dock cleats, securing the boat as it listed from side to side on the swell of the incoming tide.

The old man greeted Jack with a wave. '*Buongiorno,* Jack. *Ben tornato.*'

'*Buongiorno, Felipe. Grazie.*'

Jack stood up and turned to Emma, extending a hand to help steady her as she walked the length of the boat.

'Who's that?' she whispered.

'That's Felipe, the owner of the restaurant. He's basically the owner of the beach. Well, I mean, you can't actually *own* a beach in Italy, but the restaurant is his, as are those loungers over there on the shore, so this whole setup belongs to him. The restaurant has been here for something like sixty years. He built it way before any legal permits were required so nobody cared back then. But when the government began to implement development laws and restrictions and put planning guidelines in place, he was told that he would have to take it down. Rumour has it that he refused and said he'd blow up the cliff before he'd give up his restaurant.'

Emma laughed. 'Are you serious?'

'Apparently. He had lost his wife and son in a boating accident and the restaurant was the only thing he had left. He's a tough old bastard, so it wouldn't surprise me if the story was true.'

'Jeez, that's hard core.'

'Yep. The government eventually gave up. Probably figured that he wasn't doing any harm and they had bigger problems to solve. At the time Giglio wasn't even a popular tourist destination, so it didn't really matter. He stuck to his guns and won out. You've got to admire that.'

She followed Jack onto the dock. 'Totally.'

Felipe greeted Jack with a warm hug, slapping his back like an old friend. *'Allora, chi è la signora?'* he asked, turning to face Emma.

'*Si chiama* Emma,' Jack responded. 'Her name is Emma.'

'*Piacere, signora,*' Felipe said, extending a hand towards her.

His large, calloused hand dwarfed hers as he shook it firmly, smiling widely as he did so. He gestured for the three of them to follow him up the wooden steps to the restaurant and led them to a corner table facing the bay. He stood as they pulled out chairs and sat down, shouting something in rapid Italian towards the kitchen before he pulled out a fourth chair and joined them.

A waiter appeared with an ice bucket and a bottle of white wine.

'Oh, he's breaking out the good stuff,' Jack said, reading the label on the bottle.

'Why, what is it?' Emma asked.

'It's made here in Giglio, on this side of the island, by a small producer, just a few hundred bottles a year. It's excellent. It would easily win an award at the Italian wine awards, Vinitaly, but they don't produce enough to distribute it beyond Giglio, so they couldn't be arsed to enter the awards. Only a few places on the island sell it, Felipe's is one of them. He's a friend of the family that owns the vineyard.'

The waiter poured four glasses and stuck the bottle on ice. Felipe made a circling gesture with his hand. The waiter nodded and stuck a second bottle in the ice bucket. They never saw a menu, nor did they order anything.

Platters of food began to show up as the conversation morphed from Italian to English and back again, a delightful array of seafood dishes that showcased the freshness and flavours of the Mediterranean. The dishes ranged from wild-caught tuna tartare, stuffed zucchini blossoms, a spicy spaghetti shrimp dish that Emma couldn't pronounce and *zuppa di pesce*: a light, delicate seafood stew cooked in a tomato and saffron broth. Each of the mouth-watering dishes highlighted the bounty of the local products in a uniquely Italian way.

Felipe spoke a little English and told story after story, alternating between the two languages and asking Jack to translate when he got stuck. She guessed that Jack had heard these stories many times before so his ability to act as translator was more due to this fact than to his level of Italian comprehension. Though she could understand little, Emma sat among them, completely content, enjoying the moment, the conviviality, the rounded sounds of Italian being tossed over and back across the table. She wished she could understand more, wished that she could engage with even a little bit of Italian. She understood now why Jack was determined to learn some of the language. She would too if this kind of genuinely local experience was the payoff.

She marvelled at Jack's ability to keep up and at the obvious warmth and friendship that radiated from Felipe and Pierpaolo. For someone who returned just once a year, he was certainly warmly welcomed, and he had invited her into this world. He had pulled her in, not just to him, but to everything that he surrounded himself with here.

She looked across the table and caught his eye. He had

been watching her. He smiled a genuine smile, his eyes crinkling up at the corners.

In that simple moment, her heart felt full. It had been a long time since she had felt this from anyone, with anyone. What was it with this guy? Yes, she was on holiday; yes, they were on an Italian island; yes, she was having this great lunch with all these lovely people, having just swum through a cave and stepped off a boat. But somehow, it all felt natural. None of it felt forced or contrived. Everything felt easy with him. She didn't have to pretend to be anything or act any other way. She was just being Emma, just being herself, and it felt ridiculously freeing to do so.

A couple of hours and several bottles of wine later, the party of four broke up. Goodbye hugs were shared, and Felipe gifted a bottle of white wine to Emma, before they made their way back onto the boat.

'*Grazie! Ciao!*' was all that Emma could think to shout towards a waving Felipe as the boat motored out from the dock. 'Oh, I wish I could speak more Italian. That was fabulous, thank you!'

'*Siete pronti?*' Pierpaolo shouted back over his shoulder.

'Okay, sit tight. We're going to power our way back,' Jack said, pulling her in close to him.

'Yes, go! *Vai!*' he shouted back as the engine was powered up and the boat took off at speed.

After a fast, twenty-minute boat ride back to the marina, they clambered up onto the dock, Emma slightly dizzy from the rush of speed, wind and adrenalin. Blaine was waiting at the pier and waved in their direction, a duffel bag in his hand.

'Thanks, mate,' Jack said, taking the bag from him. 'I'll change in the bar here. Just need two minutes.'

'Okay, I'll go get a taxi.' Blaine waved to Emma before disappearing around the corner.

Jack turned to her. 'I've gotta go straight from here. Tell me you don't have plans tonight.'

'No, no plans.'

'Great. We can go back to the pizzeria for dinner if you like, seeing as all you got to sample there was garlic bread.'

'That sounds great. I haven't had pizza this whole time.'

He leaned in and kissed her gently. 'This might sound ridiculous, but I don't want to be apart from you for a minute longer than I have to. I want more of you later. I can't believe that we have to leave here tomorrow.'

'I don't even want to think about it,' she replied.

He put his hand on the back of her head and pulled her in closer, kissing her again, harder this time. 'God, you taste good. Where's your phone?'

'Here,' she said, pulling it from her bag.

'Okay, make a note of the code for my apartment. You can just meet me there. I'll be back by eight and we can go to the pizzeria straight from there. Zero-two-zero-six. It's the second of June, Italy's national day, or something. That's for the main front door of the building. The code for my apartment door is one-two-three-four. Someone clearly stopped giving a shit about security by the time they got around to coding the internal doors. I think they might all actually have the same code.'

'So, if someone wants to break into an apartment around here, they just have to enter a few key dates from Italian history or try the world's most stupid key code?'

'Basically, yes.' He laughed. 'I better get changed and catch up with Blaine. See you later.'

Her phone buzzed with a text message from Maeve.

> You've been gone abt 2yrs.
> If you don't come home soon, I'm gonna quit.
> Work sucks w/o you
> Gonna stay home and be a dog mom
> Hurry TF up! Xx

Emma smiled as she made her way slowly to the end of the street and jumped in a waiting taxi, realising just how lucky she was to be here. She needed to shower and do something with her chronically matted hair before dinner. If she was lucky, she'd have enough time for a power nap, as there hadn't been a lot of sleep the previous night and she hoped that that might be the case again tonight.

She checked the time as the taxi trundled up the hill. It was just after 4 p.m. She had to pack. She couldn't leave that until the morning. God knows how late tonight would be. No, she'd pack as soon as she got home. Pick out a cute dress for dinner and stuff everything else into her suitcase.

What time is he leaving tomorrow? I wonder if we're on the same ferry.

If tomorrow morning was going to be her last few hours with Jack, she certainly didn't plan on wasting them packing.

What time is my *ferry?*

She knew they had pre-booked tickets before

leaving Ireland, but had no clue what the departure time might be.

She resolved to check that too as soon as she got to the apartment and got back on Wi-Fi. Her stomach flipped upside down in nervous reaction at the thought of having to face the two girls the next day.

Tomorrow, Emma, she thought. *That sounds like a tomorrow problem. Stay in your happy, sexed-up bubble for tonight. You've got a dinner date with a hot Irishman and an award-winning pizza place for dinner. Doesn't get much better than that.*

She paid the driver and jogged up the hill past the church, keyed in her door code and tossed her beach bag on the floor. She dropped her still-damp swimsuit in the sink, stepped into the shower, and stood under the steaming water, her mind flashing back to the feeling of Jack's hands on her body. But as she massaged a glob of shampoo into her hair, her thoughts began to wander.

They were clearly compatible from a physical standpoint. The sex had been *phenomenal*, easily the best she'd ever had. But apart from some conversations over lunches or dinners about art or the benefits of city versus country life, and the fact that he was a very well-known and highly regarded sculptor, one who shied away from the spotlight and preferred the quiet life, she realised that she knew very little about Jack.

Frowning as she turned and rinsed, she decided that before diving into bed with him again, something she was one hundred per cent committed to, she would have to ask him a few questions.

She wanted to know more about the real Jack Bourke, the basic 'Relationship 101' stuff, before she slipped out of her dress and into his arms.

Satisfied with her resolution, she turned off the water, wrapped her hair in a towel and wiped the steam from the mirror, blithely unaware that she was getting ready for a date that wasn't going to happen.

CHAPTER SEVENTEEN

Fifteen minutes before eight o'clock Emma punched in the four-digit code for the door of Jack's apartment. The lock released and she pushed the heavy, solid door open, making her way back along the same corridor they had taken two nights prior, when he had rescued her in a state of drunken distress.

She glanced at the bed and smiled. It was neatly made with two decorative pillows at the head, in stark contrast to the crumpled mess of sheets she had woken up in the day before. She sat down on the two-seater sofa, admiring the minimalist décor and the clean lines of the furniture. This apartment was twice the size of her studio and was flooded with natural light from two windows in the living room and another in the separate bedroom.

Jack's stuff was neatly put away, his bathroom tidy, and two notepads and a laptop sat on a desk inside the window. She checked the time, her fingers drumming distractedly on the arm of the chair.

I should have asked him for the Wi-Fi code so that I could send him a message to let him know I'm here, she thought.

She pulled out her phone and opened her settings. The apartment number was displayed in the list of five available Wi-Fi networks, but it required a password.

There must be a welcome manual around here somewhere with the password.

She rifled through the stack of books on the coffee table. Nothing. A small cabinet in the hallway had two drawers, but they contained spare bulbs, batteries and a plug-in mosquito repellent.

The desk, she thought, crossing the room.

The desk looked antique and had one long drawer with a square metal knob in front. She pulled it, but it wouldn't budge. Using both hands she tugged hard, and the drawer released; the items sitting on top of the desk shuddered and shifted, the open laptop lighting up from the jolt.

The screen flashed to life, but it was the screensaver that first caught her attention.

A gloriously colourful photograph that was obviously taken in the Irish countryside; a pretty, blonde woman sitting on a ditch, smiling at the camera, clutching a grinning, cherub-like toddler, a little boy probably no more than two years old, she guessed, his Sippy cup held triumphantly aloft in the air. The background was one of green fields and stone ditches, a swathe of blue sea providing an idyllic backdrop.

She stood rooted to the spot, as she took in the photo, but it was the iMessage that suddenly flashed onto the screen from the top right side that stopped her in her tracks. It was from someone called Sarah.

> We miss you! Sam taught Bentley a new trick. So cute. See you 2mor for dinner. Hurry home!

She added a plane and a heart emoji.

Emma stood, frozen, staring at the screen.

The iMessage disappeared off to the right, the icon at the bottom of the screen now showing six unread messages.

She couldn't move. She stared at the screen, the smiling image of the woman and the toddler staring her in the face. He looked just like Jack: a mini-me.

Sarah.

Sam.

We miss you.

We.

We miss you.

For dinner.

He'd be home for dinner.

Home.

Hurry home.

We miss you.

She took a step back involuntarily, her eyes not leaving the screen. The photo was taken in Kerry, it had to be. It was exactly as Jack had described it.

Jesus Christ, she thought.

It was Valentia Island. She could make out the silhouette of the two islands in the distance. Jack had talked about them. The ones where they shot the *Star Wars* movies. This was where he lived.

Home.

See you for dinner.

He'd be home for dinner.

Her hands started to tremble, a surge of adrenalin rushing through her body. She blinked at the screen, tears pricking the backs of her eyes. She blinked again, twice, clearing her vision. The pretty, smiling, happy, blonde woman staring at her from the screen. From Kerry. From home. *Her* home. *Jack's* home.

How could this be happening? How? She had to be misreading it. This couldn't possibly be true. There was no way he could have lied to her, fooled her like this. No way he could have a family in Ireland that he'd just forgotten to mention. No. *No*. She took a deep breath and paced the length of the room.

'No, think. Think,' she said aloud.

She pressed her hands to her eyes. She felt lightheaded. This couldn't be happening.

Not again.

She paced, forcing herself to think back on the conversations they'd had. Were there any clues? Had he said something? Had she missed something? Anything?

'Fuck,' she whispered.

Then the memory flashed into her brain: an image from the night before, limbs coiled around one another. She had leaned on one elbow and suggested that they change their return flights to Dublin and stay for another couple of days. She had plenty of time off to use, and he ran his own schedule, so why not stay in Italy for a few extra, stolen days? For the first time ever she didn't care about the cost of changing her return flight. But Jack had dismissed the idea, saying simply that he had to get home, before changing the subject.

She sank down on the side of the bed and put her face in her hands. She recognised the signs by now: the pit in her stomach, the tight squeeze in her chest, they were all too familiar. She was suddenly cast back six months to the moment she had discovered Paul's affair. Even the circumstances were similar. She had found the text messages on his laptop as she had innocently searched for an upcoming hotel reservation. There had been hundreds of them ranging from PG to X-rated. She had felt the blood seep down to her feet as she scrolled and read, scrolled and read. Her hands had begun to shake as realisation sank in and adrenalin surged through her veins.

Jo had said that it was her body entering fight or flight mode. Jo, the person she had sought out after she'd slammed the door on her life and her future. Jo, who had been carrying on an affair with a married man for the past four months.

'Jesus Christ,' she whispered. 'Does everyone cheat?'

She breathed deeply as she tried to think rationally. First Paul, then Jo. Two of the people she loved most in the world. Her ability to trust had been shattered by Paul and rattled again by Jo's admission just two days earlier. And now, here she was standing in Jack Bourke's holiday apartment, staring at a photo of a pretty blonde and an adorable baby boy who looked just like Jack, both smiling at the camera, both apparently waiting for him to come home.

She put her head in her hands, her mind spinning, struggling to accept the reality of the situation. Paul and Jo had lied to her and fooled her for months, and yet here she was standing in front of more damning evidence having been apparently swept away by more deceit.

She looked around the room, her thoughts racing, her brain going into overdrive.

How had she fallen for this again? There had to have been red flags; she just hadn't wanted to see them, but there had to have been signs. Something. There was something that she had missed. She could feel it.

'C'mon, Emma, think,' she hissed.

She checked the time on her phone: 7:52 p.m.

Then she heard it. She could see him standing there at the edge of the pier talking to Blaine. 'Don't even think of emailing me when we get home tomorrow. I'm checking out for a few days and am looking forward to doing nothing until next week.' Blaine had made a comment. She couldn't recall it exactly... something about 'real life beckons'.

If Jack had nothing to do and was planning on taking a few days off work, then why couldn't he stay in Italy with her? What did he need to get back for? The realisation hit her like a gut punch: it wasn't *what* he had to get back to, it was *who*.

Her mind reeled now, her subconscious slowly started to release the observations, the thoughts, the weird feelings, the red flags that she had overlooked. She stood in his living room, the reel of visual memories of the past few days running on speed through her brain.

Apart from the time they were on the boat with Pierpaolo, he had only kissed her when they'd been alone: red flag. He hadn't kissed her or made any move towards her in front of Blaine: red flag. He had changed the subject when she'd asked about his family: red flag. He had hung up the phone that day at the marina when she got close to him: red flag.

Her mind ran back over lunch just hours earlier. What was it he had said to Felipe? 'Her name is Emma.' That was it, no clarification, no possessive pronouns.

'I wasn't his anything. I was just Emma. More red fucking flags.'

Rage began to take hold now. Her face and neck flashed red, beads of sweat breaking out on her forehead and under her arms. Her mind span, she felt lightheaded, sick.

She'd been had. Again.

She'd been taken for the greatest fool of all time, the greatest cliché of all time. She'd been a casual, disposable holiday fling, a holiday fuck far away with no evidence and no strings. He hadn't wanted to stay any longer than originally planned because he had a family to get back to. The weight of the reality was crushing. She span in a circle in the centre of the room, tears threatening.

I have to get out of here.

Her phone read 7:55 p.m. She grabbed her bag and stuffed her phone inside as she dashed to the door, pulling it shut behind her. She ran down the flight of stairs, tugged open the front door and looked left and right. The street was empty. Hesitating for just a moment, she pinpointed the location of the art festival in her head. Doing a mental map calculation, that meant that Jack would be arriving from the street on her left. She'd have to take the long way down to avoid him.

That's if he's even at the fucking festival, she thought.

What could she believe or trust now? She turned to the right and dashed around the corner, jogging down the flagstone street, her sandals slapping against the old stones. Minutes later she arrived, breathless, at her apartment. She ran quickly up the steps, tears coming now. Her suitcase was open on the floor, with everything prepacked besides the outfit she was wearing and her planned travel outfit for tomorrow.

'Thank God,' she said, tossing the travel outfit into the case.

She swept her cosmetics from the bathroom sink into her handbag and pulled open the drawer on the nightstand, adding her eye mask and lip moisturiser into the bag. She turned around in a circle.

'What else? What else?' Her voice was frantic, ratcheted up in distress.

She yanked her phone charger from the wall and grabbed her Kindle from the nightstand. Every other surface was empty.

Zipping up her suitcase, she scanned the small room one more time, slung her handbag over one shoulder and headed for the door. Her mind reeling, she made her way down the hill to the piazza, the suitcase slowing her pace slightly as it bounced and rattled along behind her.

She waved at the solitary taxi and climbed into the back, shoving her case in ahead of her.

'*Buona sera*,' the driver said as he turned the ignition in the car.

She stared at him, her heart pounding in her chest, her breath coming hard.

'*Allora, dove andiamo?*'

Her mouth opened and closed. She hadn't thought this through. She had known only that she had to get out of Jack's apartment before he got there and get out of her own before he showed up. She hadn't thought about what to do next. 'Um . . . '

The driver looked at her in the rear-view mirror and raised an eyebrow. '*Signora*, where you go?'

'Yes, I know what you mean,' she said. 'I just don't know where the hell I'm going. Sorry.' She blew out a long, deep breath. 'The marina, please.' It was the only thing she could think to say. '*Grazie.*'

He looked at her in the rear-view mirror for a moment longer.

Great, she thought. *He thinks I'm fucking crazy now too.*

Her mind raced, her thoughts in frantic competition with each other as the taxi made its way down the hill. Jack had a wife, or partner . . . a something, and a toddler, a baby . . . he was just a baby. Sarah and Sam and Bentley, all waiting for him to come home.

She felt sick again. She swallowed hard, closed her eyes and leaned her head back on the headrest. How had she ended up here again? Fooled, deceived by yet another man. But this was worse, this one had a wife, or whatever she was. This time it was *she* who was the other woman.

A cold chill settled over her and her eyes opened in a flash. She was guilty of doing the very thing she had attacked Jo over. She had got on her high horse and had accosted her for being the other woman, when in truth she knew nothing of her, or their story. She hadn't given Jo a chance to explain. She had just eviscerated her and walked out.

I'm no better, she thought.

She wiped her face with the back of one hand, stabbing her fingernails into the palm of the other, determined not to fall apart in the taxi. She checked her phone. The screen was blank, devoid of any notifications, except the time. It would remain that way until she connected to Wi-Fi again.

She wondered where Jack was right now. Had he arrived home? Had he tried to call her? Shown up at her apartment? Was he standing on the street outside her place, dialling her number, confused at her non-arrival? Or had he walked into his apartment and seen the screensaver and the message and put two and two together? Did he realise yet that he was busted?

She felt sick at the thought of it. She thought of the blonde woman smiling through the lens of the camera at Jack, sitting at home, waiting for him to get back the next day. She had mentioned dinner. She had thought ahead about tomorrow night's meal, excited to have him home. The poor woman was oblivious, just like the woman in Jo's situation. Both just carrying on with their normal lives, unaware of the web of lies and deceit they were unwittingly playing a part in.

Her stomach turned upside down and sat, heavy, weighted down with a pit of anxiety. She didn't want to know. She didn't want to hear his pathetic excuses, the usual mouthful of lies; she'd heard them all from Paul. She was disgusted, with Jack and with herself. How could she have been such a fucking idiot? The good-looking, charming artist, interested in her art.

She stared out of the window of the car. All he'd done was tell her that her art was good, her butterfly painting was special, *she* was special. She'd wanted to believe it all so badly. Paul's betrayal had rattled through her heart and soul like a train, shattering her confidence and self-belief. She hadn't painted since then, the butterfly piece being the last one she'd worked on before Paul's betrayal had broken her trust and shattered her heart into pieces. All Jack Bourke had had to do was shower her with a little praise. She'd been only too happy to believe the bullshit, to step out of her clothes and into his arms. She'd accepted praise and attention in exchange for allowing him to slip off her underwear.

'Pathetic,' she whispered.

The driver came to a stop in the piazza. She paid him and stepped from the car. The night air was still, jovial sounds of chatter and laughter being carried on the light breeze from the restaurants just a few feet ahead of her. She was back where it had all started just days earlier, but everything had changed.

CHAPTER EIGHTEEN

Emma stepped into the foyer of the hotel. Within seconds her phone lit up and emitted a series of sounds in rapid succession: pings from WhatsApp and iMessage and two missed call notifications. She opened 'Settings', scrolled to 'Blocked Contacts' and added Jack Bourke's name to the list.

'*Buona sera*,' the receptionist said in greeting, before turning her attention back to the couple in front of her.

Emma faked a smile and took the stairs up to the first floor, scanning the room as she entered. There was no sign of either Eve or Jo. She wasn't sure if she was relieved or disappointed.

'*Dio, io! Mamma mia!*' Stefano exclaimed as he ducked out from behind the bar and engulfed her in a hug. 'You stay away all this time! All these days you don't come back to the hotel or to your friends, but now you arrive!' He joined his hands together as if in prayer. '*Cos'è successo?* What has happened? You are okay?'

'Yeah,' she said slowly. 'Stefano, can I get a drink?'

He put a hand gently on her cheek. '*Certo, certo.* Come and sit here near to me.' He wheeled her suitcase into a corner, took her by the hand and guided her to a stool at the bar. 'You sit and I will make the drink.'

Moments later Stefano placed a negroni in front of her. '*Ecco.*'

She leaned forward and took a sip. 'Thank you.' She looked around the bar again, scanning the crowd. There was one large party of eight, and a few couples sitting cosily on lounge chairs, chatting intimately, each twosome locked in their own happy holiday bubble.

Stefano handed two Aperol Spritz across the bar to the waitress.

Even the fucking drinks look happy, Emma thought miserably.

'Do you know where the girls are?'

He paused for a moment, one hand leaning on the bar. 'Tonight ... tonight I think they go to a restaurant at the marina, for the last night. You will go to meet them there?'

'Oh, no, I'm just going to stay here.'

He was shaking a cocktail shaker furiously and paused, leaning across the bar towards her. 'Okay, you stay here. Is okay. You can eat here. Tell me what you want, and I will talk to the chef. *Va bene?*'

She smiled, despite her mood, wondering how much he had heard about the fallout. 'Okay, *va bene*. Thank you.'

She unlocked her phone and typed a message to Eve.

> Hi. I'm back at the hotel. Long story. I'm so sorry about everything.
> I hope you're not mad. I've been had.
> Taken for a fkng ride.
> See you later. I'll be in the bar xx

The three-dot ellipsis pulsed immediately.

> WTF? We'll be back in fifteen minutes.

Emma typed.

> No. Please don't change your plans. That'll make me feel worse. I'll see you later.

There was no further response from Eve.

'Shit,' Emma muttered. She downed the negroni. This was going to be a showdown or a shitshow. Maybe both. 'Stefano, what's the word for another again?'

He looked up from his phone. '*Un altro.*'

'That's it. Can I have *un altro*, please?'

He laughed. 'How I can say no to you with that beautiful face? But please, you must do something for me.'

'Ask me anything. Apparently, I'm here for the taking,' she said grudgingly.

He shook his head. '*Non ho capito.* I don't know what this means.'

'Sorry, just ignore me. Yes, what do you need?'

He walked around the side of the bar towards her. 'I need for you to smile. Is no good to see you sad like this. Whatever it is, this bad thing that happen. You are here, in Italy, with your friends, no?'

He put an arm around her shoulder. She looked up at him.

'Okay, thank you, Stefano. You're a good man.'

'Now I make you one more negroni, but you must stop to be so sad, *capisce?*'

'Okay, deal,' she said, as she sat back on the bar stool. 'But only because I really need that negroni.'

She heard Eve's voice from the other side of the room behind her. 'Jesus Christ!' Eve rushed towards her and engulfed her in a hug. 'If you ever do that to me again, I'll kill you. You understand? Don't ever disappear like that again. We've been worried sick about you.'

Emma had the good grace to look sheepish. 'I know. I'm sorry. It was a knee-jerk reaction. I'm sorry.'

Jo stood in front of her. 'Emma, I'm the one who's sorry. I didn't think. I just started telling you the whole story and I didn't think about what that might feel like for you. I—'

'No. Stop,' Emma said, stepping down from the bar stool. 'I'm the one who needs to apologise.' She looked from Jo to Eve. 'To both of you. I just freaked out. It took me right back to the fallout from the whole mess with Paul.'

She looked over her shoulder and pointed towards a sofa in the corner.

'Let's go over there so we can talk for a minute.'

They settled in the chairs and Emma turned to face Eve.

'Eve, I'm sorry I stormed off like that. It was a really shitty thing to do to you and I'm not trying to make an excuse, but when I heard Jo's story it just sort of triggered something in me and I was right back in that moment when I found out about Paul's affair. The whole nightmare just reignited all over again and I was back in the thick of it.'

She reached over and squeezed Eve's hand. 'But I shouldn't have run out like that. We came here to celebrate your hen party and your last few weeks of being single and I totally overreacted. I'm sorry.'

'I know you are,' Eve said. 'But honestly, Emma, I've had the best few days ever just hanging out at the beach and wandering around and yes, even eating pasta every day.' She grinned. 'Turns out my discipline is no match for fresh pasta in Italy. Jo was so mortified that she just kind of went off and did her own thing too, so we ended up just chilling out by ourselves and no offence, but I had a lovely time on my own. I never get to do this at home, so honestly, it's all good.'

Emma turned to face Jo. 'I'm sorry I freaked out. I should have stayed and talked it out with you but—'

Jo cut her off. 'Emma, I'm so sorry, I—'

'No, wait, let me finish. I'm sorry I reacted the way I did, but I'm not sorry for the things that I said. Jo, I don't know how this all started or where your head is at, but this is bigger than just you. There are two little babies involved and a wife. He has a young family, Jo.'

She shook her head and took a deep breath. It was going to be tough to voice what she wanted to say to her friend, but she felt that she had to. Someone had to.

'Look,' she continued, 'I don't know anything about him or whether this is real or just some crazy fling, but frankly, it doesn't matter. You're doing it the wrong way and you can't keep going. If this is real, and he decides that you're the one and he leaves his family, then that's on him, but you can't keep playing both sides. You being available while he's still married and living at home is really convenient because right now, he doesn't *have* to choose. I don't want to sound all judgy, but there's a better way to do this. Marriages break down all the time.'

She glanced at Eve. 'Eve, I think you're one of the lucky

ones, but about half of marriages fail, that's just a fact. But Jo, affairs only cause pain. If this is real, then you need to find out. Give him the ultimatum, make him choose. Because he can't have both, and I promise you that if you don't, this will end in disaster, and you'll be the one to take the fall.'

Jo sighed. 'I know, I know.'

'Jo, you deserve one hundred per cent of someone,' Eve chimed in. 'You deserve to be happy, in a great relationship with a guy who adores you, but it's got to be on your terms, and it's got to be exclusive. I know you, and maybe it's all hot and exciting now, but eventually you're going to want it to be real. I agree with Emma. You're going to have to be the one to step up here because right now he's got access to you, so he doesn't have to.'

A waitress approached their table.

'Look,' Emma said, 'no one is perfect. No situation is perfect, and you can't choose who you fall in love with.'

'I think that you can, actually,' Eve said. She looked up at the waitress. 'Can we get a table for dinner, please?'

'*Certo.*' She gestured towards the dining area. 'Any table you want. Whenever you are ready.'

Emma and Jo looked at Eve.

'Can what?' Emma asked.

'You *can* choose who you fall in love with, or I suppose who you don't fall in love with would be a better way of putting it.'

Jo frowned. 'You're not making any sense.'

'Okay, I'm about to get married, and in a couple of weeks I'll have a husband wandering around out there and I'd prefer if another woman didn't hook up with him. I'd prefer if, when she realised that he's married, she'd back off and go find someone else to fall in love with. We meet people all the time, but it's not like you meet someone, say hello and fall in love. There's a time lag, a time delay, and as you get to know them more, maybe you have feelings that start to develop, blah, blah, blah. What I'm saying is that at the point when you learn that that person is married, that's when you stop. That's when you hit the brakes – or should, at least. Back off. Whatever. If they are married to someone else, then the right thing to do is stop, while you can and before it goes any further.'

Jo shook her head. 'Sounds great in theory, Eve, but it just doesn't work that way. I didn't set out to fall in love with someone else's husband, that was never my intention. But as you say, we met and bit by bit we got to know each other. We were working together, not in the same practice, but in the same field, so we met a couple of times over the course of a year and slowly we got to know each other more. That's all that happened, that's all that it took. Bit by bit, meeting after meeting, it just grew. I mean, I was attracted to him from the start, sure, but I knew he was married, so it's not like I just jumped the guy. But the truth is that every time I saw him again, I felt something. Call it chemistry or spark or whatever you want, but it was real. He felt it too and it grew until it became greater than the fact that he was married to someone else. I know it sounds really shitty and heartless, but I just stopped caring about or thinking about this other woman, his wife. I wanted him more than I cared about the consequences.'

Eve sank back in the chair. 'Some pre-wedding pep talk

this is. You're really selling me on the idea of marriage right now.'

'No, that's different,' Jo insisted. 'You two are *actually* happy together. You're compatible and the best of friends. This guy, who shall remain nameless... he's just not happy with her, and she's not happy with him. They're just stuck. And when you're not happy or fulfilled, at home, at work, whatever, you start to look elsewhere for it. That's it. It's no mystery. It sucks but it's that simple.'

'It's fucked up is what it is,' Eve said. 'Why even bother getting married at all then?'

Emma raised both hands. 'Okay, okay. This is going in the wrong direction. Eve, you found your forever man. You two belong together, you're getting married, and you'll live happily ever after, okay? We don't need any last-minute doubts or jitters from you.' She looked at Jo. 'And you, you need to figure out what you're doing. You can't just keep having an affair with this guy. It's not fair on anyone and it won't end well, but you've got to drive this. The other woman is not a good look on you.'

'Who made you Dr Phil all of a sudden?' Eve asked.

Emma sighed and shook her head. 'When I left here that night, I booked an Airbnb up at the castle. I got a taxi up and was looking for the place when I bumped into Jack.'

'Jack, the sculptor?'

'Yes.'

'Ooh,' Eve said, a smile forming on her face. 'There we were thinking you were all sad and alone, but it turns out you were with he-with-the-gifted-hands. No wonder you went dark.'

Jo sat up straight and folded her arms. 'Can't wait to hear this.'

Emma blushed and dropped her chin to her chest. 'Yeah, I just sort of fell into it. Headfirst. It was hot and heavy and amazing.' She looked up at Jo from under her lashes. 'But it turns out he's married . . . or living with someone, whatever, but not single. I didn't know. I just found out tonight.'

'Ah,' Jo said, a small smile settling on her face. 'No wonder you were so quick to release me from that judgy death grip you had me locked in. So, it's a case of glass-houses and stones, is it?'

'Yeah, I suppose so.'

'How did you find out?' Eve asked.

'We'd arranged to meet at his place tonight. I got there first and let myself in. His laptop was open—'

'You broke into his laptop and *stalked* him?' Eve shrieked.

'No, of course not! I wasn't looking for anything. I didn't know he was married or partnered-up or whatever. No, I just bumped into the desk and the laptop screen sprang to life. There's his screensaver with her and this adorable little boy, a toddler. Then a message flashed up on the screen saying, "We miss you. Hurry home". Oh, and "See you for dinner".'

Eve leaned forward open-mouthed. 'Wow, that's pretty shitty. What is it with all these men?! Jesus.'

'I know. I can't believe I fell for it. I'm no better.'

'No,' Eve insisted, 'wait a minute. This is a totally different situation. You didn't know anything about him, and if he hit on you, then you're allowed to assume that he's single, cause if he's not, he's a piece of shit.'

She turned to face Jo. 'Sorry, Jo, but I'll never see it any other way.'

Jo shrugged. 'I get it.'

'Emma, don't you dare go feeling guilty for whatever happened over the past few days. This is a different beast, and you haven't done anything wrong.'

'Yeah, except fall for the wrong guy,' Emma said with a grimace.

'Welcome to my world,' Jo responded. 'Bet it was hot, though.'

Emma puffed out a breath. 'He was *fire*! It was absolutely insane.'

Eve grinned. 'Well, we did say that you needed a recovery man, right? You needed to move on from Paul the prick, and now you can. You had hot sex with a hot sculptor.'

'Hot, married, dad sculptor,' Emma mumbled.

'Yeah, well, you didn't know that, so stop beating yourself up. You did the decent thing – you went on holiday, had a holiday fling and now you can go home and get on with the rest of your life.'

'I hate to interrupt this deep and meaningful conversation, but is anyone else hungry?' Jo asked.

'Yes,' they replied in unison.

Eve stood up. 'Okay, well, this is our last night on the island, ladies, and I think we've dedicated enough of it already to talking about men, so how about we order a bottle of champagne, get some menus and get back to what this whole trip was supposed to be about. Me.'

'Let's do it,' Emma replied, grateful for the change in conversation. As they walked to the table, she faked a smile, determined not to bring down the tone of their last night. Even though her heart ached at having to walk away from what had for a fleeting moment felt so real and had been so welcome, and her ego was bruised for having fallen for the greatest deception of all time, she was glad to be here with two women who loved her unquestioningly and unconditionally.

A waiter distributed menus and a wine list as Stefano presented a bottle of Franciacorta.

'This is Italy's champagne,' he said, removing the foil covering. 'Is the best in Italy. I think you will like it very much.' He popped the cork and poured three glasses. 'I am very happy to see three friends together again and smiling. Is better like this, no?'

'Yes,' Emma agreed.

Eve raised her glass to her lips. 'Bygones, Stefano.'

'What is bygones?' he asked with a frown.

'It means that it's over, in the past. Forget about it and move on.'

'I like this. This I think I will use. Bygones,' he repeated. He turned to face Emma. '*Salute*. I am happy to see that you are happy again. Is not good to see you sad like when you come here tonight to the bar. Life it is short, no? Too short to be sad. Look at where you are.' He gestured around the room and towards the bay beyond, shimmering under the light of the moon. 'You are in Italy. Is not good to be sad.' He continued to look at Emma. 'You must choose to be happy. Is a choice. To be happy is a choice and you must choose this every day. Some days, the bad things they will happen, but then, you fix the problem, and you must choose to be happy again.'

The girls clinked glasses. '*Salute!*'

Eve looked up at Stefano. 'That's solid life advice, Stefano. Here's a crazy idea. Have you ever been to Ireland?'

'Yes, one time, many years ago. It was very green and the people they were very friendly.'

Eve smiled. 'All true. Well, how about you come to my wedding next month? You can get a flight from Rome to Dublin, it's not that expensive, and just come in for the weekend.'

'*Davvero?* You say this for real?'

Jo piped up. 'Great idea! Yes, come, Stefano! Irish weddings are a blast!'

A wide grin broke across his face. 'Tell me the date and I will try to get the days off. I will love to come.'

'Brilliant,' Eve replied. 'Give me your number and I'll send you the dates on WhatsApp.'

'*Perfetto*. Okay, *speriamo in bene.*'

Emma turned to look up at him. 'What does that mean?'

He paused for a moment, translating the phrase in his head. 'It means that we hope for the good.'

'Hope for the best,' she corrected.

'*Brava*. Hope for the best,' he repeated before disappearing back to the bar.

Eve raised her glass. 'Ladies, here's to hoping for the best. Now back to me and the wedding of the year.'

The waitress arrived to take their order for dinner. Emma picked up the menu, scanning the pasta options as Jo ordered a bottle of red wine. She ordered the *spaghetti pomodoro*, the classic tomato and basil dish, her all-time favourite. Determined to park her real feelings for their last night in Giglio, she put on a smile and toasted the bride-to-be. She was sad that the holiday was coming to an end, and sad that what had started with such promise with Jack had come to a crashing end. But as she sipped her champagne and listened to Eve's happy chatter, she knew she'd never regret any of it. She knew instinctively that she would never forget the magical few days in Giglio, but she was going to have to work hard to forget Jack Bourke.

CHAPTER NINETEEN

Six weeks later

Jack Bourke was all over the news. Not an interview, because as Emma knew only too well by now, he didn't do interviews. No, he was all over the news because he'd just been awarded the Talbot Prize in London, the highest artistic honour in the United Kingdom. It was one thing to win and hold highly esteemed awards in one's own country, but it was another entirely to be awarded the same in a different country. It was the first time that an Irish artist had taken home the coveted prize, and the black-tie affair had been covered by all the Irish news outlets.

Emma scrolled through the photos on her phone. For a man who was most comfortable in the middle of the country and dressed down, Jack Bourke wore a tuxedo well. 'Dashing' was the word that came to mind as she zoomed in on a photo of him with the Irish ambassador. She knew that smile: quietly confident. She'd seen it up close. Too close, it turned out.

She closed the news app and tossed her phone on the king-sized bed.

She turned and stared out of the window at the sprawling gardens of Carton House, a stunning, three-hundred-year-old estate in County Meath, just a twenty-minute drive from Dublin city.

The rain had stopped an hour ago. Just in time for Eve's 2 p.m. ceremony. Emma and Jo had opted to spend the night, rather than deal with late-night taxis after the wedding.

She wondered where Jack was right now. The awards ceremony had been last night. Was he still in London? Back in Kerry?

She sighed deeply. She had never really known him at all.

A loud rap on the door startled her back to reality.

'It's me!' Jo announced.

Emma crossed the room and unlocked the door.

'Hi. We—' She stared at Emma, still in her robe, curlers dangling from her hair. 'You're not ready. We're supposed to be downstairs in ten minutes.'

'I know, I know. I just need a minute.'

'Are you okay?'

'Yep, fine. I just got distracted. You look amazing.' She looked Jo up and down. 'That dress is fab. Red is your colour.'

Jo sat on the edge of the bed. 'Thanks. I won't be able to eat dinner, though. There's zero room for expansion in this dress. Champagne and strawberries will be the way to go.'

Emma laughed and uncoiled the curlers from her hair.

'So, what's going on, Em?'

'Nothing, what do you mean?'

'Emma, I read the news too. I saw him all over the papers

when I went to get coffee this morning. Don't tell me that that's not what this is about. It's okay to be hurt, you know.'

'I know.' She sighed. 'It's just . . . I don't know. It was just weird seeing him in those photos. He looks so good and . . . I just thought I knew him better than that, that he wasn't that kind of guy. I thought it had meant something for real, whatever it was. I mean, I'm not saying I'd found the one, but just that it felt, I dunno, different.'

'I know. It sucks, but you're better off finding out sooner rather than later. This way at least no one gets hurt.'

Emma slipped off her robe and stepped into her dress. She turned to face the mirror. 'No one? I wouldn't be so sure of that.'

'Yeah, must have stung to see him all over the news. Shame it wasn't for murder or grand larceny or something.'

'Jesus, your mind works in weird ways sometimes.'

Jo perched on the edge of the bed. 'Thanks. I ended it with Mark.' She sighed. 'That's his name.'

Emma spun around. 'You did? What happened?'

'It was the right thing to do. He'll never leave her, especially not while the kids are young, and I get it.' She shrugged. 'That's not my fairy tale.'

'I don't know what to say. I'm sorry, but I'm proud of you. Not sure if that helps at all.'

'No, not an ounce, but hey, what can we do? Love. What a load of shite.'

'I'm not sure that's the emotion we're supposed to be channelling today,' Emma said, leaning into the mirror.

'True. Okay, let's go and get tipsy on expensive champagne so we can suffer through the religious bit. I promised Eve that I'd help get little Robert ready to walk down the aisle with his cousin. They're tossing out rose petals or something, so don't let me drink too much.' She stood up to leave. 'Oh, and Stefano's downstairs. He's looking pretty hot in his tailored suit.'

'Don't start. The last thing I need is to get involved with another man. Can we just please go and enjoy the wedding?'

'Yep! See you downstairs,' Jo said, pulling the door closed behind her.

With a spritz of perfume, a slick of lip gloss and one backward glance in the mirror, Emma grabbed her purse, stepped into her heels and headed downstairs. She heard Stefano's voice before she saw him.

'Emma! *Sei bellissima!*'

As she reached the bottom of the sweeping staircase, he greeted her with a kiss on each cheek and wrapped her in a hug. She had to admit that it was good to see him.

'You look great! You clean up well.'

Stefano frowned and looked down at his suit. 'What does this mean?'

She laughed. 'No, it just means that you look good all dressed up.'

'Ah.' He smiled. 'Okay, okay. *Grazie.* I am so happy to see you.'

'Me too. Jo is around here somewhere. Probably at the bar.'

'Yes, yes, I see her earlier. She said that she will be at the bar all day.'

'She's not lying, Stefano. C'mon, let's get a drink.'

They walked through the foyer to find Jo perched at the end of the sleek mahogany bar. 'Champagne, bitches?'

The bartender obliged by pouring two more glasses of champagne and topping up Jo's glass.

'Here, let's get a selfie,' she said, pulling out her phone. 'Look at us all glammed up. What a handsome throuple we make.'

The elegant drawing room filled quickly with extended family and friends, the guests eager to kick off the celebrations with a quick drink before the ceremony began. Stefano, having flown in that morning from Rome, asked the barman for a Guinness, intent on explaining that this was not his first time in Ireland.

'How long is the ceremony part?' Jo asked.

'I've no idea,' Emma replied. 'It's bound to be twenty minutes or so. There's a harpist so that will fill it out a bit.'

'Oh, I didn't know she'd got a harpist. I love the harp.'

'Well, you've been kind of distracted for the past few months. Most of the details went over your head.'

'Yeah, I suppose I was. God, I was a really bad friend there for a while, wasn't I?'

'Bad? No. Absent? Yes. Do we have time for another?'

'I think so. There's an usher or something who calls us to be seated.'

Emma motioned for the bartender, who topped up their glasses. Stefano raised his pint of Guinness. '*Salute.*'

'*Salute!*' they cheered in unison as the usher arrived and announced that it was time for the guests to take their seats.

The ceremony lasted twenty-two minutes. It was simple and classy, the poignancy of the moment accentuated by the soft lilt of the harp. Eve was radiant in a fitted, off-white lace gown. Emma couldn't recall ever having seen her smile the way she smiled as she walked slowly down the aisle. She wiped a tear from the corner of her eye, a happy tear, happy for her friend having found true love, her forever man.

She leaned over to Jo. 'Do you think we'll ever find the one?'

Jo shrugged her shoulders. 'Don't know. I hope so, otherwise it'll be you and me in a nursing home together with sagging boobs and dentures. We'll have to rely on little Robert and any future kids that Eve might have to smuggle in alcohol for us. We'll need to remind each other going forward to be kind to them when they're being annoying as we'll be reliant on those brown-paper-bag deliveries.'

Emma stifled a laugh. 'You say the weirdest things at the worst times.'

Jo elbowed her in the side, nodding her head in Stefano's direction. 'Then again, maybe you've already met "the one".'

'Shh!' Emma hissed. 'Don't even start. He's sweet and cute and all, but no.'

'Okay, fair enough. Maybe I'll have a go.'

Emma coughed to cover the laugh that she couldn't stop in time. 'You're the worst.'

Twenty-two minutes and two emotional I dos later, the justice of the peace pronounced them man and wife. The crowd erupted in applause as the groom kissed his bride and both Jo and Emma wiped away tears of joy. The harpist played Pachelbel's Canon in D Major as they walked down the aisle hand in hand and stepped out into the afternoon sun for photographs.

'That got me,' Emma said, turning to file down the aisle behind the crowd.

'Yep, me too,' Jo replied. 'Okay, Stefano. *Andiamo*. This is your first Irish wedding, isn't it?'

'Yes, the first.'

'Okay, well, this is when the fun starts.'

The party spilled back into the bar, which by now had a dedicated champagne bar and a table with hors d'oeuvres and canapés. The French doors were flung open, so guests could wander out onto the gravel path and the rose garden beyond. The crowd of fifty intermingled, embracing old friends and making new ones, as toasts were made to the happy couple. The soundtrack was one of glasses clinking and loud, happy chatter as the harpist set up in one corner, providing a layer of soft melody.

Emma's phone vibrated in her purse. She glanced at the screen, but didn't recognise the number, so she hit decline and popped it back out of sight. Less than a minute later, it buzzed for a second time. She checked again. Same number. She hit ignore and stuck it back into her bag.

'Who's that?' Jo asked. She handed Emma a glass of champagne.

'Dunno. Probably spam. I get at least six of those a week.'

'Yeah, me too. I don't answer them.'

'No, I barely pick up if I know the person these days. I'm so done talking on the phone. Just send me a text. What the—' She opened her purse for the third time. 'Okay, this is getting annoying.'

'Maybe you should answer it,' Jo suggested.

The screen flashed up with a voicemail notification.

'Okay, if this is Bob in Nairobi asking me for my email address so that he can transfer twenty million, I'm going to turn off my phone.'

'That's a bit dramatic. What if he really does want you to have the twenty million?'

Laughing, Emma hit play and put the phone to her ear. 'I'm going to step outside. I can't hear a thing in here.'

Jo tapped the bar counter. 'Okay, I'll top up my glass and follow you out.'

Emma stepped out into the courtyard and pressed play.

Emma, hi, this is Blaine Taylor. We met in Giglio. I got your number from Jack Bourke . . .

The voicemail was less than a minute long. She stuck a finger in her right ear and pressed the phone to her left, her lips parting, her jaw dropping slowly. She looked down at the phone and pressed the play button a second time.

'What the . . . ?'

Jo came to a stop alongside her.

Emma looked down at her phone. 'That was Blaine.'

Jo hesitated for a moment, a confused look on her face. 'Blaine? Blaine from Italy? Jack's Blaine?'

Emma nodded. 'Yes.'

'Okay, I can't read your expression. Why was Blaine calling you? What did he say? Did you call him back?'

'No, not yet. I just . . . ' Her voice trailed off.

'How does Blaine have your number?'

'He said he got it from Jack. Jack gave him my number.'

'Okay, for the love of God, what did he *say?*' she urged. 'What's going on? Has something happened?'

Emma stood still, the phone in her hand. 'No.' She shook her head. 'Nothing's happened.' She stared down at the phone. 'But based on his message, I think that maybe something is about to.'

CHAPTER TWENTY

Emma handed the phone to Jo, who pressed play. A loud cheer broke out from the drawing room.

Jo spun around, glaring in the direction of the noise. 'Christ's sake, lads. You're at a wedding, not a football match. Hang on, I have to play that again now.' She pressed the phone to her ear, listening intently. 'Holy shit, is this for real?'

'You know as much as I do, Jo.'

'Are you going to call him back?' She handed the phone to Emma. 'You know you have to do this, don't you? I mean, there's no way in the wide earthly world that you're not going to do this.'

Everything about Blaine was measured and reserved, but his tone of voice had expressed a sense of urgency, along with a specific request to call him back within twenty-four hours.

'I know, but—'

'Whoa, whoa, whoa!' Jo held up a hand. 'No, absolutely not. You're not going to talk yourself out of this. You are *doing* this, Emma Brosnan.'

Eve crossed the gravel path towards them, holding the

skirt of her dress with both hands. 'She's doing what? What have I missed? Jesus, these photos are a dose and a half. My cheeks hurt from smiling. I need a drink.'

'You haven't had a drink yet?' Jo asked incredulously.

'I had a shot of tequila in my room before the ceremony. Okay, two. And then I pounded a glass of champagne in there afterwards. You're not supposed to look half-cut in your wedding photos, Jo.'

'Fair enough. I'll get you one now. What do you want?'

'Vodka. Rocks.'

Jo grinned. 'Right. I guess we're done with the champagne portion of this programme. Hang on.' She turned to Emma. 'Don't tell her without me, I want to hear her reaction. I'll be back in a second. I'll cut the line and tell them that it's an emergency vodka for the bride. People will understand.'

'What's going on?' Eve asked. Her veil flapped in her face. 'Can you fix this for me please? I asked my husband, but he's useless, he can't pin it properly. Welcome to the rest of my life.'

Emma giggled. 'Well, it's not like he's had a lot of practice with veils or hair clips.' She pulled the clip from Eve's hair, adjusted the veil and pinned it back.'

'Ouch! Okay, that won't be moving anytime soon.'

'You're welcome,' Emma said with a smile. 'The dress is amazing, by the way. You look phenomenal and you look so tiny!'

'Thanks. The wedding diet nearly killed me. I can't wait to have a Tayto sandwich later on tonight.'

'There are Tayto sandwiches?'

'Yep, around ten p.m. Emergency Tayto sandwich rations for the troops.'

'Genius idea.'

Jo tiptoed across the gravel in her heels, three vodka cocktails clustered in her hands. 'This gravel will wreck my shoes. Okay, ladies, here you are. Cheers, bitches.'

'Cheers! To the blushing bride!' Emma said, raising her glass aloft.

'Cheers,' Eve replied. 'I love you both, now tell me what's going on.'

'Just play it for her. Play it!' Jo urged.

'She won't be able to hear it with that racket.' Emma gestured to the four groomsmen, marching the length of the rose garden with the groom up on their shoulders and the photographer in hot pursuit.

Eve sighed as she watched the men parade through the grass. 'I'm just so happy that my wedding day turned out to be as elegant and sophisticated as I dreamed it would. Such a special moment to capture.'

Emma handed her the phone. 'Here, just press play.'

Eve's expression changed from one of curiosity to that of incredulity as the message played out. 'Are you serious?' She looked at both of them. 'He wants you to exhibit your art at an upcoming exhibition at the Mansion House. How does he even know about your art? Did you guys talk about it in Italy?'

'No, I mean, I think he mentioned it once in passing, but we didn't really talk about it in any detail.'

Eve handed the phone back to her. 'You know you have to do this, don't you? You don't say no to an opportunity like this. The Mansion House is the Lord Mayor's residence. This is a really big deal, Emma.'

Jo nodded. 'Yep, that's exactly what I said. You have to call him back. Right now.'

'Okay, I'll go call him right now.'

Emma stepped back into the drawing room of Carton House, cut through the crowd and sat on a red velvet chaise longue in the foyer. Blaine picked up after two rings.

'Emma, hi, thanks for calling me back.'

'Hi, of course. I just got your message. Sorry if it's a bit loud, I'm at a wedding.'

'No problem. I won't keep you. I know this is a little out of the blue, but here's the situation.'

He continued to explain about the upcoming exhibition at the Mansion House in Dublin city, an annual presentation of previously unexhibited rising talent that he personally hand selects each year. One of the exhibitors had just pulled out citing personal problems, which Blaine subsequently learned was code for divorce. So he had an open slot. The exhibition was in three weeks. She would need to exhibit a minimum of four pieces, and they can't have been exhibited or published anywhere previously, including having been shared online. Oh, and he needed an answer today.

'You were my first call. I do have a backup plan if you can't commit, but my preference was you.'

'How do you even know about my artwork? I don't think we even really talked about it in Italy.'

'I told Jack about the other woman pulling out and that I had to find another artist, which is not easy at such short notice. People have been preparing for this for months. He suggested you right off the bat. He sent me some shots of your work. The butterfly one is of particular interest. That caught my eye.'

'He had photos of them?' she asked, her mind spinning.

'Oh, that's right. He asked me if he could send some to himself. I didn't think any more of it.'

'I hate to sound pushy, but I'm afraid I'll need an answer right away – we're under pressure for time, as you can imagine. Do you have any questions?'

She had only one. She hesitated for a moment: she hated that she felt the need to ask it, but she did.

'Um, well, just one . . .'

'Yes?'

'Um, will Jack be there? I mean, is he a part of it in any way? Like being a judge like he was in Italy?'

'No, he's not involved. In fact, I think he's going to be abroad that week.' He paused for a moment. 'So, what's it to be? Are you in?'

Relief flooded her veins. There was no way she could see Jack again. It would have been all but impossible to refuse an invitation like this, except if he had been a part of it. There was no way she could pretend. It just wasn't who she was. But he wasn't involved. A smile broke across her face.

'Yes, of course I'm in. Who says no to something like this?'

He laughed. 'Marvellous. I'll let you get back to the wedding now. I'll send you a message shortly with a link to the website. It'll have more information about the venue, terms and conditions and all that. We can talk more tomorrow. Do you have any other new pieces?'

'No, I haven't painted properly in months. Not since—' She stopped short of mentioning the debacle with Paul months earlier. She hadn't thought of him in weeks – since she'd come back from Italy, in fact. She smiled, realising that it didn't hurt any more just to think of him. 'But I did start dabbling in something again when I got home from Italy. I think Giglio kind of inspired me a little, so I could work on those.'

'Great. The butterfly piece was quite stunning. If you focus on creating some sort of series along that basis, I think you'll be on to something. It's quite unique, which is exactly the angle you want for this project. Anyway, enough for now. We can chat again tomorrow when you've got more time. Any other questions?'

She hesitated. Her only other question had nothing to do with her artwork or the exhibition.

'Does Jack know that you called me?'

'Of course, it was he who gave me your number. He said I shouldn't think twice about it, that he'd seen some of your work and you had a very real, raw talent.'

'Oh, that was nice. Okay. Well, thank you for thinking of me.'

She could hear the smile in his voice. 'No offence, but I didn't. Jack did.'

'Right. Well, then, thank you for the opportunity.'

'My pleasure. I'll give you a call tomorrow. Enjoy the day.'

'Thanks, okay. Bye.'

She sat there for a moment, processing the conversation. Jack had thought of her. Jack had told him about her art. Jack had suggested he call her. Jack had given him her number.

Jack.

She leaned back into the soft velvet and sighed. Jack. How had she read it all so wrong when it had felt and seemed so right? She had stormed out and he hadn't followed. He hadn't even tried to find her. That told her everything she needed to know. His silence, his absence, was loaded with guilt, and it was the only confirmation she had needed.

But here he was, thinking of her, vouching for her, giving her the opportunity of a lifetime. Maybe the couple of days had meant nothing to him; they couldn't have, given his personal circumstances. It was clear now that he had only been in it for fun, stepping out of his domestic routine and throwing himself into a holiday fling. It was another country. No one need know, no one would get hurt.

She shook her head. She'd been fooled by that part, but as she sat staring at the phone in her hands, she knew instinctively that it hadn't all been in her imagination. He wasn't all bad. Okay, he'd lied about his domestic situation and that was hard to forgive, but he had meant the things he'd said about her work. He had been nothing but encouraging and positive in Italy, and it sounded like he had been just the same with Blaine, enough to convince him to offer her the chance.

Maybe that was his way of saying sorry.

She stood up to go find the girls and rejoin the party. She had three weeks to create three new pieces of art. It was an insane deadline, but one she was determined to meet. She would do nothing else for the next three weeks but paint. Blaine had said she should focus on the butterflies. Her phone pinged with the sound of an email.

'Jesus,' she whispered as she opened the link and scrolled through the details of the annual art exhibition. 'I'm going to be exhibiting at this thing. This is insane.'

She walked back through the drawing room towards the courtyard. After tonight she would do nothing and go nowhere, she would just paint. This was the kind of opportunity that one was handed once in a lifetime and for some reason Jack Bourke had decided that she should have it.

There was no way she would have believed that she was worthy of exhibiting at an exhibition of this pedigree, but if Jack believed in her enough to put her forward as a candidate, didn't she owe it to herself to believe too? She may have been fooled by his charm, but this, at least, was real. Maybe he felt like he owed her one.

She stepped back out into the sunshine, looking for the woman in white and the flame-haired siren in the red dress. She waved across the courtyard, picked up a drink from a passing waiter's tray and stepped carefully onto the gravel.

She smiled to herself.

Challenge accepted, she thought.

CHAPTER TWENTY-ONE

The exhibitors were granted access to the grand hall at 3 p.m. to set up for the exhibition, which would be open to the public from 5. Emma had taken a half-day from work and was waiting anxiously outside at 2.45 p.m. Her oversized, leather artist's case stood leaning up against her hip at the bottom of the steps. Another artist with a similar sized case arrived and stood alongside her, nodding at her in acknowledgement.

Eve and Jo had both promised to show up after work to offer some support, but otherwise, she most likely wouldn't know a soul.

Probably for the best, she thought. No fake conversations or polite small talk to make, just anonymous members of the public, wandering by, looking at and, presumably, silently judging her work. She took a deep breath to try to calm the rise of anxiety swelling inside of her.

The door to the Mansion House was unlocked and opened at exactly 3 p.m. and Emma and the other artists filed inside. They were directed down the wide corridor to a pair of white double doors. Inside were twelve stations, each with a name that designated an artist's place for the evening. Each station held four easels, already sized to house the pieces of art that the artists had declared they would showcase. A small, handwritten sign sat on her table:

Emma Brosnan. Watercolour artist.

She smiled.

Funny, she thought. In all the years that she'd painted, she'd never once referred to herself as a watercolour artist, just as someone who liked to paint. Maybe this was part of her problem, downplaying her abilities.

Her thoughts drifted to Jack as she carefully took the first piece of art from its protective case and mounted it on one of the easels. She had known little about him before she had met him in Giglio. From a distance, he had always struck her as successful, established and confident, but when she met him in person, he had struck her as just an ordinary, down-to-earth guy. He had no airs or graces and in fact tended to dismiss talk of his art-world celebrity status.

She rested the largest of the four pieces on its easel, adjusting the spread of the three legs to assume its weight and balance accordingly.

It was his confidence. That was one of the things that had attracted her, his quiet confidence. He believed in himself and his work; he didn't feel the need to prove anything to anyone, he just did what he did for himself. He was his own person.

She stood in front of her own work, staring into space, seeing nothing, her thoughts swirling like wisps of smoke in her head. They say that people come into your life for a reason, a season or a lifetime. Maybe Jack had come into hers for this reason – to propel her here to this moment, to give her the confidence to believe in herself, the push to do the thing she loved to do more than anything: to paint. Maybe that's why the universe had had them collide so intensely in Italy. She knew one thing for certain: she wouldn't be standing here right now if it wasn't for Jack Bourke. Things had ended badly between them – terribly, actually – but it had forced her hand. No, *he* had forced her hand, and now here she was surrounded by these immensely talented artists.

She blinked, her attention focusing back to the current situation, her gaze returning to the room. She took in the adjacent displays, the exquisite pieces of art. All these super-talented, creative people, and somehow, she had ended up in the middle of them.

I belong here, she thought. *I belong in this room. Maybe if I say it often enough, I'll eventually believe it.*

'Emma.' Blaine's voice came from behind her.

She did a double take. He looked very sophisticated in a dark grey two-piece suit and blue and white striped shirt.

'Wow, you look great,' she said.

He smiled. 'Thank you. You've just not seen me in a suit. This is my work armour. It's good to see you. You look marvellous.' He gave her a kiss on the cheek.

She blushed at the compliment. She had laboured for days over what one wore to an art exhibition. She'd consulted with Jo and Eve, who had made her try on eight outfits two nights earlier. They'd decided unanimously on a simple, wheaten-coloured, linen midi dress with cap sleeves which she paired with her favourite nude block heels that made her feel tall.

Eve and Jo had been perched on the end of her bed, a bottle of wine on the rug between them. 'That's the one!' Eve had said. 'You look amazing in that!'

'Are you sure?' she'd replied, twisting left and right in front of the mirror.

'Good God, woman, *yes*. And add that to the list of things you need to work on this year,' Jo had scoffed. 'Self-love.'

She skipped over Blaine's compliment now. It felt strange to be standing here alone with him. She'd only ever met him in Jack's company. Her mind raced, thoughts tripping over each other as questions reeled in her head. What had Jack shared with him? How much did he know about what had transpired between them in Italy? Did he know that they'd slept together? Was it possible that Jack had withheld that piece of information from him? As his agent he had to know about Jack's personal life, so he must have been aware that Jack wasn't free to run around the island of Giglio with another woman. But then maybe he was the kind of guy who didn't care what people did. Did he know about her sudden disappearance? Should she ask how Jack was? Or was it best to just say nothing.

'How have you been?' was all she could think to say.

His phone rang in his pocket. He took it out, glanced at the screen and silenced it. 'Sorry about that, I thought it was off. I've been good, good. Busy as usual. This time of year is always a bit of a madhouse.' He turned to face her four easels. 'Okay, let's see what you've got.'

The closest to him was the first butterfly piece she had painted, a photo of which Jack had seen in Italy and subsequently shared with Blaine. He stepped in closer and peered at the canvas and her brushstrokes.

'It's even more beautiful in real life.'

Given its abstract nature, Blaine knew that to really appreciate the piece, it had to be viewed from a distance. He glanced over his shoulder and took five steps backwards, folding his arms, with one hand resting on his chin. He didn't look at Emma, his focus was on the piece of art entirely.

'Quite striking.'

He moved silently in front of the three other pieces, all of which were extensions of her butterfly theme, walking down the line, coming to a stop in front of each easel, before walking back to her.

'Stunning, Emma. These are stunning. Well done. This is absolutely beautiful work and I'm very grateful to you for turning it out on such short notice. I'm guessing you've done little else since our first phone call.'

She laughed. 'Not a thing.' She gestured towards the artwork. 'This is literally all I've done for the last three weeks. I had a lot of holidays built up, so I took a week off work and didn't leave my apartment. I swear I looked like I lived under a bridge at one point.'

Blaine smiled. 'Well, thankfully you don't this evening. Okay, here's how this is going to go . . . '

He explained that the Lord Mayor would officially open the exhibition at 5 p.m. Several members of the press had confirmed their attendance so the event would be well documented in tomorrow's newspapers. The exhibition would remain open to the public until 8 p.m.

'If you don't have plans later, I thought we might have a drink and get a bite to eat. One of my favourite restaurants is very near here. I'd love to talk to you about representation, if you're open to that.'

'Representation?'

'Yes, I'd like to sign you as a client and represent you moving forward.'

'Sign me? As a client?'

Blaine frowned. 'Yes. What did you think was going to happen?'

She hesitated. 'I . . . well, I hadn't thought . . . about anything really. I just thought I was exhibiting here tonight. I didn't think about anything beyond that.'

'I see,' Blaine said slowly in his soft London accent. 'Okay, let's see if I can clear this up a little for you.' He cleared his throat. 'Emma, you have an extraordinary talent, a fact which I don't believe you have fully grasped yet. I realise that you have a full-time job doing something in . . .' He paused. 'I'm actually not sure what you do. It's finance or something, isn't it?' He didn't wait for her to respond. 'Anyway, none of that matters. *You*, my dear, need to paint, because you are an artist who just hasn't accepted the fact yet. I also believe that you haven't realised your full potential, and I, for one, would like to help you get there. So, what I would like to do, later this evening, if possible, is sit down and explain how this all works. By this, I mean an agent–artist contractual relationship.'

She stared at him. 'I don't know what to say.'

'Are you free for dinner later?'

'Yes.'

'Good, then let's leave it at that and we can discuss it all once this is over. Don't worry, you won't have to make any decisions tonight. I'm sure you'll have lots of questions and I'll be happy to answer them all and we can take it from there.'

'Okay,' she said slowly. 'I'm just relieved that you like the new pieces. I really didn't want to let you down.'

Blaine shook his head. 'Emma, they are incredible. I'd wager a hundred euro that they'll all sell tonight.'

'Sell?'

'Yes, all of them.'

'I didn't realise that they'd be for sale.'

'You didn't see that on the website?'

She grimaced. 'I looked at the site, but just quickly on the day of the wedding. The next day I just got stuck into painting and I kind of forgot to go back to it.'

'I see. Well, you don't have to, of course, but we get a rather sophisticated crowd at this event. They'll be mostly art collectors and the like, with some curious members of the public, but without a doubt there will be buyers here. They love to see new talent and invest in pieces before the artists go professional.'

'I had no idea.'

'So, that means you haven't thought about pricing?'

She laughed. This was becoming more insane by the minute. 'No.'

'Hmm, okay. Well, if you want my guide on it, I'd price them all the same. Keep it simple. Twenty-five hundred euros a piece.'

'Twenty-five hundred each?' she said in a high-pitched squeal. 'That's ten grand!'

Blaine smiled. 'I can see that this is going to be fun. I haven't had a real newbie – no offence – for a while. I'm used to working with more experienced artists and they're far more jaded with the world. I love your enthusiasm and excitement. You're a raw talent, and don't take my word for it. He pulled his phone from his pocket and opened his photos app. He scrolled three times and handed her his phone. 'Here, it's Jack's latest piece. They say that imitation is the highest form of flattery.'

Her mouth dropped as she stared at the photo. It was a white sculpture, a bust of a woman's head and neck, with a cluster of butterflies obscuring her eyes, forehead and the top of her head. It was the most exquisite thing she had ever seen. It wasn't a copy of her watercolour; it was Jack's own take on it. While hers was abstract, his was intensely detailed, the butterflies appearing to just balance lightly, precariously, around the woman's face. She looked from the phone to Blaine as tears stung the back of her eyes.

'Your painting was his inspiration. He'll win an award for this – I'd bet my career on that. It's his best work yet.'

She didn't know how to respond. 'I'm stunned.'

'As was I.' He turned to look over his shoulder. 'Okay, are you ready?'

She followed his gaze back towards the entrance as the double doors were thrown open. It was the moment she didn't know she'd been waiting for her whole life. It was her turn to stand in the spotlight as an artist. It was showtime.

CHAPTER TWENTY-TWO

Three hours later, exhausted and elated, Emma walked side by side with Blaine, to the long-standing and much respected Michelin-starred restaurant One Pico. Located just off St Stephen's Green in central Dublin and housed in an eighteenth-century coach house, the restaurant was discreetly tucked away in a city-centre alley. Emma knew of it only by reputation, renowned for its modern French cooking with a distinct Irish influence. She paused as she reached the entrance.

'This is the restaurant you referred to earlier? I thought we were just going for a bite to eat.'

'They have food here, so yes, this qualifies,' he said with a smile, gesturing for her to enter in front of him. 'Anyway, I thought this would be appropriate for a celebration.'

They were greeted warmly and, once they were seated, the sommelier arrived to offer them a glass of champagne.

Blaine raised his glass. 'Congratulations on your first sell-out exhibition.'

She beamed. 'Thank you and thank you again for giving me the opportunity. I just can't believe I pulled it off.'

'Well, you put in the work, and it showed.'

She looked around the elegant dining room with its curved banquette tables and well-heeled diners.

'This place is beautiful,' she whispered.

'It is.' Blaine nodded in agreement. 'I come here a lot. The food is exquisite – that goes without saying – but there's plenty of space between tables, so it's perfect for a business meeting or a private conversation.'

He reached into his slimline, brown leather briefcase and pulled out a document. 'I took the liberty of printing my standard representation agreement. You don't have to read it now, just take it with you and look it over. I figured that this evening we could have a chat and you could ask me whatever questions you might have.'

Emma shook her head. 'I can't believe this is happening. That I'm going to be represented by the same agent as Jack Bourke. This is insane!'

'You're every bit as talented, my dear, and you need to start believing that. You have a fine career ahead of you, should you choose it.'

'His latest piece – the one you showed me earlier tonight – is something else.'

'You'll find that's what happens. The more an artist practises his, or her, career, the better they become, the braver they become. It's almost like giving yourself permission to break new ground. But yes, I agree. His new piece is on another level entirely. It's very exciting.'

He took a sip of champagne and flicked through the heavy, leather wine list.

'He's worked on nothing else since he returned from Italy. He was quite obsessed; in a way I've not known him to be before this. You, my dear, made quite an impression on him. I'm just sorry that things ended... Well, it's none of my business, of course, but I'm just sorry that things didn't work out between you two.'

'Work out?'

He had the decency to blush. 'I'm sorry. I shouldn't have said anything. It's none of my business.'

The conversation was paused as a waiter came to take their order.

'No, hang on,' she continued, confused now. Did Blaine really not know about Jack's private life? Was he that private? '*Work out?* How could things have worked out between us when he's married.'

'*Married?* Who's married?'

It was Blaine's turn to look confused.

'Jack.'

He shook his head. 'Jack isn't married.'

Emma leaned across the table and whispered loudly. 'Okay, partnered, living together, whatever.'

'Emma, he's not married nor is he living with anyone, never has done. I'm not sure what you're talking about.'

The sommelier reappeared with a bottle of Chablis, making polite small talk as he opened it and poured a taste for Emma. Barely able to contain herself, she sipped the wine.

'Yes, perfect. Thank you.'

Losing her mind, she watched as he slowly poured a little in each glass. She squeezed her two hands together on her lap, waiting for the man to once again be out of earshot.

'I saw the photo, Blaine. The one of a blonde woman and a toddler. And messages saying they miss him and that she'd have dinner ready when he got home.'

She could hear the words in her head as they rolled off her tongue. She sounded like a stalker.

She watched as Blaine's expression changed. He folded his arms across his chest. 'So, that's what happened,' he said slowly. 'Okay, now it all makes sense.' He smiled at her.

Why is he smiling at me? What the hell is going on?

'Emma, Jack is not now, nor has he ever been, married. The woman in his screensaver is his sister-in-law, Michelle, and the little boy is his nephew, Liam.'

She opened her mouth to speak, but she couldn't. She sat there, immobile, her mouth agape.

The woman in his screensaver is his sister-in-law, Michelle, and the little boy is his nephew, Liam. His sister-in-law and his nephew.

Why had Jack never mentioned his nephew? He hadn't talked about his family at all, apart from that one throwaway comment about his sisters.

She squeezed the napkin in her lap.

Then again, why should he? I didn't. I never talked about the Paul situation in any detail because I didn't want to ruin the moment. What was it Jack had said? That one day ... something about staying in the moment. Shit.

Her mouth was dry. She leaned forward across the table.

'He never mentioned a nephew. If he had nothing to hide, then why did he hide it? I mean, why didn't he say something? About any of this, whatever it is.'

Blaine ran a hand across his chin. 'He didn't hide anything, Emma. He just doesn't like to talk about what happened. It's not a story that he cares to revisit.'

'Oh God,' she groaned, putting her two hands to her face. 'How wrong have I got this?'

'Very,' he replied.

'Blaine, what don't I know? Please tell me.'

Blaine sighed and placed his wine glass on the table. He hesitated for a moment before beginning slowly. 'Liam's father was Jack's brother, Michael. Michael was married to Michelle – the blonde lady you saw in the photo – and they had a three-year-old little girl called Zoe, who Michael adored. He had an executive role at Google, and they lived just outside Dublin city.' Blaine sighed for the second time and shook his head. 'About two years ago, Michael was driving to work with Zoe in the back seat. He was supposed to drop her off at the crèche before continuing on to the office. His phone rang, it was his boss, but when he went to answer it, he dropped the phone. He leaned down to pick it up but hit a kerb and lost control of the car. It was a horrific, freak accident, the car rolled over twice and ended up in a ditch. Zoe didn't make it. Michael couldn't forgive himself and took his own life a few weeks later.'

Emma gasped, her hand shooting up to cover her mouth instinctively. 'Oh my God.'

'The worst part is that Michelle and Michael weren't yet aware that Michelle was pregnant with Liam. Michael would never have left Liam behind, but he didn't know. The whole thing was just awful.' He shook his head, the relaying of the story bringing the memories back. 'Jack and Michael had always been very close, but around the time of Michael's car accident, Jack's schedule was particularly intense, and he was travelling a lot internationally for work. Jack took Michael's death really hard, and he convinced himself that had he stayed closer to Michael in the wake of the tragedy, maybe his death could have been prevented. That's nonsense, of course, but grief does things to people's psyches. Afterwards, Jack was determined to be there for Liam, so he convinced Michelle to move to Kerry. He bought them a cottage close to his house on the island and he's like a pseudo father-figure to Liam. There's nothing between Jack and Michelle, just a deep friendship and a commitment to raising Liam. That's just the kind of guy Jack is.'

She squeezed her hands into fists as her blood ran cold through her body, a pit forming in her stomach. 'Oh, God. I thought . . . I just assumed. I saw the photo and then some stupid message flashed up on the screen about being home for dinner. I wasn't stalking him, I swear. I was waiting for him at his apartment and this all happened in a few seconds. The little boy looked just like Jack so I—'

'You jumped to the wrong conclusion,' Blaine said gently. 'Liam looks just like his father, Michael, who bore a strong resemblance to Jack. It's an easy mistake to make.'

'I'm such an idiot. I just ran out. I literally ran away and blocked his number. What am I going to do?' she asked, looking up at Blaine. 'I got it so wrong. I just ran out on him and once I left Giglio he had no way to contact me. Not that he'd have wanted to with the way I acted.'

'Well, he tried,' Blaine said slowly. 'At least in Giglio he did. That much I know.'

'What do you mean?' she asked.

'He called me the night you disappeared. When you weren't at his apartment he tried calling you. Then he went looking for you. He had no idea what had happened, but he went to the hotel to see if you'd gone back there. The barman told him that you'd just left on the last ferry back to the mainland.'

'*What?*' she cried. 'The barman? Oh, God. Stefano. Shit.' She looked up sheepishly at Blaine. 'When I got back to the hotel, I ran into him, and he saw me all upset. He probably assumed that Jack was the one who upset me if he came in hot on my heels. Shit. This whole situation was a huge misunderstanding on everyone's part.'

The sommelier topped up their glasses and disappeared.

'He must have thought I was a complete freak just disappearing like that.'

'Well, no, look, this is none of my business . . .'

'What? Tell me, Blaine, please.'

'He didn't go into detail, but he shared that you'd recently been through a really bad break-up and the only logical assumption he could make was that you panicked and changed your mind, or that you simply didn't want to get into something so suddenly. Honestly, Emma, he didn't know what to think and he had no way to reach you as you'd blocked his number. All he knew is that you lived somewhere in Dublin city. He thought it best just to leave you be, but to be fair, he really didn't have another choice.'

Emma sat silently for a moment. 'But why didn't he tell me about his situation, about the little boy, and his brother?'

Blaine took a sip of wine. 'He never talks about it, not with anyone. He talked with me about it shortly after it happened and never mentioned it again. I think it still causes him too much pain. I don't know for sure, and he certainly hasn't talked to me about you, but my guess, if I know Jack at all, is that he didn't want to get into anything too heavy when he was having such a wonderful time with you in Italy. You two only spent a few days together and I'd say that he just didn't want to get into such a painful conversation and open old wounds when you had such a short amount of time together.'

He raised both hands in the air. 'But those are my words and that is my opinion, not Jack's.'

'Jesus,' she said, looking directly at Blaine. 'I owe him an apology.'

'That's a good start; but one word of advice, if I may?'

'Yes, please.'

'Apologies are far more powerful when given in person.'

'In person . . .'

'If you mean it, then it will carry far more weight in person, and I happen to know that he's at home working this weekend.'

She knew that he was right and with sudden clarity she knew exactly what she needed to do. She nodded slowly. 'Right . . . I need to go to Kerry.'

CHAPTER TWENTY-THREE

She called in sick to work. There was no way that this could wait any longer: she would have to go today. She had never minded the short walk to her local café, but today it was maddening. Was it always this crowded on a Friday morning? Were people always this annoying? Why couldn't they just walk in a straight line instead of meandering from side to side? She bumped shoulders with two women, sighing loudly in frustration each time.

She couldn't text and walk quickly at the same time, so she dictated a message to Jo and Eve using Siri. They had planned to meet for a picnic dinner in the Phoenix Park, but even though it had been her idea, she was going to have to bail out tonight. She kept the messages short, saying that something had come up and that she'd explain later. There was no way she was going to go into any level of detail regarding her half-arsed plan to hit the road for Kerry: she was already nervous enough about the idea of it and didn't need the girls piling on even more anxiety.

Ever since they'd returned from Giglio, Emma had been suggesting that they change up their normal routine of pub, restaurant, shop and instead start to spend more time exploring the natural beauty of Dublin. They'd finally done the clifftop hike at Howth, they'd met for lunches on the coast instead of their usual urban favourites, and in the run-up to Eve's wedding, they'd taken several day trips out of the city to surrounding scenic spots. She had signed up for swimming lessons, determined to overcome her fear of the water, and had convinced the girls to do a week-long beginner's sailing course next spring at the Irish National Sailing School.

Ten minutes later she rounded the corner towards the café. The queue was out the door. She checked her watch.

'Goddamn city queues,' she whispered, waiting an infuriating fifteen minutes to get a takeaway cappuccino.

She walked at speed back to her apartment.

Bad enough that it's a Friday, but it's a Bank Holiday weekend so the traffic will be even worse, she thought.

'Just grab your bag and get in the car,' she said to herself as she stuck her key in the door.

Five hours later, a road sign indicated that she was finally arriving in Caherciveen. In one of their many conversations in Italy, Jack had mentioned that Caherciveen was the closest town to Valentia Island and, after hours on the winding Irish roads, Emma had never been more relieved to arrive at a destination. She adjusted her speed to match the long trail of traffic moving slowly ahead of her, falling in line as the cars inched forward along the two-lane main street. She passed a bakery on the left, its window chock-full of Irish soda bread and homemade pies, followed by a gift shop, its display resplendent with colourful Irish tweeds and woollen knits. A pharmacy sat on the right corner, its neon green cross illuminated over the door.

With the traffic at a standstill, Emma glanced down a side street that splintered off to the right. A credit union sat on the corner, its double doors flung open, and a butcher shop with a queue of customers spilling out the door. The car came to a stop again at a pedestrian crossing as an old man with a walker shuffled slowly across, followed by a young woman with a buggy determinedly ignoring its red-faced, wailing occupant.

Emma stared ahead at the enormous cathedral that towered over the rest of the town, and wondered why a small town in rural Ireland merited such a magnificent church. It seemed at odds with the dimensions of every other building on the main street, almost incongruously so. She could feel her anxiety building as the traffic inched forward, past Willie's Wines, the local off-licence, and a double-storefront antiques shop, with all manner of crockery, silver and old mahogany furniture on display.

Mom would love to get stuck in there, she thought as she changed gears.

Increasing her speed, she passed a hardware shop selling everything from tools and mops to rat poison, followed by the fishmonger, its display case loaded with slick, silvery heaps of fresh local fish and shellfish. Suddenly, she reached the other end of town.

'That was it?' she exclaimed behind the wheel of the car. 'That's the big town?'

The road opened to a patchwork of green fields on both sides. At the crest of the hill, she spotted a sign for the

Valentia Island Car Ferry. Her stomach flipped. She must be getting close.

'What am I doing here?' she whispered.

Jack had said that his house was on the far side of the island by the bridge, so that's the direction she wanted to go. She made a right turn at a crossroad, following a sign for Portmagee, and drove in silence for the next ten minutes, her thoughts racing, anxiety simmering in her chest.

'Wow, beautiful,' she said quietly. With the town of Caherciveen behind her, the landscape was textbook rural: sparsely populated, with rolling green fields as far as she could see. Cottages dotted the swathes of land, with hedgerows and stone walls denoting ownership and boundaries. Cumulous clouds in the distance raced at speed across the horizon, powered by the strong winds coming off the south-west coast and the Atlantic Ocean. The car began to bounce gently up and down as she crossed through the bog, the tarmacadam surface proving no match for the soft, yielding peat land that lay underneath. Slowly, the fields began to concede territory to the bay, the verdant green replaced by a striking blue. As she rounded the bend she could see the bridge to Valentia Island. Her stomach flipped again.

'Here we go,' she mumbled under her breath. 'Okay.'

A white road sign with black lettering in traditional Gaelic font announced that she was arriving in Portmagee. Hesitating for just a second, Emma slowed the car and pulled off to the left, following the road into the village. Now that she was here, she was entirely uncertain of what her plan was, and needed a minute to think. She parked the car, climbed out and stretched.

The sea breeze carried the briny scent of salt water in the air towards her. She breathed it in and stretched again as she gazed around. The village was utterly charming, with a row of terraced houses painted in soft pastel colours along one side. On the other side, a string of terraced houses backed up to the bay. A half-dozen fishing boats were moored in the dock, bobbing gently in the strong breeze, emitting the unmistakable clanking, creaking sounds of boats tied up in a harbour.

It felt good to walk, having been in the car for over five hours, but she wasn't doing it for the exercise or the step count, she was trying to postpone the moment when she would face Jack. The mad idea she'd had at dinner the previous night to embark on a five-hour dash across the country seemed ridiculous right now. She needed a minute.

Strolling down the narrow footpath, she passed a café, its handwritten sign proffering homemade scones and pies. Her stomach growled just thinking about food. She hadn't had anything to eat or drink all day, except for a hastily gulped cappuccino and a fistful of raspberries in the car, but despite the hunger, there was no way she could eat right now.

She saw the green An Post sign ahead and smiled – the place that sold everything you needed, as Jack had described it. Its metal door was flung open as tourists and locals filed in and out, arms loaded with fresh bread or daily essentials, kids eagerly licking whipped ice-cream cones and delivery van drivers dodging the queue with boxes of that day's orders. The window display was full of the Skellig Islands and *Star Wars* paraphernalia, along with the requisite Irish beach holiday accoutrements – coloured fishing nets for fish that would never be captured, buckets and spades for sandcastle construction and multicoloured windmills on bamboo sticks with no purpose other than to delight little minds by spinning wildly in the Atlantic coastal breeze.

In an instant the plastic-coloured windmills transported Emma back to barefoot, carefree summer days on the Dublin coast with her sister and cousins. Picnics were homemade, consisting of ham or chicken sandwiches, bags of Tayto and slices of apple. There was something reassuring and charming in the fact that despite all the advances in technology, in thirty-something years the basic tools for a fun day at the beach hadn't changed.

She walked the length of the village, passing the church and the pubs that Jack had so accurately described to her just weeks earlier, and sat on the low stone wall at the end of the road. She stared across the bay at Valentia Island, her eyes darting across the dozens of houses tucked into the undulating hills, and realised that she didn't even have an address for him.

'Which one is his?' she mumbled.

She would have to ask for directions. Surely in a small place like this people knew where he lived, or is that just not a thing that people did – give out addresses to random strangers, which she absolutely qualified as. She decided that the Post Office would be her best bet.

She strolled back to the centre of the village, sidestepping a group of ice-cream-laden children giggling their way along the footpath. The little shop was still full of people as she made her way down the left aisle towards the butcher's counter at the back, and back up the other aisle past the shelves of fresh breads and baked goods.

What do you bring to someone when you show up unannounced to say sorry?

She slid a loaf of Irish soda bread into a brown paper bag and retraced her steps to the refrigeration section. Local goats' cheese, fresh buffalo mozzarella from Macroom, an aged cheddar and a jar of Ballymaloe relish. This would be her peace offering. Her arms full, she joined the queue of five or six, shuffling slowly forward. Before reaching the counter, she passed the DIY household section. She failed to smother the giggle when she spotted the knots of blue rope. The woman in the queue ahead turned to see the source of Emma's amusement, looked her up and down and turned back to the counter.

'What's your problem?' Emma muttered under her breath.

Balancing the bread under her chin, she picked up a length of rope. *This* would be her peace offering.

Finally, the man behind the counter nodded in her direction. 'How's it going? Will that be it?'

'Yes, thanks. That's it,' Emma replied, laying the items on the counter. 'Um, I'm looking for directions to Jack Bourke's house.'

The man's hand paused over the cash register as he looked down at her. 'We've two Jack Bourkes around here. Is it the plumber or the sculptor you're looking for?'

'The sculptor. On the island.'

'Oh, JB's house you want so. That's easy. Go over the bridge and make a left. Follow the sign for Bray Head. At the next junction make another left towards Bray Head. He's the last house on the road, a white cottage, black gate.'

'Okay, thanks. I don't even know if he's home,' she said, as much to herself as to the man behind the counter.

He looked at her again. 'You're a surprise, so are you?'

She couldn't help but smile. 'Kind of, yeah.'

'He's around all right, but I haven't seen him in three or four days so he's probably working on something new. He does that when he's working on a new piece, just gets stuck in and forgets about everything else. I can give him a call if you want to see if he's home.'

'No,' she said quickly. 'I'd rather just show up.'

'Fair enough. Is the cheese going back there too?'

'Sorry?'

'Is that what the cheese is for?'

'Yes, why?'

He smiled at her. 'He likes a Dairy Milk. If you're going to be a surprise, that won't hurt your chances.'

A voice came from deep in the back of the store. 'Mark! Phone!'

'I'll be right there,' he shouted back.

Emma reached out and picked a bar of Dairy Milk chocolate from the display.

'Do you want a bag?'

'Yes, please. Oh, do you have a paper bag or something . . . for the rope.'

'Yep.' He reached beneath the counter and pulled out a brown paper bag.

She glanced down at the length of blue rope. 'Looks a bit murdery just sitting there, doesn't it?'

'Does a bit now, in fairness. Doesn't really go with the cheese.'

Emma tapped her credit card on the terminal and gathered up the two bags. 'Thanks.'

'No bother. I might give him a welfare call later on just to check.' He grinned. 'There's a dog, too; he'll bark at you but don't worry about him. He's about as dangerous as a rabbit.'

'Bentley,' Emma said.

'That's the one.' He stepped out from behind the counter and watched her leave.

She knew exactly what he was thinking in that moment, this stranger in his shop buying rope and cheese, not knowing JB's address, but knowing about Bentley. She could almost hear him think the words: *Who the hell are you and what are you doing at JB's house?*

As she made her way back to the car, she was beginning to wonder the same thing, but it was too late to turn back now. She'd come too far, and regardless of the outcome tonight, she was going to cross the bridge to the island and play it out.

CHAPTER TWENTY-FOUR

His directions had been spot on. Emma crossed the bridge and made a left at the top of the hill, then followed the narrow road around one bend after another until she reached the crossroads. The hedgerows were ablaze with dense clusters of wild Montbretia, the fields dotted with sheep and cows grazing lazily, oblivious to the natural beauty that surrounded them. An approaching tractor forced her to pull in tight to the ditch, her wing mirror scraping through a scrub of thorny briars. She pulled back out and followed the slow curve of the road, the view opening up before her with a striking view of Foilhammerum Bay and the Atlantic Ocean beyond.

She pushed the lever to clear the windscreen, the rubber sleeves flapping back and forth, washing off five hours of road grease and dead insects. Her eyes scanned the horizon, the blue of the ocean competing with the verdant green and orange of the fields and hedges. The land continued steeply up, peaking at the crest of Bray Head; the lookout tower that Jack had mentioned sat in a dominant position, looming large over the island.

Straight out to sea, she could make out the unmistakable

silhouettes of the Skellig Islands, now arguably more famous for having been the site of the most recent *Star Wars* movies rather than as the UNESCO-recognised monastic site of historical and religious relevance. The islands sat twelve kilometres out to sea like rocks discarded from the shore, rising upwards from the Atlantic Ocean, a striking presence amid a vast sea of nothingness.

As she made the second left turn at the crossroads, she could see the white farmhouse straight ahead, nestled into the foot of Bray Head, the last house on the island. She felt her heart rate increase with nervous anxiety as questions flooded her mind. What if he wasn't home? What if he didn't want to see her? What if he was really mad at her? What if he had someone else there? What if he was busy working and didn't want to be interrupted? What if he just didn't want her showing up unannounced?

She took a long, slow breath, adrenalin pumping in her veins as she pulled up at the black gate. The bread and cheese suddenly seemed like a stupid idea, totally insignificant in the scheme of things, and the rope ... well, that was just downright weird. What had she been thinking? Even if he was at home, she'd have to leave that in the car. Stupid idea. In fact, this whole thing was a stupid idea. She hadn't thought it through at all.

'Fuck,' she whispered. She leaned her head on the steering wheel.

Maybe she should just turn around, do a three-point turn right here, and hide out in the room she'd booked as a precaution in Portmagee.

Her hand paused over the gearstick, the engine turning over quietly as she suddenly let out an almighty shriek. The yellow lab came from nowhere and stood tall up against the gate, inches from the driver's window, his barks echoing through the car, clearly unimpressed at the unannounced visitor.

'Jesus Christ!' she exclaimed, her heart pounding with fright. She clutched her hand to her chest. 'Bentley.'

The door of the garage adjacent to the house was thrown open. Jack stepped out into the early-evening sunshine, squinting as his eyes adjusted to the light.

Faded denim jeans, a white T-shirt and a worn, stained half apron around his waist was testament to the fact that he was working. His hands were white with plaster dust. He shielded his eyes with one hand and looked in her direction.

He wasn't smiling.

Emma turned off the ignition and stepped from the car. Bentley went nuts, his barks echoing across the fields.

'Bentley, down!' Jack said. He walked across the gravel driveway and put a hand on his collar. 'Down, Bentley.'

The dog obeyed and sat obediently at his feet.

'Well, I'll be damned,' Jack said slowly. 'You're the last person I'd have expected to see here.'

Emma grimaced as he held open the gate. 'I'm sorry for showing up unannounced like this. I just took a chance.'

Bentley loped up to her, sniffed her clothes and licked the back of her hand.

'Bentley, sit. How did you find me?'

'I asked at the Post Office.'

Jack raised his eyebrows. 'A city girl dropping into Portmagee unannounced asking for directions to my house. That'll get some traction.'

'Why?' she asked.

'No one ever comes here. I don't bring anyone here.'

A gasp caught in her throat. 'Oh God, sorry ... I didn't think I—'

'No, I just don't invite anyone here, ever. This is my retreat from the world. It sounds a bit dramatic, I know, but when you're on the road so much and on display publicly, which I hate, there's nothing like coming home to a place like this with no one to bother you and no one looking for you. The people around here don't take any notice of me. I'm just JB, just a regular guy, not some well-known sculptor, and that's the way I like it. I have to deal with all that shite when I'm touring or whatever, but not around here. Here I'm just a guy with a dog.'

He paused, his hand absentmindedly scratching Bentley's head. He gave a small smile. 'Although, I do recall telling you that you should come see for yourself one day, so technically you *were* invited. I just never thought you'd show up, especially after the way you disappeared in Italy.'

Emma smiled nervously. 'I know, I can explain. I swear. This was a bit of a surprise to me too, to be honest. I just decided last night to take a chance on you being here, and I made something up at work about not feeling well and I jumped in the car before I lost my nerve.' Her eyes went to his apron. 'Were you working? I can come back later if you're busy.'

The smile had retreated. 'I was just finishing up. It's dinner time, isn't it, Bentley?'

Bentley stood up, his tail wagging in confirmation.

'C'mon, Bentley, let's show Emma the studio.' He turned to face her. 'You've come this far; you might as well come inside.'

Bentley led the way to what she had mistakenly assumed was a garage. She gasped as she stepped inside. The entire interior was pristine white, including the stained-white poured-concrete floors. Shelves lined the walls with dozens of pieces of work, each at varying degrees of completion. Raw materials were stacked neatly to one side, a long work bench ran down the centre of the room and an empty wall to the right was home to photographer's lights and umbrellas, presumably for photographing the finished pieces.

'This is amazing. You have everything you need right here.'

Jack shrugged. 'Well, you saw how long it took to get here. You kind of have to be properly set up.'

She stood admiring his work, her eyes darting from one piece to the next. She came to a stop in front of the butterfly piece 'This is amazing. I saw a photo of it last night. It's even more impressive in real life.'

He pulled off his apron. 'You saw a photo of it? How—'

'Blaine showed it to me, last night at the Mansion House. Jack, can I just say—'

'Oh, that's right, last night was the exhibition. How'd it go?'

'It was amazing. I sold all four pieces, and I know I have you to thank for that.' She took a step towards him. 'Really, thank you. Blaine told me that you sent him the photos of some of my pieces and you told him that I was good. That's the only reason he offered me the slot.'

'No problem. He needed someone at the last minute, and I was happy to recommend you. I'm glad it worked out.' He put the lid back on a large plastic tub and stuck two metal tools into a bucket of water.

She leaned over the butterfly sculpture. 'Blaine said this is your best work yet. I can see why.'

Jack shrugged. 'It ought to be. It's all I've done since I got back from Italy. I blame you.' He glanced over at her and grinned. 'I haven't been able to get it out of my head.'

'What? Italy?'

'Well, yeah, that too. But it was your butterfly piece I was referring to. I'm not surprised you sold out last night.'

Is he changing the subject again? she wondered. *Not wanting to talk about Italy, turning the conversation back to the exhibition last night? Well, I'm going to have to force the agenda. I came here for a reason.*

Jack wiped his hands on a towel. 'We were just finishing up for the day, weren't we, Bentley? Time for a treat, isn't it?'

Bentley gave a gentle half-bark in agreement.

'C'mon inside, I'll make us a drink.' He paused. 'Unless you have to be somewhere else?'

'No, not at all. I booked a room in Portmagee, so I must check in there at some stage, but I'm in no hurry.'

'Where are you staying?'

'Um, the bed and breakfast at the pub and restaurant. The Bridge Bar.'

'There's no panic. There'll be someone at reception until around nine o'clock. Let's go, Bentley.'

Bentley bounded to the door, his tail wagging furiously from side to side in anticipation of his evening treat. They crossed the driveway in silence behind him, their footsteps crunching in the gravel. Jack pushed open the front door and stood back, gesturing for Emma to go first.

'Wow!' she exclaimed. 'This is stunning.'

The entire ground floor was open plan: a staircase stood to the left, and on the right was the living room with a cavernous open stone fireplace against the opposite wall. The floors were original wood planks, softened with the patina of age and decades of foot traffic. The walls were rough plaster, a soft shade of off-white with eclectic art breaking up the white spaces. Cosy, lived-in sofas and armchairs were nestled around the room, with floor and table lamps positioned beside or behind each one, the lampshades in a pale grey slightly off-kilter, lending a casual air to the room. A bookcase to the right of the fireplace held a haphazardly stacked collection of books. Irish linen and wool throws were tossed over the backs of chairs, testament to the wild south-west Kerry winters. Nothing about the place was perfect, and as a result it was perfection in itself.

Straight ahead running left to right was the kitchen and dining room, shrouded in natural light from multiple windows and a set of double doors that led to the walled garden behind the house.

'Gin and tonic?' Jack asked.

She followed him to the kitchen.

'Yes, sounds great. Jack, this place is unreal,' she said, turning in a circle to look around.

'Thanks. It was a lot of work; still a bit to do, but it's home. I love it.'

'I can see why. It's totally deceiving from the outside. It looks like a cute cottage, then you come inside and it's this amazing, contemporary space. It's like something out of a magazine. Do you cook, too?' she asked, her gaze falling on the large cream-coloured Aga stove.

'Yep. You have to when you live in a place as remote as this. There aren't any food delivery options.'

'I suppose.' She ran her hand over the dark grey countertops. 'Is this granite?'

'No, porcelain. Apparently, it's more sustainable and durable than granite. I didn't have a clue. Had to get a little help with the kitchen.'

'Well, someone gave you good advice,' she said, admiring the warm, inviting space.

'Have a seat.' He indicated towards the oversized kitchen island.

She pulled out a bar stool and watched as he opened a cupboard and took out a dog biscuit for Bentley, whose tail was thumping against the tiled kitchen floor. Jack placed two square crystal glasses on the table, pulled some ice from the freezer, and sliced a lemon. He held up the bottle of gin for her to see.

'Skellig Six Eighteen. It's the local gin, made just in the road in Caherciveen.'

'What does the six eighteen stand for?'

'It's the number of steps to get to the top of the Skellig island just off the coast there.'

He waggled a paring knife in the direction of the Atlantic Ocean.

'I saw them – the Skelligs, I mean – driving over from Portmagee. It's just stunning here, a kind of wild beauty.'

He placed a glass on the counter in front of her.

'Yeah, it's raw. That's what I love about it.'

She twirled the glass in her hand. 'I owe you an apology,' she said quietly.

'I can't possibly think what for.'

She looked up to find him staring directly at her. Her mouth went dry. He wasn't going to make this easy.

He leaned back against the sink, folded his arms, his T-shirt stretching across his chest, and crossed one ankle in front of the other. He didn't drop his gaze. Bentley sat at his feet, his head tilted expectantly, as if he too was waiting to see what would happen next.

'This should be good,' Jack said, with the beginning of a half-smile.

CHAPTER TWENTY-FIVE

Her pulse was racing. She could feel the slight tremor of nerves in her hand. She placed the crystal glass on the kitchen island and took a deep breath. She had come all this way, playing this conversation out in her head a thousand times over the course of the hours-long journey. He had to know that she had come to apologise, to explain, but he was just standing there waiting for it. He wasn't going to let her off the hook. He hadn't swept her up in his arms at the mere sight of her. He hadn't said he was so glad she had come. There hadn't been any epic Hollywood, cinematic moment.

No grand gesture. Nothing.

But neither had he thrown her out or turned his back on her.

She realised suddenly that she likely had one shot at this and if she knew anything about him it was that he was a straight shooter who said what he thought and meant what he said. The only way through this was to be blatantly honest. She couldn't look at him.

Here goes nothing, she thought.

'Jack, I'm so sorry. I totally jumped to the wrong

conclusion.' Once she started, she couldn't stop, the words flowing like a torrent from her mouth. 'I was waiting for you to show up and I bumped against the desk thing and your laptop was open and it sprung to life. I saw your screensaver of this beautiful blonde woman and a little blond boy who looked so like you, and it stopped me in my tracks.'

He opened his mouth to speak.

'No, wait, please. Let me finish before I lose my mind.' She cleared her throat. 'A message flashed up on the screen. It said, "we miss you" and then something about you being home in time for dinner the next night. I wanted to throw up. I assumed she was your wife, and he was your little boy, and I thought everything had been just lies between us. I overreacted completely, I know that now, but at the time I couldn't think straight. I think it was a combination of the situation with Paul and then Jo confessing to her affair, and it was all just too much. I seriously wondered if *everyone* was cheating. I saw the photo and the message and put two and two together and got nineteen.'

She paused for a breath, trying her damnedest to fight back the threat of tears.

'I honestly didn't know what to think . . . All these images flashed through my head, and I thought that the whole time you'd been married, or whatever, and that the whole thing was all lies and meant nothing, so I grabbed my things and left. I didn't want to see you and I guessed you'd show up at my apartment, so I went back to the hotel.'

'I know.'

She looked up at him now.

'Of course I went to your apartment. You weren't at my place like we'd planned, so I went to your place. I thought you were just running late, but I met one of your neighbours who saw you leaving with your suitcase. I didn't know what the hell was going on, but I figured that the only other place you'd go would be back to the girls at the hotel. So, I took a taxi there and asked the bartender if he'd seen you. He told me you'd left on the last ferry. He looked at me like he wanted to kill me. I didn't know what his problem was, but I knew I wasn't going to get anything further out of him. I tried your number again, but you had me blocked at that point – nice move by the way, that felt pretty shit – so I had no way to reach you. I even went so far as to ask at reception if the girls were in their rooms, but she called both rooms and there was no answer. I assumed that they'd left with you, so I'd officially run out of options.'

'I know. Blaine told me.'

He stared at her, his eyes not leaving hers. 'I assumed that what we'd had in Italy had all been in my head. I had no idea why you'd left, but I figured you'd changed your mind. I thought it was something to do with your break-up and that it was too soon for something else ... for *someone* else. I thought you'd just freaked and wanted out.'

He shook his head. 'I felt really stupid, that I'd read too much into it, whatever *it* was, and that I was ridiculous for even thinking that it might be more than just a holiday fling. But I don't do flings, that's the problem and it's probably why I'm still single. They're fucking exhausting.' He ran a hand through his hair. 'All these games, all this pretence and fake shit. I've no time for it. If I don't connect with someone on a real level, then I'm just not interested. I thought I had that with you, then you just took off. I didn't sleep that night. I kept running over everything in my head like a crazy person. I thought I'd see you at the airport in Rome or that maybe we'd be on the same flight together. Then I got back to Kerry and everything you'd said about Dublin and the city and city life and not being outdoorsy and all that stuff, it all ran through my head, and I figured it was just pointless. So, I pulled up the photo of your butterfly piece and got lost in that, and I let go of the idea of you.'

He came around the side of the island and stood in front of her. 'I had no idea that you'd jumped to some crazy conclusion and thought that the whole thing had been fake, or that *I'd* been deceitful. That must have been awful, and it couldn't have been further from the truth.'

A tear streaked down her cheek.

'This is all my fault, Jack. I completely freaked out. It was like PTSD or something. I panicked. I can't tell you how sorry I am.'

He lifted his hand and gently wiped her cheek. 'So, it looks like we're both guilty of the same crime. You jumped to the wrong conclusion about that photo, and I jumped to the wrong conclusion about why you disappeared.'

She looked down at the floor, trying desperately hard not to break down in tears.

Hold it together, Emma, she thought. *Don't ugly cry now. Not now.*

He leaned one hand on the island. 'I'm glad Blaine told you. About the photo, that is. I'm sorry that you thought I'd been playing you and that they were my family. Well, they are, but not in the way you thought.' He sighed. 'I can't imagine what that must have felt like. And I can see why you might think that. My brother and I looked alike and

Liam is the image of Michael. I wasn't hiding anything, I just don't like to talk about it. I dunno, maybe I need to do therapy or something, but I still can't talk about it. I don't even like to think about it, to be honest. It's too painful.'

He turned around and leaned back on the island alongside her. 'Michael was my best friend. We were really close and when he—' He sighed. 'Like I said, I really don't like to talk about it. It was only a couple of years ago and I feel that pain every single day. Some days I'm mad as fuck at him for doing what he did, other days I'm just crippled in pain at the thought that he felt there was no other way out.'

Bentley shifted and came to settle at his feet, as if he could feel the pain that Jack was sharing.

'I decided that the only good thing I could do was to be there for Michelle and Liam. She doesn't have any family, so I moved them down here and they are a part of my life in the biggest way.'

'I know,' she said quietly. 'I told Blaine what I'd done, and he explained everything to me. Once I found out that I'd got the whole thing so wrong, I knew that I had to see you, so I jumped in the car this morning and just drove here.'

She turned her head to look up at him. 'I'll do anything to prove to you how sorry I am. I was so wrong. I know that now.'

'Well, I'd like nothing more than to believe that the time we spent together did actually mean something to you, so—'

'Of course it did. I loved every minute of it, and I've missed you so much since I fucked it all up and ran away like some dramatic *Gone with the Wind* character.'

Jack frowned. 'I've seen *Gone with the Wind* and I'm pretty sure there were no laptops and screensavers and messages throwing Scarlett O'Hara off her game.'

Emma laughed, despite the desperate clutch on her heart. 'Fair enough.'

'So, as I was saying, I'd like nothing more than to believe that you're sorry and that this,' he gestured with both hands now, 'that this was real.'

'It was,' she insisted. 'I swear it was. It was all real.'

'Okay, well, you're going to have to prove it to me.'

'I know.' She nodded furiously, her heart pounding in her chest. She wanted nothing more than another chance with him. 'I will, I promise.'

'If you're serious—'

'I am.'

'Jesus,' he laughed. 'Will you calm down and let me finish.'

'Sorry.'

'If you're serious, you're going to have to do your penance here. Do time, as they say in the movies.'

She looked at him, confused, a small frown forming between her eyebrows.

He shifted his position, leaned his back against the counter and rested both hands on either side. 'That's the choice. If you're serious and you want to see what this really is, get to know me better, then you're going to have to stay here for the entire weekend. In deep country. Surrounded by fields and sheep and the ocean. With no fancy wine bars, no fancy shops, no fancy brunches. Just you, me and Bentley in this small, remote cottage and nobody else for miles. That's a tall order for a city slicker like yourself. It's Friday night and there's nowhere to go and nothing to do.'

He looked out of the window towards her car.

'Did you pack a bag?'

'Yes.'

'Anything remotely *outsidey* in it?'

She smiled. 'Honestly, I have no idea what I packed. I just stuffed a few things in there this morning before I left. 'Are you being serious right now ... about me staying the weekend?'

His expression softened. 'I've never been more serious about anything in my life, and I've never wanted anyone like this.'

He swung around, stood in front of her and leaned in towards her, his arms on either side of her on the island. 'I know this is crazy and we've only spent a few days together in Italy, but I haven't been able to get you out of my head. When Blaine told me that he'd been in touch with you I was out of my mind jealous. Not of Blaine, but of the fact that he got to talk to you, to be with you. I've thought of you every single day since we left that island. Hour after hour. I thought we were done before we'd even really started, but it didn't matter; I still couldn't get you out of my head. And I know that you're a city girl and I'm a country boy, but now that you're going to be a hot-shot artist, maybe you could consider spending some time in the country. You know ... for inspirational purposes.'

She stepped towards him, stopping inches from his face, feeling braver – hopeful, even – for the first time in months. 'I'd only be doing it for my art, of course. It'd have nothing to do with the fact that you're here.'

'No, I get that. You'd be driving five hours across the country and forgoing your fancy restaurants and bougee brunches for walks down country lanes and evenings by the fire. *Huge* sacrifice.'

She smiled up at him, her heart pounding in her chest. 'I never thought I'd say this, but walks down country lanes and evenings by the fire have never sounded so appealing.'

He took her into his arms and kissed her gently. He pulled back slowly, his eyes locked on hers. 'You know what, Emma Brosnan? I think there's a good chance we'll make a country girl out of you yet.'

Acknowledgements

The act of writing the book is done, for the most part, in solitude, but it takes a village to bring it to life and get it into your hands. I'm lucky to have a very lovely and hugely supportive village!

Thank you to my wonderful agent, Elizabeth Counsell, for your unwavering support and enthusiasm, and for being such fun to work with. I look forward to many more of your brilliant ideation-stage brainstorming sessions.

Thank you to the dedicated and talented wider team at Northbank Talent Management – I hope we get to work on many more books together.

Thank you to my brilliant editor Tilda Key for believing in this story from the beginning and for pushing me outside of my comfort zone to add a little heat! This book is infinitely better as a result of your input.

Thank you to the wonderful Zoe Carroll for carefully guiding the drafts through to the final iteration. I'm hugely grateful for your patience and kindness.

Thank you to my very talented copyeditor, Alison Tulett. I look forward to working with you every time, knowing that the story is in great hands, and you'll whip my oversights and hodgepodge grammatical errors into shape.

Thank you to the lovely Rebecca Roy for your keen observations and your attention to detail.

Thank you to the team at Hachette Ireland, with special thanks to Elaine Egan and Siobhán Tierney, in tandem with Mark Walsh at Plunkett PR – it's always so fun and such a pleasure to work with you when publication day comes around.

Thank you to my fabulous sisters Martina and Angela, for putting down real books in order to read the first draft of mine. It always starts with you two.

Continued thanks to Uncle Ger and Eileen for scouring the bookshops in Cork City and doing a little rearranging of the book displays when no one is watching.

Thank you to my wonderful friend Cathy Roth for reading the first draft and for convincing me that the 'hot scene' worked.

Thank you to the one and only Starr, my lovely findoutologist friend for running the numbers and holding me accountable to the goals!

Thank you to the Irish writing community for being so graciously supportive of Irish writers, including the team at Writing.ie, Rick O'Shea Book Club Group, BooKPunK, and the many bloggers for spreading the word.

Finally, thanks to you the reader. I hope that you enjoyed the journey to the gorgeous island of Giglio. It exists in real life and is truly spectacular, and I only hope that I managed to do it justice. If you enjoyed the book, I'd be very grateful if you'd leave a review on Amazon or Goodreads, so that others might consider reading it too. And if you feel inclined, I'd love to hear from you directly:

◼️ Catherine Mangan

◯ catherinemanganauthor

✕ @cath_mangan

Fall in love with a sun-drenched holiday romance

Lily flees New York to travel to her best friend's wedding on the sun-drenched island of Ischia – but there's more to the secluded island than she'd ever imagined. Sparkling seas, breath-taking beaches and delicious food should be the perfect cure for her broken heart – and then local, Matt, shows her the true magic the island has to offer and how Lily can help save it.

Escape to the Italian coast and get swept away with the perfect summer romance

When Niam's life falls apart, her sister invites her to tag along on a work trip to the sun-drenched Italian coast, but she soon finds that she never wants to leave. With help from her new-found Italian friends – and the possibility of romance on the horizon – can she make her new life in the sun a success?

Escape to an Italian island and fall in love with this irresistible holiday read

Junior travel writer Katie has landed the assignment of a lifetime on the idyllic Italian island of Ponza. But when her best friend is injured, she's stuck for a month – juggling a demanding boss, a distant boyfriend and an intriguing local chef. As island life draws her in, Katie must decide what she truly wants before it's too late.